Dark Water

Dark Ship

Dark Horse

Dark Shadows

Dark Paradise

Dark Fury

DARK SHIP

A Ryan Weller Thriller

EVAN GRAVER

THIRD REEF
PUBLISHING LLC

Dark Ship

www.evangraver.com

ISBN-10: 1-7338866-1-3

ISBN-13: 978-1-7338866-1-1

This is a work of fiction. Any resemblance to any person, living or dead, business, companies, events, or locales is entirely coincidental.

Printed and bound in the United States of America

First Printed March 2018

Published by Third Reef Publishing, LLC

Hollywood, Florida

www.thirdreefpublishing.com

Dedicated to:
Antonio "Tony" Vesuvius Forte

You challenged and motivated us.
Even at your lowest, you inspired us.
Your twelve years on this earth were not enough.
We love you and miss you.

CHAPTER ONE

José Luis Orozco considered cocaine, tequila, subordinates to do his bidding, and the ever-present rotation of beautiful women to be the luxuries of command. One such creature was under his desk right now. He kept pushing her hands away from his crotch. While he wanted nothing more than to relax into his chair and feel the warmth of her mouth around him, he had to finish this meeting first.

He needed to take retribution for their *jefe muerto*—dead boss—Arturo Guerrero. Orozco wanted the killers dead. Better yet, he wanted them brought back to Tampico, so he could torture them. His gaze drifted to the massive Russian leaning against his office wall, a bounty hunter he'd hired to track down the *asesinos Yanqui*—Yankee assassins—Ryan Weller and Mango Hulsey.

Suddenly, Orozco's hand shot out to clamp onto the edge of the desk and his eyes closed.

"Are you all right, *Patrón?*" Eduardo Sanchez asked, even though he could see the woman's bare feet sticking out from under the desk and knew exactly what she was doing. His boss had a habit of mixing business with pleasure.

"*Sí, sí,*" Orozco groaned, trying not the let the excitement show on his deep brown face. The creases around his mouth gave the appearance of a perpetual frown, accented by the shape of his long goatee. He kept his mustache, beard, and hair trimmed close to the skin.

His men did not dare utter another word. Beside Orozco's right hand was a massive stainless-steel Smith and Wesson Model 500 revolver with rubber grips and a laser sight. He'd shot more than one man in a fit of anger, and no one sitting around the desk wanted his head turned into a canoe.

Orozco pushed the woman's hands away. She laid her head in his lap, and he stroked her silky, black hair. Again, his stare fixed on Grigory Dmitri Morozov, who was examining a statue of *Nuestra Señora de la Santa Muerte. Our Lady of Holy Death*, colloquially known as *Santa Muerte*. The idol, a cross between the Virgin Mary and the Grim Reaper, wore a hooded cloak and carried a scythe. Her face was a grinning skull. Orozco considered *Santa Muerte* to be his patron saint. He often prayed to her for guidance.

Morozov smiled, laying his lips back and baring his teeth in the snarl of a feral hound. Even the man's canines stuck out like the fangs of a ferocious hunter. Most did not know his real name and referred to him by his nickname, *Volk*—the Wolf, Orozco did the same. He was one of the few men Orozco feared.

Volk was a monster. At six feet, six inches, he weighed nearly three hundred pounds. Hardened muscle packed his frame. The only fat was around his midsection. His arm and chest muscles stretched the fabric of his dress shirt. He wore his blonde hair swept back off his forehead. The blue-eyed Russian reminded Orozco of a beefier Dolph Lundgren, when Lundgren fought Sylvester Stallone in *Rocky IV*.

"Give me an update," Orozco said.

"*Patrón*," Sanchez pleaded, "let me send some *sicarios* after them. We can take care of this with our own assassins. We do not need this *puta* stinking up our business."

Orozco smiled in agreement. The bounty hunter was a whore, but Orozco's voice held a warning. "Do not bring this up again, Eduardo. Our *sicarios* are good for killing in Mexico but not in the United States. We have enough heat on us already because of Guerrero. Volk will keep us from being associated with their disappearance."

"*Si, jefe*, but—"

The cartel leader cut him off by wrapping his fingers around the grip of the fifty-caliber revolver. He wasn't in the mood for insubordination. He wanted this meeting to be over. The damned woman's hands were insistent. Ignoring them as best he could, he said to Volk, "Tell me how you plan to do it."

Volk pushed a lock of his blond hair behind his ear. "They work for a company called Dark Water Research."

"We know this, *Lobo*," Orozco snapped. He used the Spanish version of the Russian's nickname. "Guerrero knew this and didn't kill them. Now we need revenge, and I'm paying you for results."

The Russian nodded, unaffected by the temperamental Mexican. "Mango Hulsey is living on a sailboat at the Dark Water Research facility."

"Again, this much we know," Orozco shouted angrily. He brushed away the woman's hand.

Volk ran a finger over the statue's scythe, letting the tip linger on the scythe's point. He picked up the statue to examine it more closely.

"Put that down!" Orozco roared, snatching up his revolver and aiming it at Volk's head. The laser sight painted a dancing red dot on the Russian's forehead.

"*Neechevo srashnava,*" Volk said in Russian. *No harm.* He set the statue down, aligned as before, and looked at the shorter man. "Ryan Weller is traveling with a Homeland Security agent in Atlanta, Georgia. I sent a team after him. They will take him when they have the chance. Then they will go after Hulsey."

"*Excelente.*" Orozco rubbed his hands together. "I want to drag their bodies through the streets as an example to anyone who wishes to mess with the Aztlán cartel." He couldn't keep the girl's hands off him, and he couldn't stand it any longer. "All of you leave. Now!"

When the room was empty, Orozco leaned his head back and thought about his rise to power while the woman pleasured him. After the *asesinos Yanqui* had killed Arturo Guerrero and escaped, war had enveloped the city. Street fights, car bombs, long-range assassinations, and drive-by shootings had punctuated the power struggle for leadership of the Aztlán cartel and ownership of Tampico, Mexico.

José Luis Orozco declared himself the victor.

Before Guerrero's death, Orozco had been third in command. Guerrero had liked Orozco because the man worked hard, handled himself with confidence, was unafraid to get his hands dirty to accomplish the job or to keep his men in line. Because of these attributes, Guerrero had placed Orozco in charge of his cocaine distribution network. Orozco increased shipments and sales, which pleased the cartel boss. What did not please Guerrero was Orozco's opposition to his scheme to start a war with the United States and retake what many believed to be Mexico's rightful heritage, the land stolen during the Mexican-American War and the Treaty of Guadalupe Hidalgo. Guerrero believed the U.S. had unjustly started a war with their country and forcibly took more than half of Mexico's land. Orozco didn't care about ancient history, only about the money he could make from the sale of drugs, firearms, and slaves across the border in the United States.

When word of a gunfight at Guerrero's isolated compound had reached Orozco, he'd been one of the first to arrive to provide backup, and he'd coordinated the city-wide manhunt for the murderous *pendejos*—assholes.

Orozco had no love for Arturo Guerrero, but he needed to take retribution against anyone who came into his territory and killed one of his own. His eyelids fluttered as he braced his hands on the desk, the fingers of his right hand wrapping around the pistol's grip. He imagined the thrill of killing the *gringos* as he lost himself in the woman's caress.

CHAPTER TWO

Ryan Weller shoved his hands into his trouser pockets. He rolled his neck and leaned against the wall. A steady flow of people exited U.S. Customs at Atlanta's Hartsfield-Jackson Airport. They paid him no attention as they streamed past him, stuffing documents into pockets and excitedly speaking in myriad languages. Ryan was fluent in English and Spanish and knew a little French, allowing him to eavesdrop on their conversations.

He checked his watch again and glanced over his shoulder at Floyd Landis. The Department of Homeland Security agent was on the far side of the crowd, arms crossed, sipping coffee, and scanning the crowd. His dark eyes met Ryan's. Landis motioned with his head to continue searching the crowd.

Ryan turned away, frustrated. They were waiting on Aaron Grose. His flight from Belize had arrived at the same time as two others. Ryan glanced at his watch again and scanned the lines. He shifted his feet, feeling the pinch of the patent leather oxfords. He longed for the comfortable fit of his normal attire: shorts, a T-shirt, and his well-worn boat shoes.

He spotted his man as Aaron glanced around at his fellow passengers, gauging the distance to the booth where his passport would be checked and stamped. Like most travelers, Aaron fidgeted with a smart phone, scrolling and pecking at the screen. Ryan caught Landis's eye, and motioned toward their quarry.

Landis nodded and moved through the throng of people to stand beside Ryan. He was here because Ryan had asked him to help with an investigation into the international arms dealer, Jim Kilroy. Kilroy had supplied the Aztlán cartel with weapons for their attempt at starting a war for the desert Southwest, which many Latinos still considered part of Mexico. It irritated Ryan that no one wanted to do anything to stop this guy. No one wanted to talk about him in conjunction with the illegal firearms brought into the U.S. by the Mexican cartel. Just because Kilroy had contracts with the U.S. government didn't make him a good guy. And if Aaron Grose was in bed with Kilroy, that made him guilty by association.

Aaron stepped to the customs booth and handed over his passport. The uniformed TSA agent took the passport and fanned through it. Ryan knew from studying Aaron's passport photo and from watching countless travelers pass through customs that she was verifying the image of the five-feet-ten-inch white male with brown eyes and blond hair matched the man standing in front of her.

Aaron flashed a smile at the agent. She smiled back, then ducked her head to look at the stamps in the booklet.

Ryan moved closer to hear their conversation.

"Says you've been in Belize for the last five years," the TSA agent said.

Aaron leaned on the counter and gazed at her. She was a slightly overweight woman with light ebony skin. Her black hair was braided and piled high on her head. "Yeah, Tamica,"

Aaron said, reading her name tag. "I own a scuba diving resort on Caye Caulker. I run charters to every country in the region. You should come down sometime."

"I don't scuba dive, Mr. Grose."

"I tell you what, Tamica." He slid her a business card, embossed with the name Caye Caulker Adventures. "You call this number, and I'll make sure you have a free stay."

The woman used her hand to cover her smile and hide her embarrassment, but she still took the card. "Thanks, Mr. Grose," she managed to say.

"Call me Aaron."

With a little too much honey in her voice, she said, "Anything to declare, Aaron?"

He grinned again. "Nope, just heading to Wyoming to see my family."

Tamica stamped his passport before sliding it under the plexiglass divider.

Aaron slipped the passport into his back pocket and walked past Tamica's booth. He gave her a parting smile and turned to find Ryan and Landis staring at him.

Landis pulled out his gold-and-blue Homeland Security Investigations badge from his pocket. "Mr. Grose, I'm Floyd Landis."

Aaron glanced from one man to the other. Landis, in his fifties, had a slight paunch with short, steel-gray hair and hard, dark eyes set into a weathered face. He stood eye-to-eye with Aaron. Ryan was taller, six feet, with brown hair going shaggy around the ears. His green eyes stared at Aaron with curiosity. Both men sported dark suits. Landis wore a tie.

"Who are you?" Aaron asked Ryan.

Landis tucked his badge into his pocket and said, "Ryan Weller. He's a civilian contractor. We need to speak with you in private. Follow me."

"Am I being arrested?"

"Mr. Grose, we want your full cooperation. Now, you can come nicely, or I can slap some cuffs on you. We can make a scene about you being a threat to national security. Which would you like?"

Ryan nodded at Tamica. "I'm sure your new friend would like to see you go peacefully."

Aaron glanced over his shoulder. Tamica was watching them. He flashed her a reassuring smile, then turned to face Ryan and Landis. "I'll go quietly."

Landis led the way. Ryan carried Aaron's backpack and towed his rolling suitcase while following them through a series of hallways. They escorted Aaron to a small room and told him to sit in a chair. When he'd taken a seat, Landis closed the door.

Landis and Ryan continued down the corridor to another room. A computer monitor played footage of Aaron's tiny holding room, which was cramped even further by a desk shoved into one corner, the chair Aaron was sitting in, and a second chair beside the desk. As they watched, Aaron switched seats, so he was facing the door. He spent a few minutes staring at the door, then looked at a watch on his left wrist. He fiddled with the watch for several minutes.

Ryan asked Landis, "How long are you going to let him stew?"

"Until I get bored." Landis poured coffee into a paper cup. He sipped the steaming liquid as he watched the monitor.

Thirty minutes later, Landis heaved himself out of the chair and poured more coffee. He filled two more cups. To Ryan, he said, "Put some cream and sugar in your pocket and carry these."

Ryan did as instructed, following Landis to the holding room. Landis pushed open the door and held it for Ryan. Ryan nudged the door closed with his foot as he stepped inside.

CHAPTER THREE

Aaron Grose watched the civilian contractor shove the door closed. He said, "Hope you have someone out there to open the door after it locks."

"You better hope you get to walk out that door," Landis responded. "It might be a one-way trip to Gitmo for you."

"I've been to Cuba several times, but I have no desire to go to prison there," Aaron said, clearly puzzled.

"Then you'd better cooperate," Landis said.

Ryan set a cup of coffee on the desk and deposited a handful of cream and sugar packets. Aaron picked up two sugars and dumped them into his cup. He crossed his legs and sipped his coffee.

Landis sat down in the empty chair. Aaron watched Ryan lean against the wall in the far corner of the room. To Aaron, the man in the corner was the more dangerous of the two. He had an edge to him, a hardness in his lean, muscular body. He reminded Aaron of the American special forces troops who sometimes came through his dive shop while on leave from conducting operations in Central America.

When Landis moved, Aaron got a glimpse of a pistol butt.

He couldn't see a gun imprinted in Ryan's clothes, either along his waistline or under his shoulder. He tried to relax. The closeness of the three bodies had increased the room's temperature. A trickle of sweat rolled down his temple. Aaron shifted in the chair and glanced up at the ceiling. In the corner, above Ryan, an all-seeing electronic eye winked back at him with a flash of red light.

To break the silence, Aaron pointed at the camera and asked, "Who's watching us?"

Landis leaned forward, ignoring the question. "Mr. Grose, how long have you operated a business in Belize?"

Aaron smiled. "Twelve years." He was trying to remain calm. "Look, maybe I should call my lawyer."

"I'm afraid we can't let you do that," Landis said. "You're being held on suspicion of terrorism."

Aaron rose abruptly as he shouted, "Terrorism!"

Landis stood up. "Calm down, Mr. Grose."

Ryan didn't move from his corner. Aaron glowered at him, unnerved by the man's nonchalance.

The two men stared at each other until Ryan pushed away from the wall and took a step forward. Menace laced his words. "Sit down, Aaron." In the small room, the step had brought them nose-to-nose.

Aaron backed up. His knees hit the edge of his chair and buckled. He dropped heavily onto the thinly padded steel.

Ryan continued. "Who're you going to call? Trisha, your sister? She's a real estate lawyer. She can't help you. Or maybe you'd like to call your business partner?"

Aaron's eyebrows arched. "Who?"

Ryan leaned in closer. "Come on, Aaron. We know you're helping Jim Kilroy move illegal weapons."

Aaron gulped. "Jim's a resort developer."

Ryan said, "Jim Kilroy's one of the largest arms dealers in North, Central, and South America."

Aaron's jaw dropped open. "No way." To help recover from his shock, he picked up his coffee and sipped it slowly. Ryan retreated to his corner.

"It's a fact, Mr. Grose," Landis affirmed.

"Jim is just an investor in my business. I'm not involved in the weapons trade, so why am I here?"

Landis crossed his arms before speaking. "Number one, you haven't paid U.S. taxes since you left the country, and you owe the U.S. government quite a chunk of change. Our figures indicate you owe about half a million dollars in back taxes, interest, and penalties. All those are compounding daily, Aaron. Every minute you waste sitting here is another dollar in fines. Number two, we think you know more about Jim's business. We want you to give us information on his whereabouts and his movements. We also know you're friendly with his wife, Karen. Press her for information if you can."

"This is blackmail!"

"This is you playing ball, Mr. Grose," Landis said. "We want information on Jim Kilroy's gunrunning operation. You want to get your business out of hock with the IRS. We can work hand in hand, or we can do things the hard way. If we don't get information, you lose your business."

Aaron balled his hands into fists. His blood surged through his veins and pounded in his temples. His vision blurred. He took a deep breath, knowing a fistfight in the confined office space would result in his being arrested. Two steadying breaths later, he said, "And if I play ball?"

Landis glanced at his partner, then back at Aaron. The agent had a hint of a smile on his lips. "You give us actionable intelligence, and we'll wipe the slate clean. Then you'll need to start paying taxes on your future income."

"What if I can't get any actionable intelligence?" Aaron used his fingers to make air quotes around actionable.

"We want intelligence that will lead us to Kilroy's network," Ryan said. "We're going to take him down. We're going to stop him from selling weapons." He stepped forward and leaned down to face Aaron. "Your business partner arms gangs in El Salvador, who rape and murder young children, and Colombian cartels, who manufacture cocaine. He sold weapons to the Mexican separatists who started a bombing campaign in the U.S. last month. I'm sure you've heard about that. Kilroy's weapons are in every country in this hemisphere, Aaron." The name came out like it tasted bitter. "We're going to take him down and send him to jail. You're going to help us."

Landis glanced up sharply at Ryan.

Aaron stared in disbelief. "Jim helped me start my resort. He's a developer. I've worked with him for years. I would know if he was an arms dealer. He's not, he's just a resort developer."

"Yeah, he's a developer," Ryan said sarcastically. "He just uses his resorts to launder his dirty money. He's probably using yours, too." He stabbed an accusatory finger at Aaron. "He's a criminal and you're his accomplice."

"No, I'm not!" Aaron shouted. "I don't have anything to do with guns, and I know every penny that goes in and out of my place. I am not a criminal, and neither is Jim."

Ryan gazed implacably at Aaron and sipped his coffee. Aaron noticed Landis was staring at his contractor. He tried to wrap his mind around the information being dumped on him. The men seemed earnest, yet the only real fact Aaron could pin down was that he was up to his neck in IRS debt.

He concentrated on what he knew about Jim Kilroy. The man had inherited several commercial properties in Florida, among them a world-class golf resort. He had used these as leverage to buy and develop more properties. He now owned hotels in New York City, Florida, Mexico, Costa

Rica, Panama, the Dominican Republic, and both the U.S. and the British Virgin Islands. He had once famously tried to build a resort on Jost Van Dyke but was quickly shut down by environmentalists and the government. Jim had always been good to him. He'd helped him start his resort when he was just a young dive instructor looking for the next thrill in life. If he had a best friend it would be Jim's wife, Karen.

He scuffed the toe of his shoe on the bare concrete floor. He wanted out of this room, out of this airport, and out of this trouble.

"What can you tell us about Jim's boats?" Ryan asked.

Aaron looked up. "He's got a one-hundred-and-twenty-five-foot Alaska crab boat he converted into a luxury mother-ship for a Viking sportfisher and a couple other small boats."

Landis took a notepad out. "What's the name of the boat?"

"*Northwest Passage*."

"What about Karen?" Ryan asked. "Can you press her for information?"

"I can't."

"Why not?" Ryan asked.

"She went to New York City a few weeks ago. She had a fight with Jim and went to see her mother. I haven't spoken to her since she left."

"Call her. Go see her," Ryan said.

"How would that work?" Aaron used his fingers to make a pretend telephone and held them to his ear. "Hey, Karen, your husband's an international arms dealer. Got anything to tell me, so I can spill it to the feds?"

"Okay, anything else?" Landis asked.

"No," Aaron barked, clearly annoyed. "Look, I run a scuba diving resort on Caye Caulker. I see Jim, maybe, once every six months. Karen comes by more often. I take her diving.

But, like I said earlier, I haven't seen her around because she went to New York City to visit her mother."

"Okay, Mr. Grose, here's what's going to happen," Landis said. "You're going to walk out of here and go see your family. You're going to get that sister of yours to hook you up with a good tax lawyer. Then you're going to go back to Belize and run your resort." Landis pointed his thumb at his companion. "In a few weeks, Ryan will come down to your resort and spend some time diving and taking in the sights. You'll introduce him to Kilroy."

Aaron looked over at Ryan, "Do you dive?"

Ryan smirked.

"That boy is part fish," Landis said stoically. "He was Navy EOD."

"I don't know what that is," Aaron said, puzzled.

"It means he disarmed bombs underwater for the U.S. Navy," Landis said.

Explosive Ordnance Disposal was one of the Navy's most rigorous programs, a grueling year long course of diving, ordnance disposal training, parachute, small unit tactics, and firearms skills. They operated in the harshest environments to disarm and dispose of all manner of explosive devices from car bombs to underwater mines.

Aaron sat up straight, shrugged his shoulders, and said, "Come on down. I can't guarantee Jim will be there." He crossed his arms and stared at Ryan. "Hope the government's paying for your rooms, because I'm not footing the bill."

"I'll take care of it," Ryan replied.

Aaron looked at his watch. "Are we done here? I missed my connecting flight to Salt Lake City. I need to book another one, and, apparently, I have to find a lawyer now."

Landis pulled an airline ticket from his jacket pocket. He set it on the desk and tapped it with his finger. "You're on the next flight out."

"You never had any intention of sending me to Gitmo," Aaron exclaimed.

"Oh, no, Aaron," Ryan said. "We have every intention of sending you to Gitmo. You're complicit in the illegal arms trade by involving yourself with Kilroy. I'm going to make sure you go to prison."

"But I'm not, and you know it." Aaron knew he sounded like a little kid. All he needed was to stamp his foot to complete the tantrum.

Landis stood up and walked to the door. He jerked it open and pointed outside.

In the hall, Aaron picked up his backpack and grabbed the handle on his luggage. "How the hell do I get out of here?"

CHAPTER FOUR

Ryan started to step through the closing door after Aaron. Landis placed a hand on his chest and shoved him backward before slamming the door shut. Ryan stumbled and felt himself driven into the chair Aaron had just occupied. He looked up at Landis and read the anger on the man's face.

It echoed in his words. "What the hell was that? You're a liaison, not a one-man wrecking crew. I agreed to go down this rabbit hole with you, but you're out of line. Your behavior is making me seriously reconsider the DHS's relationship with Dark Water Research—and specifically your involvement."

It was the flippant answers given by a criminal and the fact that no one seemed to care if Jim Kilroy spread machines of death across the globe that had set Ryan off. Giving a little grief to Aaron Grose had been satisfying.

"I apologize, Floyd."

"Are you trying to piss me off?" Landis growled. No one called the DHS man by his first name. He made it quite clear he didn't like people saying it, and he didn't like being associated with a barber in Mayberry.

Ryan crossed his arms. "I'm trying to bring down an international gun dealer."

Landis sat down in the other chair. He leaned forward and rested a forearm on the scarred top of the desk. "Look, you're a good guy, Ryan. You were a standout sailor, an excellent EOD tech, and you did this country a real service by taking out Arturo Guerrero, but you're getting into something above your pay grade. Kilroy has government contracts, and that gives him some protection. If he screws the pooch, we can nail him to the wall. Until then ..." He trailed off and leaned back in the chair. "This whole thing makes me feel dirty. I don't care about a guy who doesn't pay his taxes—there are worse criminals out there—and we both know he isn't helping Kilroy sell guns."

"You don't care about Kilroy?"

"I didn't say I didn't care. I said I can't do anything about it. Let's go home and forget about this mess."

Ryan looked the man in the eyes and lied, "All right, Landis. You got it."

CHAPTER FIVE

Ten years ago, the commercial dive and salvage conglomerate Dark Water Research had purchased an old airplane hangar from the U.S. Navy base in Corpus Christi, tore it down, and reassembled it on the south bank of Industrial Canal in Texas City, Texas, the heart of the U.S. oil industry.

As part of their expanding operations, DWR handled many of the U.S. government's ship husbandry needs, infrastructure contracts, maintenance of submarine communications cables, and undersea pipelines. With DWR's wide presence above and below the ocean, several of the alphabet agencies had asked them to observe and report if they came across any maritime security issues. The DHS had taken this one step further and asked DWR to perform investigations, and provided them with a permanent liaison, Floyd Landis.

When DWR president Greg Olsen answered the phone in his second-floor office of the now state-of-the-art airplane hangar, his DHS liaison, Ryan Weller who asked, "Did you see the video?"

"Yeah, I saw it." Greg had watched the real time interview

of Aaron Grose on his computer.

"What did you think?" Ryan asked.

Greg pressed the speaker button on the phone and said, "I think there's a few things this guy isn't telling us."

"Probably," Ryan replied. "Is Mango there with you?"

"Yeah, he's here. We're on speaker." Greg looked over at Mango Hulsey, a former member of the Coast Guard's Maritime Security Response Team, a direct-action unit specializing in counterterrorism and law enforcement.

Mango leaned over the speakerphone. "He knows something, but he might not know that he knows. You know, bro."

Ryan laughed. "Really?"

"Are you headed back?" Greg asked.

"No, I'm going to New York City."

"New York City!" Greg and Mango both echoed.

"What are you, some city slicker?" Mango effected a Texas twang.

"No," Ryan said, still laughing. "I want to talk to Karen Kilroy. Is there anything DWR needs me to handle while I'm up there?"

"Not that I know of," Greg said. "If there is, I'll give you a call. Is Landis going with you?"

"No, he has other things to do."

Greg shook his head and rubbed his temples. Since boarding Guerrero's pirate vessel and finding out Jim Kilroy was supplying the cartel with weapons, Ryan had been fixated on finding the gun dealer and ending his operations. "Ryan, what's going on?"

"I'm going to New York, just like I said."

Greg let out a long sigh. This wasn't the guy Greg had known in the Navy. Something had changed. While Ryan's methodical planning and attention to details still shone through, he was becoming more rogue. Operating by the seat of his pants was going to get him killed.

Mango asked, "What happened to Aaron?"

"We put him on a flight to Salt Lake. Floyd told him I would visit his place in Belize in a week or so. Better pack your bag."

Greg said, "As head of this operation, I think I need a little R&R myself."

"The more, the merrier," Ryan said. "Set it up."

"I will. Talk to you later." Greg hung up the phone and rubbed his hands together. "Company trip to Belize."

Mango sat down on the other side of Greg's desk, propping his left leg on another chair. He swung the right up, crossing his prosthesis over his left ankle. He'd lost the leg about six inches below the knee during a ship boarding incident in the Persian Gulf. "Are you going for the fun of it or because Ryan needs a minder?"

"That's what I hired you for. But to answer your question, both. I'm not sure what's going on with him, or why he's so fixated on Kilroy."

Mango nodded. "I can't say that I blame him. Kilroy needs to be put out of business."

"You support his vendetta?"

"I don't know if it's a vendetta, but he believes he's doing what you hired him for."

Greg shook his head. "I hired him to work with Landis."

"Landis points him in a direction. That direction right now, bro, is Belize. Are we going to have Chuck fly us down?" Mango referred to Chuck Newland, DWR's resident pilot.

"No, I think we need to take *Dark Water*." Greg meant DWR's Hatteras GT63 sportfishing yacht. "It would be nice to have our own base of operations. If Kilroy escapes by boat, we'll be able to give chase."

"I agree," Mango replied.

"I've got some work to do. Can you start preparing *Dark Water*?"

"Yeah."

Mango left the room as Greg busied himself with paper-work. In truth, he just wanted to be left alone. He did have plenty to do, but he felt overwhelmed by running the business. He'd hoped to ease into operations and learn things from the bottom up. That plan had changed the day his father and mother were killed when a car bomb detonated at the Texas Governor's Mansion. The attack had been part of Arturo Guerrero's plot to pressure the United States into returning Aztlán.

Greg had accompanied his father and grandfather to many jobsites over the years and had begun working as a diver when he was eighteen. He'd worked for DWR during the summers while earning a bachelor's degree in marine engineering at Texas A&M. After graduation, he had enlisted in the Navy, went through the training pipeline to become an EOD technician, then attended officer candidate school. While he enjoyed the Navy, he'd planned to return to DWR to take over the DHS operations. That plan had not come to fruition either.

He pushed his wheelchair to a window overlooking DWR's marina, which contained many of the company's work vessels as well as *Dark Water* and Mango's Amazon 44 sail-boat, *Alamo*. Under the window was a low cabinet. A Barrett 98B bolt action sniper rifle chambered in .388 Lapua with a NightForce NXS scope sat on the cabinet beneath the window. The gun rested on the two legs of its bipod and the point of its butt stock. Greg ran a finger along the stock to wipe away a speck of dust. He'd begun shooting the gun for sport, enjoying the thrill of precision shooting. Punching holes in paper at long distance was about control, and it was one of the few things in life he felt he *could* control.

Greg locked his fingers behind his head and stared out the window.

With his father dead, he had been forced to recruit a new employee to handle the DHS operations. Greg was more than willing to take on the task, but his paralysis limited what role he would play in those activates. He had enjoyed piloting *Dark Water* across the Gulf of Mexico to rescue Ryan and providing support for the Tampico operation. He wanted to do more of it, but as president of DWR, he needed to focus on running the business, not chasing bad guys.

More than anything, his injuries depressed him. An accident had severed his spinal column at the T-10 level, just below his belly button. Helping Ryan was better than being stuck in an office. He hated being limited by the loss of his legs. There were many things he could do, but he had a tendency to focus more on the things he could not. Walking was a superhuman power.

Greg let out a deep sigh and picked up his phone to call his grandfather.

Cliff Olsen answered on the first ring.

"Can you come to the office?" Greg asked.

"What's the matter?"

"I need to speak with you."

"Fine," Cliff huffed. "I'll be there in an hour."

Greg called DWR's Chief Operating Officer, Shelly Hughes. When she answered, he told her to join him in his office in sixty minutes. She agreed and hung up.

Greg set the cell phone down beside the rifle and continued to stare out the window. Beyond the small harbor was Industrial Canal, leading into Galveston Bay. An oil tanker crept along the Texas City Dike, roiling the muddy brown waters of Texas City Channel. He knew the dike would be packed with boaters, swimmers, and fishermen utilizing what locals called "the world's longest man-made fishing pier."

Cliff was the first to arrive. He was in his seventies, and

the sun had turned his creased skin into leather. He wore his normal uniform: a white cowboy hat, black jeans, a Western-style snap shirt, and alligator-skinned cowboy boots. His fingers were stained yellow from decades of smoking.

"How are you, son?"

"Good, Grandpa."

"What do you want to talk about?"

"Let's wait until Shelly gets here."

Cliff sat down and fished his cigarettes from the left breast pocket of his shirt. He stuck one between his lips but did not light it.

While they waited for Shelly, Greg filled the octogenarian in on the latest DWR news.

Shelly arrived ten minutes later and dropped wearily into a seat beside Cliff.

Cliff took his cigarette out of his mouth and raised his eyebrows.

Greg looked from one to the other.

Shelly gave him a go-ahead motion with her hand. "Well?"

The paraplegic took a deep breath. "I don't want to be president anymore."

Cliff snorted. "I can't say it's a surprise."

"What are you going to do?" Shelly asked.

Greg shrugged.

The old man pulled the cigarette from his mouth and looked Greg in the eyes. "You can't be an operator forever."

Greg rolled a pencil between his fingers and scratched at a chip in the paint with a thumbnail. "I don't want to be stuck in this office either."

Shelly said, "I've known you long enough to know that you've got something in mind."

The two had met during their freshman year at Texas A&M. They quickly became study partners and had been in an on-off relationship since. They'd been "on" since Greg's injury. He watched her run a hand through her light brown hair, then said, "I want to continue working, just in a different role."

Clifford exhaled smoke through a yellow-toothed smile. "Just say you want to be Ryan's driver and get it over with. I understand, son. It's the allure of the action."

Greg knew his grandfather would understand better than anyone. Cliff had run operations as a Navy UDT in the last months of the Korean War and later became one of the first SEALs into Vietnam. He then ran several covert operations for the CIA during his tenure as head of DWR.

"I want to help Ryan," Greg said. "If I'm helping him, I can't give my full attention to my job here. When we got back from the last op, things were chaotic. There's another op brewing and I want to be part of it. I don't want the business to suffer."

Shelly shook her head. "You need to take better care of yourself. Last time you were sick for a week after you got back. You were dehydrated and had the start of a pressure sore on your butt. You have to be more careful."

"I know. I know." Greg held up his hands in defense.

Clifford ashed his cigarette in a small tray on Greg's desk. "Sure we can't change your mind?"

"Ryan and Mango are going to Belize when Ryan gets back from New York. I'm going to drive them down in *Dark Water*."

"Who's going to take your place?" Shelly demanded.

"I've invited Kip Chatel to interview," Greg replied.

Shelly said, "Do you mean Admiral Kip Chatel from Boeing?"

"Yes."

Cliff whistled. "Shooting for the stars, son."

"He's coming tomorrow. I want you guys to show him around."

CHAPTER SIX

Ryan Weller watched the front door of a five-story brownstone facing West Ninety-Seventh Street on New York City's Upper West Side. He'd flown to the Big Apple from Atlanta, rented a car, and was now on the trail of Karen Kilroy.

Jim Kilroy's development company had a boutique hotel just steps away from the New York Stock Exchange, and Ryan had hung out in the lobby or on the street for two days before the doorman threatened to call the police.

Now he was outside her mother's house. He'd sighted the trophy wife when she pulled the curtain back to look down on the street. Ryan had waved at her and motioned for her to come out. She hadn't looked out the window since.

While he waited in the rental car, he studied her social media pages and the information Landis had reluctantly given him. Karen had attended Columbia University. She'd left with a bachelor's in advanced clinical social work, with a concentration in international social welfare. Part of her student loans had been forgiven when Karen volunteered for the Peace Corps. They'd sent her to Costa Rica to teach English.

She had met her future husband while visiting his resort outside of Playa Hermosa. Not long after, she left her position with the Peace Corps and moved in with Jim.

Ryan scanned the street, watching vehicles, bicyclists, and pedestrians move up and down the narrow corridor. "Man, I stick out like a sore thumb here," he muttered. "She probably thinks I'm a cop."

This might have been easier if he had taken the Homeland Security badge Landis had tried to give him. Ryan had rejected it, several times. He didn't want to be a Fed with all the rules and laws and bullshit that carrying a badge entailed. He didn't want to work for the government again.

Deciding not to prolong his stakeout, Ryan swung the door open and levered himself out of the car. He didn't like sitting around waiting for the action to develop. The late August heat reflecting off the pavement and buildings caused beads of sweat to pop out on his forehead. A kid on a skateboard zipped past. Ryan continued across the street and up the steps of the row house, where he pressed the call button for the apartment.

An elderly female voice came through the intercom speaker. "May I help you?"

"Hi, Mrs. Thorpe, my name's Ryan Weller. I need to speak with your daughter, Karen."

There was a long pause before the voice came back. "She's not here."

"Mrs. Thorpe, please open the door. I'm tired of waiting for her to come out, and she knows I'm here."

The door buzzed, and he pulled it open, taking the stairs two at a time to the third floor, to knock on the apartment door.

Karen Kilroy, a platinum blonde with artificially enhanced breasts and a deep tan, held the door open and swept her hand out in a gesture of invitation. Ryan stepped into the foyer and waited for her to close the door. She locked the deadbolt before leading him into the living room.

Adella Thorpe sat in a white wingback chair. She was thin and frail with short white hair. Age and sickness had wrinkled her skin. Liver spots dotted her arms and hands.

"What can I do for you?" Karen asked.

"I'd like to speak to you about your husband," Ryan said.

"What about him?"

"Can we speak privately?" Ryan glanced over at Mrs. Thorpe.

"You may say what you wish right here." Karen sat but did not invite Ryan to do so.

Ryan looked around the ornately furnished room. Nothing appeared newer than the Victorian Age. The room appeared to be a time capsule from the day the brownstone had been built. He suspected much of the furniture was custom-made. All of it was in immaculate condition and smelled like mothballs and hand sanitizer.

"Okay." Ryan cleared his throat. "Jim is involved in the illegal weapons trade."

"You don't speak ill of someone's husband." Adella Thorpe's voice was soft and hoarse.

"I'm not speaking ill of him, Mrs. Thorpe. I know he deals in illegal weapons. He sold weapons to the Mexican separatists who bombed the buildings in Austin, Phoenix, and Los Angeles last month."

"Is this true, Karen?"

"Mother." Karen's tone was patronizing. "Don't believe everything you hear." She stood and pointed at the door. In a firmer voice, she said, "Please leave." She walked past Ryan to the foyer and opened the front door.

Ryan laid a business card on a small round table, beside a flower-filled vase and a set of keys. Karen looked at the card then at him with a hint of amusement in her eyes.

The door slammed behind Ryan as he stepped out. He went to the car. The hot leather attempted to burn his skin through his thin dress pants. Feeling boiled alive by the steamy interior dampened his mood further at not accomplishing anything during his confrontation with Karen. The New York traffic didn't help his disposition as he drove back to the hotel.

Deep in the hotel's concrete parking structure, the heat wasn't as bad. Ryan was thankful for the relief as he walked toward the elevator. He noticed a dark SUV gliding up the entrance ramp and turning toward him. Automatically, he moved closer to the row of parked cars. He heard the vehicle's engine roar as it accelerated. Headlights snapped on and aimed right at him.

He dove onto the hood of a red Hyundai and jerked his feet up as the silver Ford Explorer brushed past. Using his momentum, he brought his legs up over his head and somersaulted off the car. Hoping to land on his feet, but misjudging the landing, he dropped off the edge of the car and crumpled to the ground, landing hard on his side, and grimacing as pain shot through the ribs he'd bruised in Mexico.

The pain didn't distract him for long. He glanced up to see the SUV backing toward him. The passenger had his window down, a long, black silencer aimed at Ryan. He rolled under a high-clearance Ford pickup, then, instead of rolling all the way to the other side, Ryan stopped halfway and rolled back out the side where he'd started. The Explorer continued backward, passing Ryan.

Gaining his feet, Ryan wished he was wearing something other than his slick-soled oxfords. He kept low and ran between the cars, angling for the stairwell. As he passed a thick support column, he tripped over a man's foot when the man stuck his leg out from behind a column.

Instinctively, Ryan thrust his hands out in front of him.

His right hand hit first, and the wrist gave as it took the full weight of his body. He slammed down on his right shoulder and continued the roll to his right.

The man leaped from behind the column and landed on Ryan, pinning Ryan on his back. Ryan recognized the two small wooden handles and the thin metal wire of a garotte in his assailant's hands but brought his left wrist up and stopped the wire from tightening around his neck. Ryan jerked his knee hard into the man's crotch and at the same time delivered an open-handed heel strike to the man's face. The man deflected the blow and kept trying to wrap the garotte around Ryan's neck.

The wire dug deep into his skin and sawed through to raw flesh. Blood flowed freely down his arm. With his right hand, he delivered repeated blows to the man's face. The wire was forcing his wrist tighter against his neck. The pressure was slowly crushing his windpipe. His attacker planted his knee on the inside of Ryan's right thigh, effectively immobilizing his leg. Garotte put all his weight on Ryan's leg and drew back his other, slamming it forward into Ryan's groin. The blow didn't have much power, but it still took away what little breath Ryan's had left.

Tires screeched. Out of the corner of his eye, Ryan saw the Explorer come to a stop on the other side of the parked cars. From his vantage point, all he could see was a set of combat boots stepping out of the SUV.

Garotte drew his leg back to hammer Ryan's groin again. Ryan shifted his attention back to Garotte. The pain of the wire biting through his wrist was excruciating. He extended the fingers of his right hand, forming a slight cup. With all his might, he smacked Garotte on the ear in a thunderclap strike. Garotte immediately dropped his weapon and grasped the side of his head. Ryan knew the strike could rupture an eardrum, turning an attacker temporarily deaf and disoriented. Garotte moaned as he sat up straight. Ryan punched him in the windpipe. His assailant let go of his ear to clutch his throat. The strike was hard enough to crush the throat and, as Ryan rolled away, he knew he'd killed the man. It was only a matter of time before he suffocated to death.

Ryan came up in a crouch behind the closest car. The guy in combat boots was approaching, a silenced pistol clasped in both hands. He stopped at the grotesque sight of Garotte's purple face and bulging eyes. Combat Boots swung the pistol to the left, his eyes tracking with the sights.

Ryan fired his body straight up, shoving the heel of his hand between Combat Boot's outstretched arms, and slammed it into his jaw. The man's teeth shattered as they crashed together. Combat Boot's head snapped back, and his knees gave out. As his assailant crumpled to the ground, Ryan dashed for the stairwell door.

The door bounced off its stops as Ryan tore through it and up the first flight of stairs. He heard rubber shriek on pavement as a vehicle accelerated. He waited, hands on knees, sucking in big lungsful of air, and shaking from the adrenaline. He's just killed a man and badly injured another, and he had no idea why.

After ten minutes of silence, Ryan crept down to the door and peered through the small window. He couldn't see anything out of place and eased the door open. There was no one around. No man sucking his dying breaths through a crushed throat, no shattered teeth, no discarded pistol. Nothing. The only sign that an assault had taken place was the blood dripping from Ryan's wrist. He checked the wound. The wire had bitten deep into his flesh in a straight, thin line. If he held his hand out and flexed his wrist down, he thought he could see bone. His stomach lurched, and he quickly hyperflexed his wrist toward the elbow to close the wound. Pulling his tie from his suit coat pocket, he wrapped it around the cut and did his best to tie it off. Done with his makeshift triage, he punched the elevator button and stood with his back to the wall until the doors opened and he could step inside.

In his room, he went straight to the bathroom and ran water over the cut. "What the hell was that all about?" he asked the empty room while wrapping his wrist in a hand towel. He needed stitches to fix the deep cut. He changed into cargo shorts, a polo shirt, and a pair of worn boat shoes. He hurriedly packed his suitcase, then used the automated checkout on the television to close his room account before carrying his suitcase downstairs. He climbed into the rental car and headed for an urgent care center.

When he left the clinic, he had twenty stitches and a tightly wrapped white bandage to close his wound. The nurse gave him instructions for care, and the doctor signed a prescription for antibiotics and pain killers.

All Ryan wanted was a cold beer and a cigarette, and to know who was trying to kill him.

CHAPTER SEVEN

It was close to sunrise when Ryan finished picking up his prescriptions. He turned in his rental car and ordered an Uber. When the white Chevy Malibu arrived with a Middle Eastern man behind the wheel, Ryan hopped in and ordered the driver to make a few extra turns on the way to the Holiday Inn on Sixth Avenue to see if he was being followed. He wanted to leave Manhattan altogether, but he also wanted to be close to Karen's townhome if she decided to call. He'd give it one more day and then he was going back to Texas

Outside the hotel entrance, he satisfied his nicotine craving and watched for parked cars with occupants, or other suspicious actors. Done with his smoke, he checked in with a bleary-eyed, overweight woman behind the counter, bought a cold beer and a water from the small store, and went up to his room. After filling a plastic cup with beer and thinking about how cheap the hotel chain was for not having actual glasses in the room, he swallowed one of each of his pills. He ignored the "do not mix alcohol and antibiotics" warning on the pill bottles and washed them down with the beer.

Ryan shucked off his shorts and shirt, finished the beer,

and curled up under the covers. He was asleep within minutes.

The ringing of a phone brought him out of a deep sleep, and he fumbled for his cell phone. "Hello?"

"Is this Mr. Weller?" a female voice asked.

"Yes," Ryan sat up in bed.

"This is Karen Kilroy. You left your number with me yesterday."

"Uh, yeah, I did," he managed to stammer out in surprise.

"Do you know where the Cambria Hotel is?"

"Not really. I'm not from New York."

"It's on West Twenty-Eighth, between Sixth and Seventh."

"Okay."

"Meet me at the rooftop bar at nine this evening."

"Okay." Before he could ask more questions, the line went dead. He glanced at his watch, surprised to see it was almost five now.

At eight, Ryan sat at the inside bar adjacent to Cambria's rooftop lounge. A baseball game played on the television. Three people chatted in a circle at the far end of the room. Through the massive sliding glass doors, he could see the Manhattan skyline. On the open-air roof, white wicker chairs with black cushions were neatly aligned around black wicker tables. Several wicker couches faced the glass railing with an excellent view of the setting sun as it dropped below the skyscrapers.

He was partway through his second Stella Artois when his phone vibrated in his pocket.

"Hey, babe," he said in greeting.

"Where are you?" his girlfriend Emily Hunt asked.

"Manhattan."

"Why are you there?"

"Chasing a lead." He stepped out to the roof and sat in a wicker chair, sinking deep into the cushions. His gaze roved over the high rises, and he marveled at the round wooden water tanks that dominated the rooftops. He propped a foot on the wicker coffee table and took a sip of beer.

"Is everything okay?" Emily asked.

"Everything is fine." He glanced at his wrist. He'd put on a long-sleeved dress shirt to help cover the bandage.

"Are you sure? Shelly called me and said you were on a personal vendetta."

Ryan took a deep breath and closed his eyes as he let it out. "I'm working a case."

A waitress appeared at his side, and he considered ordering a third beer but decided to wait until Karen arrived. He covered the phone, told the waitress he was expecting company, and described Karen to her. She pocketed the Andrew Jackson he handed her as she walked away.

"Who are you meeting?" Emily asked when Ryan put the phone to his ear and told her he was back.

"The wife of the man we're tracking down."

"Ryan ..."

He could hear the displeasure in her voice. He'd been a hero not long ago. Now he was a rogue element on a vendetta, and the women were gossiping behind his back. Or Greg was using them as a conduit to express his displeasure.

"Everything is fine, Em. I'm going to talk to this woman and then get on a plane to Texas. From there, we're going to Belize."

"Just you, or you and Mango? Why isn't he with you right now?"

Ryan gazed out at the stunning view of the city. The buildings were ablaze with lights as far as he could see. "Greg, Mango, and I are going to Belize to meet with another source. That guy is supposed to put us in contact with our man." He didn't want to spell it all out, because he didn't know who was listening. After last attack night, he had to be on his toes.

"When are you leaving?"

"Shortly after I get back."

Her voice dripped with honey when she asked, "Do you have time to make a layover?"

Ryan laughed. "Absolutely!"

"Call me when you know your flight schedule."

"Will do, babe. I'll talk to you later."

"Bye, sweetie."

He hung up the phone and rolled his beer bottle around in his hands. He wasn't nervous about meeting Karen, but he didn't enjoy interviews or stakeouts. This was outside his purview. He was a diver, an explosives expert, a carpenter, and a sailor. He could talk to beautiful women, and he'd done his fair share of it, but this was something other than a date. He sipped his beer again. DWR had eyes everywhere and they were tasked with "see it, report it." He was the direct-action arm of the company. To him, action meant actively doing something, not poking around the edges with Aaron Grose and hiding out in a car to ambush a woman tending to her sick mother.

He was ready to get into Jim Kilroy's space and poke him. In the grand scheme of things, stopping one dealer wouldn't end the illicit arms trade. Another would crop up to take Kilroy's place, or two, or three. If history taught any lessons, it was that eventually arms dealers made a mistake and they were forced out of business, or arrested, or found dead with a bullet in the brain pan. It was Kilroy's time to find a new line of work.

Ryan shifted in his seat and fiddled with his phone. He'd downloaded an app that would allow him to record on his Android device. He plugged in his headphones and tested the system.

Twenty-five minutes later, the waitress delivered Karen Kilroy to Ryan's seat. She wore a black cocktail dress which she smoothed across her bottom as she sat in the chair beside him. Karen ordered a Cosmopolitan and Ryan ordered a third Stella. The waitress moved around the outside bar collecting empty glasses and bottles before returning inside. More patrons had arrived.

Ryan discreetly clicked on the recording app and draped his earbuds over the chair arm. He hoped they didn't pick up too much background noise. "What can I help you with, Mrs. Kilroy?"

"Call me Karen, please." She took a deep breath and blew it out through puffed-up cheeks. "Jim and I had a fight a couple of weeks ago. I left him and came up here."

"What did you fight about, Karen?"

She fixed her pale blue eyes on him, and Ryan understood Jim Kilroy's attraction to her. "I found out he was an international arms dealer."

"How long have you been married to him?" Ryan asked incredulously.

"Five years, next month. I knew Jim was a resort developer and had properties all over the Caribbean, but I didn't find out about his other business until I overheard one of his phone calls." She laid a hand on Ryan's. "I swear I didn't know he was supplying Arturo Guerrero's men."

She amused him. She was a well-educated woman, yet she spoke like a young socialite and added a bit of New York flavor, which made her sound like a sorority girl. He knew better than to underestimate a well-educated woman married to an international arms dealer.

"What was the phone call about?"

"He was talking to a man named Darren. Darren was supposed to make a delivery, and something happened which made Jim irate. I've never heard him tear someone down like that." She shook her head.

"And you confronted Jim about it?"

She stiffened and squeezed her eyes shut. After a moment, she said, "Yes."

The waitress set their drinks on the table. She smiled at Ryan and asked if he needed anything else. Ryan shook his head and the waitress moved away.

Karen leaned close to him and whispered, "Someone has a fan."

Ryan almost choked on his beer.

"Do you have a girlfriend?" Karen asked. "You're not married. You're not wearing a ring, anyway, and you have no tan line where a ring would be. What's your story?"

"I have a girlfriend," he replied.

Karen smiled coyly. "A good-looking guy like you probably has them waiting in line."

"I can only handle one at a time."

Karen laughed, leaned back in her chair, Cosmo in hand, and crossed her slim, tan legs. She took a sip while peering across the rim at Ryan.

Trying to get back on track, Ryan asked, "What happened when you confronted your husband?"

Karen took another drink and set the glass down on the coffee table. She leaned close to him. "He told me the truth. He supplies firearms, explosives, tanks, missiles, and even medical supplies to those who need them. He explained that at various times he works for the rebels and, at others, he works for the governments. It depends on the direction the wind is blowing and who's willing to pay the most money.

"I was angry at him and ran home to my mother. I was coming anyway. She's been getting radiation. She has cervical cancer, Ryan, and it's awful. Did you see how frail she looks?"

Ryan nodded.

"She's been through such a difficult time lately. I had to come back, even if I wasn't mad at Jim. I talked to my mother about it. She said it was just another part of his business. It is just business, isn't it? He has contracts, and much of what he does is legitimate. He sells guns like some sell cars, or houses, or blenders."

"People don't kill each other with blenders, Karen."

Her mouth turned down in a frown. "I see what you mean." She took another sip of the Cosmo. Ryan watched her lips curve over the rim of the martini glass again. She tilted her head back and drained the last bit of liquid, then waved the glass at the waitress.

When the waitress arrived, Karen said, "I'd like another and get him a beer as well."

The waitress looked at Ryan, who nodded. He watched her walk away, enjoying the sway of her hips under tight black dress pants.

"She's a looker. No doubt she'd give you her number."

"I don't doubt she would." He already had it in his pocket. She'd handed it to him before Karen arrived. "Tell me about Darren. What kind of business does he do for your husband?"

Karen tapped a manicured pink fingernail against her front tooth as she thought.

Ryan prompted again, "Tell me exactly what Jim said to him over the phone."

"My goodness." She frowned again and looked away to the horizon beyond the endless water barrels. "Let's see; I was going down to Jim's office at our home in the Bocas del Toro islands. That's in Panama, on the Caribbean coast. We have such a beautiful place there. Every morning I walk on the beach and say hello to the children. I teach English at one of the schools when they need help. It's wonderful.

"I wanted to tell Jim about the lobster we were going to

have for dinner. I'd just caught them myself. I love to scuba dive. Do you dive, Ryan?"

"Yes."

"Wonderful! It's so lovely, isn't it?"

"It is, Karen. Keep going."

"He left his office door open, which was unusual. I guess he thought I was going to be gone longer than I was. I heard him arguing with this Darren fellow. Jim was extremely upset because Darren hadn't made a delivery to some men in Colombia. He must have reassured Jim everything would be all right, because Jim quieted down and told him he'd better get the job done because he had another shipment ready to go out. This one was bigger than the Colombia one. Jim said it was the biggest arms deal he'd ever made. Something about Santo Domingo."

She stopped talking when the waitress placed their drinks on the table.

Ryan smiled at the waitress. She had a hippie name— Autumn, or Rainbow, or Flower. He couldn't remember.

"Anyway," Karen continued, "Jim told Darren the shipment must go out on time, or there would be repercussions. I don't know if he was talking about himself or Darren. I was frightened, Ryan. I'd never heard Jim speak about gun dealing or weapons. He doesn't like guns and said so many times. He doesn't even want the security guards at our resorts to carry them. He says it sends the wrong message to our clientele.

"I confronted him after he got off the phone. I asked him if he was selling weapons. He said not to worry about it, that it was just business. I didn't believe him. Not after he was so adamant about not having guns around. If he's selling guns and he gets caught, they can put him in jail, or take all his assets. I know. I read up on it. Google can be absolutely terrifying if you ask questions you don't really want to know the answers to."

She stopped to take a drink and catch her breath. Ryan took a swallow of his beer, giving her time to stew over her thoughts, or collect the ones rattling around in her brain, then asked, "When's the shipment going out? The big one."

"I'm not sure. Jim said something about going to Belize to meet Darren. We have a property on Caye Caulker—it's a partnership, really. It's the only place in Belize that I know Jim goes. I go there at least once a month to scuba dive. The owner, Aaron, and I are close friends."

Ryan tried to remain relaxed. The dominos were starting to fall. Karen had just connected Jim Kilroy to Aaron Grose in his gunrunning scheme. "Does Aaron help Jim deal guns?"

"I know Aaron really well. We helped him start a diving resort called Caye Caulker Adventures. He's a super good guy. I can't imagine him dealing guns with Jim. Maybe he does. I don't know." She sipped her drink again.

Ryan kept silent and let her fill the void.

"Aaron was teaching diving at a resort in Cozumel when I met him. He tried to get in my pants. He is such a looker. Kind of like you, all rugged and handsome. You both have the same roguish smile. Well, I took him to meet Jim because I knew he and Jim would get along. Jim wanted him to guide us down in Belize. Aaron said he didn't know much about Belize, and that he had a job. Jim told him to quit, so he did. He was looking for something new and we were a way for him to move on. At that time, we were living on our boat, *Northwest Passage*. Aaron moved aboard, and we went down to Belize.

"Jim was scouting for property down there, and well, Aaron fell in love with Cay Caulker and decided to build a dive resort there. Jim wanted to help, of course, and gave Aaron an excellent deal on financing. Aaron has done really well for himself and has been paying Jim back, with interest."

Talking and drinking seemed cathartic for her.

She glanced at her watch. "Oh, my. I promised Mother I wouldn't be gone long. Here I am, talking up a storm."

Ryan leaned close to her and she jumped when he placed a hand on her arm. "It's fine, Karen."

She pulled away. "Sorry, I need to go."

"Will you be all right? Can I call you a taxi?"

"No, no, I'll be fine." She stood. "It'll take more than two of those weak drinks to do me in."

Ryan rose, too. "Thanks for talking to me."

They headed toward the elevator.

"You won't arrest Jim, will you? He says he has the protection of the U.S. government."

"He may enjoy that protection now, but one day the political winds of fortune will change, and he won't be so lucky."

She cast her eyes down and clasped her hands together in front of her. "Oh, dear. I suppose you're right."

Ryan pushed the button to call the elevator. "Karen?"

She turned to face him.

"Should we see each other again, please forget we ever had this talk. Forget you even know me."

"What an odd thing to say."

"Wouldn't it seem odder if you were to recognize me, and had to explain to your husband how you told a stranger about his business?"

"I don't suppose he'd approve."

Ryan nodded. "Good night, Karen."

"Good night, Ryan Weller." She giggled conspiratorially and stepped into the elevator.

Ryan returned to his seat, and the waitress immediately approached. Ryan ordered another beer and watched her work. Her nametag had said Arielle. His thoughts turned to Emily Hunt, a tall, lithe Viking princess with hair the color of ripened wheat and cornflower-blue eyes.

She was the lead investigator for Ward and Young, a major

insurance provider based in Tampa, Florida. Part of his earlier investigation into the theft of sailboats had put Ryan in her office. They'd hit it off, and she'd spent time on his sailboat before he and Mango sailed into harm's way in the Gulf of Mexico in search of the Aztlán cartel's pirate ship.

The waitress placed his beer and the check presenter on the coffee table. He laid a DWR company credit card inside the card sleeve. She disappeared with his plastic and returned with more slips of paper and his card. He signed the receipt and sipped his beer until it was gone. Then he left a cash tip and the napkin with her phone number on it under his empty glass.

CHAPTER EIGHT

Summer sun baked the mountains and valleys around Dubois, Wyoming. Temperatures hovered in the mid-seventies, but to Aaron, the sun on his bare skin felt like tropical heat. Thinner air at higher elevations let the sun burn the skin as quickly as it did at the equator. Aaron sat in the shade of the porch roof that spanned the length of the long, low ranch home, thinking about his current predicament.

He had some money saved up, and he'd had a good run owning a first-class resort, one he'd built with his own hands, carving a niche into the dive-and-adventure market in Belize. It would be tough to walk away. He could buy a sailboat and get lost in the South Pacific.

His mother laid a hand on his shoulder, startling him. "Is everything okay, dear?"

"It's fine, Mom." He patted her hand and took the glass of lemonade she offered him.

"I'm so glad you're home. I tried for years to get your father to let me come see you in Belize. He said if you weren't man enough to come home, then there was no need to spend money to go see you."

"I'm sorry, Mom. I should have come home and ..." Aaron trailed off. As soon as he'd walked in the door, his father was on him, badgering him about not coming home, about running away, about living in a foreign country, and how scuba diving was not a good career choice. Clay deemed Aaron's time wasted for not helping with the family's farm.

"I know why you left. I understand." She patted his shoulder again.

He looked in her eyes and saw pain from years of torment. She, too, had endured his father's wrath and the years of separation. He was about to say more when the telephone rang inside the house.

"I need to get that." She turned away and went through the front door. A minute later, she was back. "It's for you, dear."

Aaron rose. "Thanks, Mom, I'll take it in the study."

Sinking into the overstuffed leather chair, he could smell the years of whiskey and cigar smoke oozing from the walls. He'd loved this room as a child, this room where his father would pay bills or tell stories about Aaron's grandpa and great grandpa, about the wars they fought and the lives they lived. Aaron had wanted to live as big as they had.

He picked up the receiver. "Hello, this is Aaron."

"Aaron, this is Commander Larry Grove. How are you?"

"I'm good. Can I ask you a favor?"

"Sure, what can I do for you?"

"I need to know about two guys: Ryan Weller and Floyd Landis. They're trying to get me to help them break up a gunrunning scheme." Aaron pictured the man at the end of the phone line. Grove was a member of the Navy SEAL's elite Naval Special Warfare Development Group, more commonly known as DEVGRU, formerly SEAL Team Six. He was a tall, lean man with a broad smile, blond hair, and ice-blue eyes. He had earned the nickname Iceman. Not only did he look like

Val Kilmer's character in *Top Gun*, but he was also cool under pressure. Aaron had met Larry last year when Larry and several of his SEALs had shown up at his resort for some down time after a training exercise with the Belize Gang Suppression Unit.

Grove sighed. "I can tell you that I know both of these gentlemen. Landis is a Homeland Security agent, and Weller's a true warrior. I served with him in the Navy when he was in Explosive Ordnance Disposal. He got out after getting shot in Afghanistan. He works for Dark Water Research in Texas City, Texas, and coordinates jobs for Homeland with Landis as his handler. If these dudes are stepping on your toes, you better be paying attention."

"Do you remember meeting Jim Kilroy when you were in Belize?"

"Yes." The phone went silent as Grove came to understand the situation. "When did you find out?"

"Two days ago," Aaron replied. "Weller and Landis cornered me in Atlanta after I cleared customs and they threatened me with tax evasion if I don't inform on him." Aaron went on to detail the whole encounter, then asked Larry for advice.

Larry said simply, "Do what they ask, Aaron."

CHAPTER NINE

Greg Olsen and Mango Hulsey found Ryan Weller in the workshop of Ryan and Mango's office. The unit was in a small commercial complex close to downtown Texas City. It consisted of a large office which Ryan had claimed when he was first hired, two office cubicles at the front entrance, one of which Mango occupied, and the garage in the back. The garage contained a workshop, gear lockers, a compressor for filling scuba tanks, and a large well-stocked, walk-in gun vault.

On the workbench in front of Ryan was a carton of Camel Blue cigarettes. To his left he'd stacked eight of the ten packs in a row of four, two high. He had the ninth in front of him and the tenth sat off to the right. An unlit cigarette dangled from his mouth.

He didn't look up as they approached.

"So much for quitting," Mango scoffed.

Ryan ignored him and continued sliding the plastic wrapper over the top of the ninth pack. When he had it positioned where he wanted it, he used a small line of glue to secure the wrapper back in place.

"Whatcha doing?" Greg asked.

"Packing for the trip."

Greg shook his head. "You know they sell cigarettes in Belize, right?"

"Yeah." Ryan finished sealing the pack and slid off his stool. He went to a locker and pulled a small electronic device from it, then returned to the workbench and sat back down. Greg bumped his wheelchair's footrest into Ryan's stool and stretched his body to see what Ryan was working on. Mango positioned himself on the other side of his teammate.

"You guys are blocking the light," Ryan growled.

Greg said, "Excuse us for being interested in what you're doing, employee."

Ryan reached for an architect's lamp. He positioned it over the small device. Next, he used a jeweler's screwdriver to remove a small panel from the pager-sized component. He replaced the tiny battery and screwed the cover back down. After tightening the last screw, he rotated the device and turned it on. It took several minutes before the screen read *Connected*. Ryan used a small slidable keyboard to type a message.

A minute later, Greg's phone buzzed with an incoming text message. He read it and smiled, shaking his head. "No. I won't do what you just suggested."

"What did it say?" Mango asked.

"He told me to screw myself."

"Nice, bro." Mango laughed. "What is that?"

"The latest in high-tech satellite tracking and communications," Ryan said as he powered it off. "It can leave a GPS trail, send an S.O.S. to the GEOS International Emergency Response Center, or send a burst message like I just did."

He dumped the cigarettes out of the tenth pack and slid the device inside, then cut off a cigarette near the filter and slid it in on top of the device. Pulling it out, he trimmed it a little more. He was able to fit two full cigarettes into the pack, and the rest he cut to fit. Then he glued the pared down smokes into their normal shape as they would be seen in the pack. When the quick-set glue had dried, he slid the butts into the pack and arranged the silver foil over them to make the pack appear unopened. He sealed the outside cellophane wrapper with a reusable gum substance.

"Very cool," Mango said. "You'd never know there was a communications device in there." He picked up the pack and compared its weight to a pack from Ryan's neat stack. "The weight is off with both of them. What's in those?"

Ryan smiled. "Party favors."

"Do tell," Greg said.

Ryan began packing the loose packs into the carton box. He put the communicator in next to last. He held up the last pack. "This is the only actual pack of cigarettes in the carton."

"Someone's going to check those," Mango said. "They'll know you screwed with the packs."

"I'm not going to worry about it," Ryan replied, sliding off the stool. He lit the Camel hanging from his lips and turned on the exhaust fan.

Greg pointed at the bandage on Ryan's arm. "What happened to your wrist?"

"Cut myself shaving."

Ryan's flippancy annoyed Greg. "Seriously?"

"No, some dudes jumped me. One tried to run me over, one tried to shoot me, and the other tried to strangle me with a garotte. I got my arm in the loop and got this little souvenir." He held up his arm.

"Why'd they jump you?" Mango asked.

Ryan took a long drink from a cup. "I've been trying to figure that out myself."

"When did you get back?" Greg asked.

"About two o'clock this morning. I was too wired to sleep and came here."

Mango inquired, "How did it go with your new lady friend?"

"I'll let you guys listen to the tape." Ryan retrieved a two-liter bottle of Mountain Dew from the refrigerator and refilled his cup. He grabbed several slices of cold pizza before he shut the door.

He led them into his office and used his laptop to play the digital recording of his conversation with Karen Kilroy.

When the recording ended, Greg asked, "Do you know who Darren is?"

Ryan finished chewing his mouthful of pizza and washed it down with soda. "Landis made some calls. His name is Darren Parsons. He's worked for Kilroy for several years."

"What's the plan from here?" Mango asked.

"We know Parsons and Kilroy are making a shipment of some kind," Ryan said. "According to Karen, it's the largest Kilroy's ever done. It sounds like it might be leaving from Belize. I don't have any straight answers. Aaron Grose is going to give us more information when we get down there. Speaking of which, has anyone made flight reservations?"

Mango said, "Greg says we're taking *Dark Water* to Belize."

"I think we're going to need a base of operations and the use of a boat," Greg justified. "It'd be better to have something we can all get around on."

Ryan wiped his hands on a napkin. "Are you up for this? I don't want you to get sick again."

Mango cut in. "Don't you have a day job?"

"I quit." Greg crossed his arms and challenged both men with hard stares.

"What did Shelly have to say?" Ryan asked.

Greg crossed his arms. "I hired Kip Chatel to be DWR's new president."

Ryan asked, "The same Kip Chatel we served under?"

"Yes, after he retired from the Navy, he went to work for Boeing. He was moving up the management ladder there, and I thought he would be a good fit for us. I had Shelly and Cliff show him around, and he said he'd take the job."

"All right." Ryan stared back. "Are you still the boss?"

"I own the controlling interest in DWR, so yes, I'm still your boss."

Mango watched the standoff with a grin on his face.

"Okay." Ryan broke the staring contest. "Did you know the world's second largest barrier reef is off the coast of Belize?"

"Have you dove there?" Mango asked Ryan.

"I was there briefly when I was sailing around the world. I dove the Blue Hole and a few sites around Ambergris Cay."

Ryan used a legal pad to make a list of what they would need for the boat trip. When he got to guns, Greg leaned over and looked at his scribbles.

"I forgot to tell you about some cool new toys I picked up." Greg pushed his wheelchair toward the gun locker.

Ryan and Mango followed. Once inside the garage area, Ryan flipped on an exhaust fan and lit a cigarette.

"Come on, bro," Mango chided. He'd been on Ryan to quit smoking since the day they'd met.

Inside the small concrete gun vault, Greg picked up a KRISS Vector carbine and handed it to Ryan. Ryan racked the slide back on the tan-and-black weapon to check the chamber for a round. When he saw the chamber and magazine were empty, he brought the stock to his shoulder and looked through the holographic sight. "Nice piece. It's unique."

"Yes, it is," Greg replied. He took the gun back and wrapped his right hand around the pistol grip. He pointed with his left index finger at a boxy area just forward of the trigger. "This is where they hide their recoil mitigation system. Instead of having the standard recoil spring that drives straight back through the buttstock, like the M4, the spring is housed vertically in front of the trigger, which drives the recoil down, helping to keep muzzle rise in check when shooting on full automatic, or during rapid fire in semi-auto mode." Greg thumbed the magazine release and the empty mag dropped out. He held it between his thumb and forefinger. "This beauty takes Glock mags. In this case, nine-millimeter. Standard capacity is seventeen, plus one in the chamber."

Mango picked up another KRISS. "When do we get to shoot 'em, bro?"

"Whenever you want. I have three of these and a pistol version in .45."

"We should add these to our loadout for Belize," Ryan said.

"That's what I got them for," Greg said.

"Cool." Mango sat down and began feeding nine-millimeter hollow-point cartridges into magazines.

Ryan stretched and yawned. "It's been a long day. Let's get out of here."

In truth, he was tired from the late-night flight to Tampa, the short day with Emily, and another red-eye to Houston. He'd been up the better part of thirty hours.

"I'm going with you," Greg said. "I have to drop Mango off at his boat."

"I caught an Uber here," Ryan said. "My Jeep is still at DWR."

"I know," Greg said. "You woke me up when the alarm went off, and I checked the cameras."

The three men went out to Greg's Chevrolet SS. The four-hundred-and-fifteen horsepower, four-door sedan had a six-speed automatic transmission with paddle shifters and custom controls for Greg to operate the gas and brakes with his hands. Greg liked to drive it hard and fast. It never took long to cover the short distance between Ryan's office and DWR, and even less time to traverse the twelve miles to their home on Tiki Island.

When Greg's grandfather had recruited Ryan to help run DHS operations, Ryan was living on his thirty-six-foot Sabre sailboat, *Sweet T*, in Wilmington, North Carolina. Upon moving to Texas, he'd bunked with Greg at Greg's Tiki Island home until he could move his sailboat to Texas. Mexican pirates had sunk *Sweet T*, and Ryan continued to live in his friend's house while he searched for a new boat.

Greg settled into the driver's seat. Ryan broke down the wheelchair and put it in the backseat. When Ryan slid into the passenger seat, Greg held up a pistol version of the KRISS Vector. It had a clear, extended magazine loaded with blunt-nose hollow-point .45 rounds.

"What are you going to do with that?" Mango asked, leaning forward between the two front seats.

"I'm using it for protection." Greg grinned. He shoved the gun between the driver's seat and the center console and fired up the engine. He bumped the transmission in reverse and backed out of the parking space. Ten minutes later, they were at DWR and cleared through the security gate.

After dropping Mango off, Greg drove west on a blacktop top feeder road flanked by a canal on the left and a field of oil storage tanks on the right. As he approached State Route 197, Greg slowed just enough to look both ways for traffic, then gunned the engine and turned left without stopping.

Ryan glanced over his shoulder to see a four-door Ford pickup truck with oversized off-road tires and a lightbar turn out of the tank farm's driveway. He kept watching the truck in the passenger side rearview mirror. Vehicles like it were commonplace in the oil fields and refinery parking lots. This one was barreling down on them.

Greg jammed the hand control down, and the sedan accelerated away from the pickup. Ryan glanced at the speedometer. They were doing almost seventy miles per hour.

Ryan looked down when his phone chimed with a text message from Emily asking if he had safely returned to Texas. He was in the middle of thumbing a promise to call her this evening when he felt Greg tap the brakes. He glanced up to see a pickup pull out of a turnoff in front of them on the east side of the road. There was another truck hidden by the first, which Ryan could only see when the lead truck pulled away. Instead of turning to go north, the truck swung into the southbound lane and stopped. The second pickup pulled its front bumper up to the rear of the first, effectively blocking all four lanes of traffic.

They couldn't use the shoulder to go around the trucks, not with water-filled ditches running along both sides of the blacktop. With no other option, Greg slammed on the brakes. The car's tires screamed in protest as they started to slide on the pavement. Greg spun the wheel hard in a U-turn.

Through the driver's side window, Ryan saw the Ford closing on them. Smoke poured off the right-side tires as the Chevy SS leaned harder on them. The acrid stench of burned rubber filled their nostrils.

The back window of the sedan exploded as gunfire began to hammer the car. Ryan watched the big Ford veer into their lane in an attempt to hit them head-on. More bullets slammed into the car. Side windows burst, and glass cascaded onto the two men. A shot sent the passenger side mirror spinning off the Chevy. Men leaned out the side windows of the four-door Ford and aimed more guns at them.

Greg strung together curses as he ducked behind the wheel. He had extensive evasive driver training and was putting all his skills to work, but three trucks full of shooting guns made his efforts almost worthless. Ryan snatched up Greg's KRISS Vector and used the barrel to knock out the remaining glass from his side window. Leaning out, he began pumping lead at the oncoming truck.

The two vehicles aimed straight at each other now, and the gunfire had died down. Ryan guessed it was because the men didn't want to hit their companions in the other vehicles. Greg's hand mashed the accelerator, and he used the paddle shifters to keep the engine's RPMs high. The big V-8 roared in protest.

Ahead of them, the truck's massive steel bumper grew larger in the Chevrolet's fractured windshield as they engaged in a high-speed game of chicken. Ryan brought the rifle barrel down a fraction and fired at the truck's front tires and grill. Two bullets found their mark in the front left tire. The tire lost pressure, and rubber shredded off the rim, causing the truck to veer into the ditch. Its front end slammed into the mounded earth, sending a cascade of dirt and water into the air. The rear tires lifted off the ground with the impact and twisted the truck sideways when they bounced back against the berm.

The Chevrolet fishtailed as Greg accelerated away from the hail of bullets. "What the hell?" he screamed. "Those guys just killed my car!"

"We can get you a new car." Ryan twisted around in the seat. He watched as the driver and passenger of the wrecked Ford ran to the other trucks. The blocking trucks made K-turns and fled the scene.

"No, screw that. Those guys came after us on purpose. What's it all about?"

"I don't know, but if they're after us, they're probably after Mango." Ryan grabbed his phone from the floor, where it had fallen during the wild maneuvering, and dialed Mango's number. It went to voicemail. He dialed Jennifer, Mango's wife. It went to voicemail. Ryan redialed Mango's number. Voicemail picked up, and Ryan started in. "We just got ambushed. Stay inside and undercover. We're coming to you."

Greg must have known exactly what Ryan was thinking, because he accelerated to a breakneck speed considering the steam pouring from under the hood and the flop of rubber from a flat tire. Even though the car was equipped with run-flats, the self-sealing system could not accommodate two pencil-sized bullet holes. The flat tire caused the car to slew from side to side as he drove. He turned onto the access road leading to DWR and pushed the car to its limits.

It seemed to take forever to reach the gates to the DWR compound. The guard stepped out and looked over the car while pushing his ballcap up on his head. "Evenin', Mr. Olsen, seems like you're havin' some car trouble."

"Skip it, Tommy, just let me in," Greg snapped.

"Yes, sir." The guard slapped the button to open the gate and saluted.

Greg ignored the gesture and leaned out the window. "Tommy, if any strange vehicles come charging in here, try to stop them."

"With what, Mr. Olsen?" Tommy asked, holding his arms up in exaggerated questioning.

DWR had never hired armed security, believing the presence of security alone was enough to prevent theft and destruction. The isolated nature of DWR's compound was also a deterrent.

"Keep your head down and run away if someone tries to crash the gate."

"Yes, sir," Tommy said, a quiver in his voice.

Greg gunned the engine and felt the front right tire slide on the pavement before it began to roll. He managed to limp his car into his designated parking space.

"Can you get your chair?" Ryan asked, kicking open the door.

"Yeah. Go." Greg waved.

Ryan hopped out of the car carrying the KRISS Vector with a fresh magazine Greg had produced from the glove box. He glanced at the shattered and bullet-riddled vehicle and wondered how they'd survived. He ran toward Mango's sailboat. The blue, steel-hulled Amazon 44 sat beside *Dark Water*, a Hatteras GT63. In the evening sunlight, both boats gleamed bright and clean.

"Mango," Ryan yelled.

Mango appeared in the Amazon's cockpit and looked for the man calling his name. He turned slightly, held his arms out from his body, and shrugged.

Then he ducked down as a shot rang out. The bullet whined as it ricocheted off steel.

Ryan threw himself flat on the ground and brought the pistol up. He scanned for the shooter, knowing the weapon he had in his hands was useless against a long-range sniper.

CHAPTER TEN

G reg Olsen pulled the titanium frame of his wheelchair from the back seat. He drew it across his chest, careful to avoid smashing it into the steering wheel, and set it on the ground outside the car. Next, he reached back for the rear wheels and cushion. He placed these in the front seat and reached for the frame again. He unfolded the chair's seat back then pushed the right side tire's quick release axle into the frame's axle tube and did the same for the left side. He loved the push-button quick releases on the rim's axles, which allowed the tires to slip on and off with ease. He positioned the chair beside the car and locked the brakes, tossed the cushion on, and transferred from the car's leather bucket seat to the wheelchair. The entire process took him seven minutes. He'd timed it on several occasions.

The report of a gunshot made him stop. He knew Ryan wasn't carrying a rifle, and Mango had a stainless Mossberg Marine twelve-gauge shotgun on the sailboat as well as his Glock 17 pistol. Neither of those firearms made the distinct sound he'd just heard.

Greg raced across the massive aircraft hangar converted

to DWR's headquarters. The elevator was still on the first floor where he'd left it. The doors slid open when he punched the *UP* button. A minute later he was on the second floor, pushing hard for his office. He habitually carried a Sig Saur P320 concealed on his body, but he needed more firepower for the current threat. Inside his office, he opened a cabinet drawer and pulled out two loaded magazines for the Barrett 98B.

The elevator was waiting for him, and he rode to the rooftop deck. Greg knew there was only two possible directions the sniper's bullet could have come from. Both would involve infiltrating an oil tank farm—either the one directly to the west, which didn't have the best line of sight, or the one across Industrial Canal. The latter was where he believed the shooter was hiding. He set the gun's bipod on the counter of the outdoor kitchen used to serve a hot lunch to DWR employees every Friday.

Before he began scanning for the sniper, he looked over the edge of the building and saw Ryan lying on the pavement. He was halfway between the building and Mango's sailboat, and totally exposed.

Greg could not see Mango, so he called his cellphone.

Mango growled, "What the hell, bro?"

"Any idea where the shot came from?" Greg asked.

"No, and I don't want to poke my head up for him to get a second look."

"Keep down, and I'll try to spot him."

"My guess is he's across the canal to the north."

"Copy." Greg put the phone on speaker and set it on the counter.

———

RYAN LEAPED to his feet and sprinted toward the cover of the boat docks. The sniper's rifle boomed again. He dove to the ground, rolling to avoid scraping his hands and shins on the coarse blacktop. His still-sore shoulders and ribs screamed at him. His wrist began to bleed while sending daggers of pain up his arm. The gun sounded again, and the pavement in front of Ryan's face exploded. He clamped his hands to his eyes as he writhed on the pavement.

———

GREG HAD NOT SEEN the shot come within a hair's breadth of hitting his friend. He was busy scanning the rooftops of the oil storage tanks across the river. He'd narrowed the location down, based on the booming echo of the rifle's report.

Police sirens floated on the stiff eastern breeze.

Across Industrial Canal, two- and three-story oil storage tanks sprouted out of the ground. Each tank had a stairway curving up its flank. Greg watched for movement, running the scope quickly over the tops of the tanks. He stopped on a light gray tower at the edge of the canal. A shooter lay sprawled under a gray tarp. Greg might have missed it except for a corner of the tarp flapping in the breeze, exposing a jeans-clad leg and a black shoe. Greg took a second to examine the sniper hide. The tarp had been stretched to cover the man and the gun, forming a small tent over the scope and barrel. Greg was thankful the shooter had chosen to forego a silencer, by doing so, given away his position.

Greg focused his scope's crosshairs on the center mass of the prone man. Factoring the wind, humidity, and angle of flight for the bullet, Greg made the calculations in his mind and matched them to the dope card taped to his gun's stock, where he had recorded detailed performance data based on the aforementioned factors, allowing him to adjust his scope hold based on previous shots at the same distance.

He inhaled, allowed half a breath to escape, and held the rest. Between beats of his heart, he stroked the trigger.

The big gun bucked against his shoulder. Across the river, the covered lump twitched once and stopped moving. Greg watched through the scope and said, "I got him!"

"Keep your eye on him," Mango said. "Ryan's hit. I'm going after him."

Greg took his eye off the scope and looked for his friend. He found Ryan lying on the pavement with his right hand clamped to the side of his face, a crimson stain turning his neck and hand red.

Greg pressed his eye to the scope again. "Shit!" The tarp flapped in the breeze, and the sniper had disappeared.

CHAPTER ELEVEN

Mango ran across the lot and dropped to his knees beside Ryan. "You okay, bro?"

"I got something in my freakin' eye." Ryan continued to press the palms of his hands to his eyes to stop the pain.

"Hang tight, buddy. We need to stop the bleeding. Let me take a look."

Ryan rolled onto his back and pulled his right hand away from his face. Chunks of asphalts had sliced open spots on his cheek and forehead. Both wounds bled freely but were not life-threatening.

"Can you open your eye?"

Ryan raised his eyelid and grit ground against his cornea. It felt like a small boulder had lodged itself behind the lid. Tears flowed as his body tried to wash out the foreign debris. He closed the eye and rolled to a seated position.

"Come on, bro, let's get you cleaned up and see if we can flush out your eye."

"What about the sniper?"

"Greg nailed him." Mango helped Ryan to his feet, and

they walked across the lot to the restrooms on the first floor of the DWR building. Ryan washed his face, then positioned his eye under a trickle of water to help flush out whatever was causing the abrasion. Mango went in search of a first aid kit.

The water did not help. After Ryan toweled his face off, Mango cleaned his two cuts with hydrogen peroxide and applied bandages to them.

Greg parked in the door to watch the proceedings. His cell phone rang. "Hello?"

Even without the speaker on Ryan could hear the conversation.

"Mr. Olsen, this is Tommy at the gate. There's an ambulance and two police cars who want to come in."

"Send them to the hangar, Tommy."

"Yes, sir."

Greg shut off the phone and clipped it to his belt. "We're about to have company."

Ryan, Mango, and Greg went out to the parking lot and watched the three vehicles come to a stop at the front entrance. Ryan used his left eye and kept his right covered with his hand. It felt better to have it covered. He was unsure if the slight blurriness in his left eye was from washing it out, or if he was getting old.

Two uniformed officers, one male, and one female, stepped out of a Texas City Police Department Ford Explorer after shutting off the light bar. Two men exited an unmarked Dodge Charger, and a man and a woman scrambled from the ambulance.

"What's the emergency, Detective Schlub?" Greg asked.

The barrel-chested man with a bushy mustache reminded Ryan of a short Tom Selleck, a Magnum P.I. wannabe. He wore blue jeans and a blue-and-red checkered dress shirt with the sleeves rolled up to his elbows. On his hip was a Heckler and Koch USP 9, two spare mags for the gun, and a set of handcuffs.

His partner was tall and lean, with a long, sloping nose on a narrow face. He was dressed in an ill-fitting gray suit. His jacket bulged around his handgun.

"Mind if we have a word, Greg?" Tom Selleck asked.

"Better bring the medics," Greg said. "Ryan has something in his eye."

The woman paramedic motioned for Ryan to sit down on the ambulance's back bumper. She pulled on a pair of latex gloves and used a flashlight to look in Ryan's eye.

Ryan read the nameplate on her shirt. "See anything, Lucy?"

"I see some grit. Have you tried flushing it?"

"Yes. Nothing came out."

"I want to flush it again." She produced a small bottle of saline with a tube on the end, and had Ryan lie on his back. Holding up his eyelid, she squirted liquid into his eye. After a short flush, she let go of his eyelid. "Any better?"

Ryan fluttered his eyelid. It still felt like closing it on a gravel pile. "No."

"You need to see a doctor to get those pieces out. What got in your eye?"

"Asphalt."

"How did that happen?"

Ryan sat up and covered his eye with his hand. "I tripped."

"The same way you got the cut on your wrist?" She pointed at the blood-stained bandage.

"No, I cut myself shaving."

"Very funny." Lucy unwrapped the bandage and examined the sutured wound. After cleaning off the fresh blood, she rewrapped it. Noticing Ryan digging his palm into his eyes, she said, "Try not to rub it. The grit can scratch the cornea."

Ryan asked, "Did you guys check on the truck in the ditch on 197?"

"We did," Schlub said. "There wasn't anyone in it. Plenty of blood, though."

Lucy packed away her kit then tried to flush Ryan's eye again. The grit didn't move. She handed him a towel to wipe off his face.

"Thanks, Lucy." Ryan stood.

"You need to see a doctor," she replied as she repacked her kit.

Detective Schlub and his partner stepped over as the paramedic put away her kit. Ryan thought the partner defined the term hatchet-faced.

"Some party you went to, Greg," Schlub said, pointing at the ruined sedan.

Greg deadpanned, "I think they were gunning for us."

"You like to crack jokes, Mr. Olsen?" Hatchet Face asked, his tone low and menacing. "I don't think it's very humorous when someone starts shooting up my district."

"Calm down, Joe," Schlub said. "Didn't you see that poor car over there? Looks like Greg was the one getting shot at. Greg Olsen, this is Detective Joe Schroeder."

"Nice to meet you, Detective. This is Ryan Weller and Mango Hulsey. Ryan was with me in the car."

"We need statements from both of you," Schroeder said.

"If you don't mind, George," Greg said, "I'd like to send Ryan to the doctor to get his eye looked at. I'll give you a statement, and you can get his later. I'll have him come down to the station."

"Very accommodating of you." Schlub pulled a small spiral notepad and pen from his shirt pocket.

"I'll drive you, Ryan," Mango volunteered.

"Take him to see Doctor Foster," Greg told Mango. "I'll call him and let him know you're coming."

. . .

DOCTOR FOSTER FLIPPED Ryan's eyelid inside out and used water and a cotton swab to clean a speck of asphalt off the back of the lid, then used a fluorescein stain to find two specks on the cornea. Both the lid and the cornea were flushed with water and stained again before the doctor declared Ryan's eye debris-free and flipped the eyelid down.

Ryan squeezed his eyes shut before blinking rapidly. "You got it."

The doctor clapped Ryan on the back. "Glad to be of service."

Back outside, Ryan told Mango to drive to the oil storage field across the canal from DWR. Ryan showed the guard his DWR badge and said, "We're checking a pipe for a potential leak."

The guard, accustomed to seeing DWR personnel passing through his gate, waved them through. Mango wove his way through the clusters of tanks to the canal, where they climbed up to the sniper's hide and knelt by the gray tarpaulin. It was held down at the two rear corners by two-pound cloth bags filled with steel shot. Two more weighted pouches lay askew at the head of the tarp.

A Knight Armament M-110 semi-automatic sniper rifle lay on the steel roof beside a spotting scope. A stain of red blood marred the otherwise smooth surface.

"Greg hit him at least," Mango said.

"Yeah, he must be slipping. Guess you need to work with him some more." Ryan lay down behind the gun, careful to stay out of the blood pool, and peered through the spotting scope. The gun was aimed at the spot in the parking lot where Ryan had cowered. He guessed the sniper had dialed in the scope for Mango's boat, and when the sniper had shifted to shoot him, he didn't properly adjust for windage and distance.

Ryan climbed to his feet, rolled the rifle and spotting scope in the tarp, and carried them down to the truck. "I was hoping this guy would give us a clue as to who's hunting us."

CHAPTER TWELVE

The Hatteras had two staterooms, one in the bow and one on the starboard side. Both had their own attached heads. On the port side were two bunk rooms with two beds each and a shared head. The V-berth stateroom and bathroom had been modified for wheelchair accessibility, and Mango had claimed the starboard stateroom. Ryan didn't mind the bunk room. It had more room than his old sailboat. He tossed his backpack on the bunk and dropped a duffle bag full of clothes on the deck. He stored the clothes in drawers under the bed, along with personal hygiene items.

Greg used a small lift to lower himself down the stairs to the stateroom level from the salon and rolled into the stateroom. He carried two bags of his own and had a third strapped to the back of his chair. As he passed Ryan, he said, "Being a paraplegic requires a lot of extra crap."

Ryan leaned on the stateroom's door jamb and watched Greg maneuver around the small room. He was at a loss for words when Greg commented on his disability. "You sure you're up to this trip?"

Greg spun around to face Ryan. "I spent a lot of time on

this boat picking your ass out of the Gulf of Mexico last month. Pretty sure I can handle a few days to Belize."

"You could always fly down and meet us."

Greg shook his head. "No way."

Mango jumped in to defend Greg. "Come on, bro, the man says he's good to go."

"Leave it to the gimps to stick together."

Greg and Mango both flipped Ryan the bird.

"I got more gear to load, so you guys enjoy your party in here." Ryan grinned at them before walking up to the salon. "Freakin' gimps," he muttered.

Mango leaned out the stateroom door. "I heard that, ya able-bodied jerk."

They loaded scuba tanks, dive gear, boxes of food, water, and beer, along with guns and ammunition. They stored the last items lockers concealed beneath bunks and in canisters built to look like plumbing in the engine room. These smuggler's holds kept prying eyes from seeing the weaponry. Many countries considered the possession of firearms a jailable offense. While the men preferred not to break the law in their host countries, they also wanted to protect themselves from others who would do them harm.

"You boys leaving so soon?"

Ryan looked up the stairs from the stateroom level to see George Schlub standing in the Hatteras's salon. The detective wore jeans and a black vest over a navy checked dress shirt. "We're going down to Belize."

"Belize." Schlub shook his head. "Well, that's real nice, fleeing the country during an investigation. Belize is an extradition country."

"We have our own work to do, Detective," Ryan said.

Schlub looked around the salon, taking in the opulent finishes. "Nice boat you have. I never understood why they call it a salon when its spelled saloon."

"We're all confused about that one," Greg replied.

"What did you call it in the Navy?" Schlub asked.

"Captain's quarters," Mango quipped.

"Good one." Schlub turned to Ryan. "You haven't been to my office like Greg promised."

"Did Greg give you a statement?"

"Yes." Schlub nodded.

Ryan said, "Then that's how it went down."

"I'd like to hear it from you." Schlub leaned against the kitchen island and crossed his arms. "I'd like to hear how you got gravel in your eye. Rumor has it there were dueling snipers out here. Did you find the guy shooting at you?"

"We didn't," Ryan said.

"Would you tell me if you did?"

"Want a beer?" Ryan asked.

"No, I'm on duty."

Ryan popped the cap off a beer. He took a long swig. "Look, Detective, what did Greg call you, George?" Schlub nodded. "George, we have no idea who came after us. I'd tell you if I did. The sniper was gone when we found his hide, but he left his gun behind. Greg winged him. It was a fair fight, and he got away."

"That was police evidence. You tampered with a crime scene."

Ryan eyed the detective while he took another pull from his bottle. "No, George. It's a Homeland Security issue."

"I didn't realize you were a DHS agent."

"I'm not. We do enough work for the government that they consider us a national security interest. I called a DHS agent I know, and he took the gun off my hands."

"You're pulling that shit on me, huh?" Schlub shook his head. "I'm watching you Dark Water types. I don't need any more violence in my town than the normal drugs, murders, rapes, and suicides."

"Well, George, I can't make you any promises," Ryan said. He sipped the beer and watched the detective.

"Did Homeland tell you anything about the gun?" Schlub asked.

"No prints and no trace."

"No NICS?" Schlub asked, referring to the FBI's National Instant Criminal Background Check System, which potential gun buyers are processed through before they can purchase a gun from a licensed dealer.

"Nothing. Which doesn't mean anything. We know illegal weapons come into this country every day."

"Or," George said, "they bought it from a private seller."

"The gun was clean," Ryan said. "It's never been in the system. There were no prints on it."

"None on the cartridges?" Schlub asked. "That's where most people slip up."

"No, and the ammunition was a standard, off-the-shelf brand."

"What about hair and fibers?"

Ryan motioned Schlub to join him in the cockpit. Schlub leaned against the stainless-steel ladder to the bridge. He fished a stub of a cigar from his pocket and chewed on it while Ryan lit a cigarette. Ryan let out a stream of smoke and said, "The guy was lying under a gray tarp on that oil tank over there." He pointed out the tallest tank across the canal. "I rolled the gun and spotting scope into the tarp and took it to San Antonio for examination. They found standard cotton clothing fibers from cheap stuff at Walmart."

"Are you kidding?" Schlub asked. "This sounds too good to be true."

"I wish I was, Detective. This guy's a ghost. I want to know who's shooting at us just as much as you do, if not more."

Schlub looked at Greg and Mango, who were listening silently to the exchange. "You guys all on the same page?"

"Yes, we are," Greg said.

"What's happening in Belize?" Schlub wanted to know.

"Dive trip."

Schlub pulled the cigar stub from his mouth and rolled it in his fingers while staring thoughtfully at Ryan. He dropped the cigar into his pocket. "You boys be safe."

"We will, George. If we're not here, your town will be a little safer."

Schlub cocked his head. "That's one way of looking at it."

CHAPTER THIRTEEN

Volk watched José Luis Orozco scream at him. "You said you would kill him! You have not kept your promises! They were supposed to be dead. *Muerte*! *Muerte*! *Muerte*!" With each shouted word, his fists banged like gavels on the oak desk.

The giant Russian sat beside Eduardo Sanchez. Both were across the desk from Orozco. Volk was quickly tiring of the little man's antics and firmly believed he was in control of the cartel only because he was the most ruthless member. Close to the man's hand was his big revolver and a mirror with a small hill of cocaine on it. Each time Orozco had slammed his fists onto the desk, a small white cloud had blossomed from the pile. Volk was pleasantly surprised to see there were no hookers in the room with them. It was unimaginable that this tyrant would remain in power for long. Nevertheless, he was in control and paying the bounty hunter's bill.

Hatred burned in the cartel leader's black eyes. He grasped his goatee in a fist at the base of his chin. Two inches of hair stuck out the bottom of his hand and he stroked the hair several times in a soothing gesture.

"Calm down," Volk said. "You give yourself stroke."

"Calm down, *Lobo*? Calm down?" the man shouted. "I'm paying you a fortune to eliminate these men, and you've been thwarted at every turn."

"Hey, *Patrón*, dis Russian don't need to be in our business," Eduardo said. "We take care of our own. I tell you dis from da first day. We don't need no help."

"You know, what, Eduardo, you're right. *Lobo,* you need some competition. I'm going to offer a reward for *dos Yanquis*." He leaned forward, placing his forearms on the desk. Volk's expression did not change. "Two million dollars to the man who kills these *asesinos*."

"I will pass da message, *jefe*," Eduardo said as he stood.

"You want an international manhunt?" Volk asked.

"It might be better than what you've done so far."

"I will kill them. You pay my fee plus two million dollars."

Orozco shook his head. "I'll pay the bounty to whomever kills Ryan Weller and Mango Hulsey. If it's you, I'll pay you two million dollars."

"You pay me what you owe me," Volk thundered. He knew better than to do business with these hot-blooded Mexicans. These drug dealers were volatile and prone to mood swings. Instead of letting him do his job and track down the men he wanted killed, Orozco was changing the game and the terms of their contract. Volk leaned forward in his chair.

Orozco laid his hand on the pistol. "I will pay nothing for your failure. You can compete for the money like everyone else."

Volk ignored the pistol and stood. He strode to the office door and threw it open. "I take your money, and you pay me what you owe." He slammed the door as he walked out.

CHAPTER FOURTEEN

Juan Comacho stepped inside the dark interior of The Pitbull, a bar frequented by roughnecks, divers, and refinery workers in Texas City. He walked through the crowd and found a seat on a stool at the end of the bar. He watched the men shoot pool, drink beer, play cards, and pump quarters into the jukebox. Kid Rock screamed about being an illegitimate son of man. Comacho ordered a beer and sipped it while picking out his target.

A man in a DWR polo shirt and jeans sat at a table drinking with a woman Comacho decided was a hooker. She wasn't even a pretty one. He ordered two of what the man was drinking and ambled over to the table. He set a beer down in front of the man and told the hooker to beat it.

"What do you mean, bub?" the man demanded.

"I want to talk to you. After I get done, you can talk to the ... the lady."

The woman stood and snatched the full Bud Light off the table.

"Hey!" the man yelled.

"Leave it. I'll buy you another one." Comacho sat down across from the guy.

"Damn right you will." The man crossed his arms. His face turned sullen. "Whatcha want?"

Comacho set the other beer bottle on the table. "Here, have it. I didn't drink out of it."

The man grabbed the bottle and drained half of it. Comacho, who had watched him guzzle at least six bottles of Bud Light before he'd walked over, shook his head. No wonder the guy was talking to that girl. He had on his beer goggles.

"Whatcha want?" the man demanded again when he set down the bottle.

"Information. I'll make it worth your while." Comacho glanced around the bar. For two million dollars, he figured Texas City was now home to the world's largest hitman convention. He laid a folded one-hundred-dollar bill on the table under his palm and tilted his hand just enough for the guy to see it.

"Kinda information?" the guy slurred.

"Where did DWR's Hatteras go?" Comacho asked.

"The what?" He looked genuinely puzzled.

"The big sportfisher that was sitting at Dark Water's docks this morning. Where did it go?"

He shrugged. "Hell, if I know."

"What about Ryan Weller, Greg Olsen, and Mango Hulsey?"

"Oh, those guys." The man's eyes narrowed. The fog of booze seemed to clear away. "Got any more of those Ben Franklins?"

Comacho nodded. He pulled a second bill from his pocket.

The guy shrugged and drank his beer.

Comacho dug deeper and pulled out three more bills. He

kept them under the table and fanned all five for the man to count.

"Assholes went to Belize. Like they're on vacation, or some shit." He took a hit from the bottle. "I bust my ass all day long humping string to rigs, and all I see them do is ride around on that damned boat. You know what I mean? Like they're too good to work."

Comacho ignored the tirade. This was why he'd picked this drunk. He'd just looked disgruntled and he was. "Where in Belize?"

"Don't know." He shrugged.

Comacho flagged down a waitress and ordered two more beers. When she brought the long necks, Comacho told her he would pay his new friend's tab. She smiled and returned several minutes later with the bill. Comacho paid cash and left all five bills under his beer bottle. He had no doubt they would more than pay for the man's evening dalliance.

Walking from the bar, he glanced around once more. A foreign man sat in a corner, talking to another DWR worker. Money had a way of making people talk. These guys had no secrets to hide. Comacho thought they probably didn't even know there was a bounty for two of their coworkers.

Outside, Comacho climbed in his car. He started it and turned on the air conditioner, thankful for it sucking the humidity from the oppressive air. He drove across town to a hotel where he used a prepaid cell phone to dial his cousin, Andreas Zavala.

"*Hola, tipo, como estas,*" Hey, dude, how are you? Zavala asked.

"*Muy bien.*" *I'm good.* Comacho continued in Spanish. "Our friends are headed for Belize."

"Where?"

"I don't know. They're in a blue-and-white Hatteras sport-fisher named *Dark Water*. It shouldn't be hard to find."

"I'll have my *playadores* watch for it."

Comacho knew Zavala's beachcombers didn't look for shells or treasure, but parcels of drugs dropped by Columbia narcotics traffickers at set points to be picked up by their Mexican counterparts. Changing tides and weather conditions sometimes carried the packages away from the rendezvous location. They floated into the mangrove thickets and beaches along the Belizean coastline where the *playadores* recovered them and passed them on to Zavala.

"Good. I'll be there in twenty-four hours. We'll find these men and collect our bounty. We have some competition though. There's a Slavic-looking *güey* in the bar pumping a DWR guy for information, just like I did."

"He probably works for Volk. We'll need to move fast."

They spoke for a few more minutes before Comacho hung up the phone. He took out the battery and the sim card then carefully destroyed both. He dumped the pieces in separate trash cans on his way into the hotel.

CHAPTER FIFTEEN

Northwest Passage laid off Caye Caulker and dropped anchor. Jim Kilroy left the aft bridge and walked down the stairs to the main deck. A crewman helped attach the lift sling to the thirty-two-foot, yellow-and-white Yellowfin center console boat. Jim held the sling in place while the crewman scampered to the crane and maneuvered the boom over the boat. Jim attached the crane hook to the sling. He pointed his index finger into the air and made a circular motion with his wrist.

The crane operator followed Jim's signals to lift the Yellowfin from its blocks and swung it over the side of the boat. Jim pointed to the water and swiveled his wrist again. The crane lowered the Yellowfin gently into the water. Jim already had rubber fenders hanging off two cleats on the starboard side of the boat's hull to keep it from bumping into the transporter.

Jim climbed down into the center console where he fired up the twin three-hundred-horsepower Mercury Verado outboard motors. He let them idle while he unhooked the lift sling. The crane operator raised the sling out of the way.

Putting the engines in gear, Jim eased away from *North-west Passage* and steered toward land. He left the helm long enough to pull in the two fenders.

When Aaron Grose had told Jim that he wanted to build a dive shop and hotel on the small island, Jim had jumped at the chance to own part of a dive resort. At the time, Jim and Karen were traveling the eastern coast of Central America, sampling the diving and fishing on an extended honeymoon.

He smiled at the memory of himself, a forty-four-year-old man wooing a twenty-four-year-old girl. She was beautiful—still was—and he'd fallen in love with her the moment they'd met. She didn't need much persuasion to get into bed and then into a bridal gown. He'd introduced her to diving, and she'd become a passionate enthusiast of the sport. She, in turn, had introduced him to Aaron Grose.

Jim pulled the Yellowfin along the Caye Caulker Adventures' dock. He tossed out the fenders and shut off the motor. A dive guide, standing on the dock, caught Jim's line and tied the boat off with a few quick turns on the dock cleat. Jim sprang to the dock and tied off the stern line.

"Is Aaron here?" Jim asked the guide.

The man answered in a thick Australian accent. "I saw him not long ago, mate. He's up in the dive shop."

Jim appraised the resort's two forty-six-foot Newton dive boats and the fifty-foot Viking fishing vessel, used for private fishing and diving charters. As he walked up the dock to the beautiful forty-room hotel and dive center, Jim recognized other small craft belonging to a few locals he knew.

The hotel was built in an L-shape with the short leg of the L to the south and the long leg running parallel to the north/south street along the front of the property. A separate building to the north, on his right, housed the dive center and shop, one of the largest in Belize. Aaron handled everything from new open water students to technical divers going below the open circuit recreational limits. In the center of the layout was a luxurious pool equipped with a water slide, a swim-up bar, and a lift for handicap persons. The pool had a maximum depth of twenty feet and tapered up to three feet deep at the bar. The extra depth and size of the pool allowed for the resort's confined water dive training needs. Surrounding the pool's azure waters were swaying palms, and thatched-roof cabanas dotted the property.

Jim continued up the walk, past long rows of shiny, aluminum dive tanks being filled by a compressor, and into the dive shop. Air conditioning and the smell of rubber and wet neoprene hit him. He took a deep breath and continued past rows of buoyancy compensating devices, racks of wetsuits, dive skins, masks, and countless other gear used to enjoy the underwater world.

He found Aaron in the shop's cramped office. Jim leaned on the door jamb and asked, "Hey, Aaron, how are you?"

Aaron looked up sharply, his eyes wide. A look of fear crossed his face. It was gone almost as fast as Jim recognized it. If he hadn't been staring right at Aaron, he would have missed it.

"Goo ... good," Aaron stammered. "Karen got in last night."

"Great, I can't wait to see her."

Aaron laid down his pencil and leaned back in his chair. "I don't know what happened between the two of you. She was pretty upset, but she said she's come to terms with whatever she was mad about."

Jim nodded. "Good."

Aaron sat forward in the chair, placed his elbows on his knees, and put his face in his hands.

"You okay?" Jim perched on the edge of the desk.

The dive shop owner looked up. "Yeah, I need to make a little money on the side."

"I thought the resort was doing good."

Aaron smiled. "It is, but I have some extra expenses. I haven't been paying U.S. taxes, and I need some cash to bargain with them."

Jim rubbed the back of his neck and pondered the situation. If Aaron owed the IRS then he, by default, owed the IRS. "How much do you need?"

"I'm not sure, probably five hundred k."

Jim snorted. "You don't owe that much in taxes."

"Taxes, and some debt from buying the Viking. You know, get back to square one. If I have the money, I can bargain with them, maybe get the amount knocked down."

"You won't need to bargain with them as much as you think."

"Look, Jim, I know what you're doing on the side. I'd like to get in on the action."

Jim leaned in close, his voice low and menacing. "What the hell are you talking about?"

"The guns you're hustling."

Jim looked Aaron up and down like he'd just seen him for the first time in his life. "I don't know what you're talking about. Are you accusing me of running guns? I thought we were friends."

Aaron shrugged and picked up the pencil. "Does Karen know what you do in your spare time?"

Jim came off the desk and took a step forward, his finger poking the air in front of Aaron's face. "You little snot! I took you in and helped you build a thriving business. Now you're willing to tear it all down for money! Go ahead and burn. I hope the IRS rapes your place because I'm done."

Aaron's voice rose with indignation. "Good! I don't need any illegal activity at my resort anyways."

Jim held up his hands in frustration. "Who do you think owns this place?" He leaned down to come face-to-face with

Aaron. "Me, that's who! I own everything you have. All I have to do is call the note, and you're sunk, mister."

"Good, then you'll be the one with the tax problems, and I'll be free and clear. I'll call the IRS right now." Aaron reached for the phone.

He clamped his hand on Aaron's wrist. "Don't be an asshole!" Jim's face reddened with anger. "You're not dumping this on me. You're the one who didn't pay your taxes."

"Then cut me in on the action, Jimmy. I'll be a good boy and fall back in line."

"You really think I'll cut you in?"

Aaron stared up at Jim. "Honestly, I don't want any part of it. Just don't bring it to my resort."

Jim released Aaron's wrist and stepped back. "If you don't care, why the big stink?"

"Because I thought we were friends, Jim, and as your friend I'm going to tell you what happened to me in Atlanta."

Jim looked puzzled. "What happened in Atlanta?"

Aaron motioned for Jim to sit, and he did. He was more curious than anything. He hadn't laundered money through Caye Caulker Adventures since its first year of operations, and no gun sales took place on the resort grounds. He did meet Darren Parsons there, but meeting a person wasn't illegal, nor could it be pinned on Aaron.

After a quick drink of water, Aaron leaned back in his chair. "I got picked up by a Homeland agent and a private contractor right after I passed through customs. They took me to a little holding office and told me I was going to Gitmo for aiding and abetting a terrorist. Then they told me you were running guns all over the globe. And to top it all off, they told me I owed back taxes and they'd look the other way if I introduced the contractor to you and acted as their snitch."

Jim rubbed his chin. "Who's the contractor?"

"Some guy named Ryan Weller. He works for a company called Dark Water Research."

"I've heard of them," Jim said, crossing his arms. "What the hell is a guy from a commercial dive and salvage company doing snooping around here?"

"Something about you supplying guns to the Aztlán cartel. He got in my face and told me he was going to take you down. I could go down with you or rat you out."

Jim scratched his chin again. "When are you supposed to introduce us?"

"He's supposed to come here, but I haven't seen him yet," Aaron said. "I told them I had no idea when or if you would show up."

"But you'll let me know when he does?" Jim asked.

"Absolutely."

"Okay," Jim said, standing up. "I want you to play both sides of the fence on this. Pass them enough intel to get you clear on the tax debt, but not enough to put me in jail."

Aaron nodded. "Jim, did you really supply the cartel?"

Jim sighed. "Yes, I did. I had no idea what Guerrero was planning. I just supply the weapons."

Aaron shook his head.

Jim opened the office door and stepped out. As he closed the door, he said, "Stick to the dive business, son. It won't get you killed."

Jim walked along the path toward the pool in the shade of the mature palms. He and Aaron had always had a good business relationship. Aaron paid his bills on time, and yes, Jim had laundered money through the resort in the beginning. Even though Aaron had built the resort into a profitable business, the margins were thin, making it hard to hide the cash Jim had passed through the books. The dive shop might have been the largest in Belize, but the dive industry was a fickle beast, hinging on tourist dollars and the economy. An old joke sprang to mind. Know how to make a million in the diving industry? Start with two.

At the end of the hotel's short leg were two suites, one on each floor overlooking the docks, a small beach, and the azure waters of the Caribbean Sea. Jim jogged up the steps to the second floor and knocked on the door of the suite. He turned to look over the pool while he waited. When the door opened, Karen stepped into his arms.

She broke the kiss and cooed, "Oh, I've missed you, Jim."

"I missed you too, honey. I'm sorry I didn't tell you."

"I know you were just trying to protect me, sweetie, and it's just business."

"That's all it is," Jim affirmed.

She kissed him passionately and pressed her body to his. In his ear she whispered, "Come in. I've got some business you need to take care of."

CHAPTER SIXTEEN

Darren Parsons sat at the small bar just off the lobby of the Caye Caulker Adventures hotel. The hotel was one of the nicest on the island, with clean, modern rooms, fast Wi-Fi, and best of all, in Darren's opinion, a full-service bar and restaurant. He had a bottle of Belikin beer in front of him and a plate of whole, fried red snapper and French fries. A baseball game between the Cleveland Indians and the Texas Rangers played on a large flat screen. Another showed ESPN's SportsCenter, and a third ran a looped montage of diving, snorkeling, and fishing video footage and pictures taken by the guides at Caye Caulker Adventures.

Darren set the empty beer bottle on the bar before motioning for the bartender to bring another. The lithe young woman brought him a cold replacement and asked if he needed anything else. He was about to say yes but decided he should hold his tongue. There were plenty of women available to him. He didn't need trouble with the hotel staff if she turned down his indecent proposal. He'd learned in his travels throughout the world that there were always women willing to do whatever he asked, albeit for a price. He'd learned to gauge who would be willing and who would not.

Darren's fifteen years in the Army had allowed him to experience a wide variety of exotic locals and women, and his thirst for sex hadn't diminished since he'd become a private contractor. On the contrary, he could afford better quality women and more exotic fetishes.

He was a few days early for his meeting with Jim Kilroy, because there was a woman on the island who accommodated his tastes, but he put his plans on hold when he saw Kilroy had arrived early as well. His boss had a grim set to his mouth. Darren had also learned it was best to let sleeping dogs lie.

The fish was excellent, and he left half the fries and a stack of bones on the platter. After signing the room check, he took his beer outside. From past visits, he knew Jim and Karen always booked the second-floor suite and he moved carefully to avoid being seen by them as he walked to the dock.

"Who owns that sportfisher beside Jim Kilroy's boat?" Darren asked a dock hand.

"I don't know, suh."

Darren watched as three men boarded a small rigid hull inflatable, which had been launched from the sportfisher's extended foredeck, and headed toward the island. The driver ran the RIB up to the Caye Caulker Adventures dock.

"Hey, da dingy dock be over der," the dock hand said, and pointed.

"We need to unload this dude, then I'll park over there," an athletic man in his early thirties said. "Won't take long."

A man with an artificial leg hefted a wheelchair onto the dock, and then Athletic Guy and Artificial Leg helped a third man maneuver from the boat to sit on the edge of the dock.

The two men climbed out of the boat and lifted their partner into the wheelchair.

"You good?" Athletic Guy asked Wheelchair Man.

"Yeah," Wheelchair Man replied, busily adjusting himself in the chair.

Athletic Guy, who had done all the talking and had the use of both legs, jumped into the RIB, and ran it over to the dingy dock while the other two moved up the dock toward the hotel. Darren sipped his beer as he watched them. They had a casual but coiled tenseness to them, despite their disabilities. He had seen many injured men in his line of work. His profession caused those injuries.

"I need to watch those guys," Darren said to himself as he lifted his beer bottle to his lips.

CHAPTER SEVENTEEN

Ryan Weller ran the RIB up on the beach and raised the motor. He locked it in place and used the bow line to tie the boat to a post already knotted with half a dozen dinghy painters. He walked across the short stretch of beach and stepped up on the seawall.

"Feels good to be back on land," Ryan said.

"I don't think Greg's seawheels have worn off yet," Mango said. "He's all over the place."

"Greg's always all over the place," Ryan replied, laughing at his buddy.

Greg gave Ryan the middle finger as the three men strolled along the palm-lined sidewalk to the resort's office. They checked into their rooms then congregated at the bar. Each ordered a margarita.

"Too bad you can't get to the swim-up bar, Greg. We could be sitting with the ladies," Ryan said with a grin.

Greg handed his margarita to Ryan. He rolled out of the bar, across the pool deck, and, at the last second, did a wheelie off the edge of the pool before splashing into the water. Several people gasped audibly and ran to see if he was okay. Ignoring the stares, he left his chair floating by the side of the pool and swam over to the bar where he hauled himself up onto a stool. The bartender, a slim brunette, looked at him in shock.

"Three margaritas." Greg held up four fingers as a joke.

From the side of the pool, Ryan said, "You're an idiot."

Greg laughed. "That will teach you to say stupid stuff."

While they were retrieving the wheelchair from the pool, Mango nudged Ryan and whispered, "It's your lady friend."

Ryan glanced to his left to see Karen Kilroy walk over to the pool, drop her sarong on a chaise lounge, and dive head-first into the deep end. Seeing her made him think of Emily, and he missed her. She would love to dive Belize's barrier reefs with him.

After she had accompanied him to the Florida Keys on his sailboat and then dropped everything to join him in Texas for a few days after his return from Mexico, Emily's boss had told her no more vacation days. That had been a month ago, and she'd hardly had a day off since.

When he'd left her apartment to go to Belize, she'd told him to stay out of trouble and to come back safe. It was a promise he wasn't sure he could keep.

CHAPTER EIGHTEEN

M oses Tillett swept his hand over his short hair. In his
old age, it was more gray than black. His bloodline
was a mix of Miskito Indian and African slaves brought by
the Spanish. As a young boy, he'd walked across Caye Caulker
when there was nothing but sandy paths and a few driftwood
huts. Now he used a cane to help him shuffle along the hard-
packed sand of Front Street. He passed Caye Caulker Adventures and turned into a small alley. To his left, a vine-covered
wall separated the resort from an apartment complex. He
smelled blossoming flowers combined with salt air and suntan
lotion as he walked to the end of the sand and gravel track.

He stopped at the seawall and looked down at the gin-
clear water lapping the rocks. Tiny fish darted among the
rocks and played in the gently lapping water. He lifted his
gaze to the two boats anchored side by side, a giant ship with
an aft superstructure and a blue-and-white sportfisher.

Leaning on his cane, Moses stepped sideways onto the
seawall before he maneuvered himself along the ledge to the
resort's wall. He grasped the wall and swung his leg around it.
The old man had to stand there, legs straddling the fence, and

caught his breath. He moved his trembling left leg around the wall and stepped off the seawall. Flowering bushes and palm trees provided shade and cover for his clandestine activities. He walked along the beach to the dinghy dock and stopped to admire the small boats. Some had durable plastic bottoms, some metal hulls, and others were made of wood. Several were nothing more than inflatable rubber rafts with oars.

From one end of the island to the other, he'd been on the move, and he was ready for a nap and a meal. Suddenly, he no longer felt the strain of his years. A smile crossed his creased face as his eyes found what he'd searched for all day. A RIB floated in the crystal-clear liquid, leaving a shadow on the sand beneath it. Painted on its nose were the words *Dark Water*. Moses rewarded himself by pulling a plastic bottle of gin from his pocket and taking a healthy slug.

"Moses, what've I told you about sneaking onto the property?"

The old man turned to see Aaron Grose standing behind him.

"Sorry, Mista Grose."

"I told you, Moses, I'll give you a job."

"Mighty generous, Mista Grose."

"Come on. You want something from the kitchen?"

"Yes, suh."

Aaron Grose accompanied the aged Miskito toward the rear entrance of the kitchen. Moses watched the few guests he could see who were not in the shadows of the setting sun. He saw a man in a wheelchair and a man with an artificial leg. He did not see a third man with them. Still, Moses felt elated. He had found the boat and the men his boss was searching for.

Aaron instructed the cook to fix Moses a hamburger and fries.

Aaron Grose was one of the few men who treated Moses

like an equal and always offered him a job. Moses preferred to sit in the shade and nurse his bottle. He was an old man. He had no desire to wash dishes, clean up after white tourists, and say, "Yes, suh, no, suh."

Moses finished his meal before slipping out of the kitchen. He walked a few blocks to the small home he shared with his son's family. Pulling a cell phone from his pocket, he dialed a number on the mainland.

"*Weh di go aan*, Moses?" *What's up,* Moses? Andreas Zavala spoke in the broken English of Belizean Kriol.

"De be here on Caye Caulker at da Caye Caulker Adventures."

"*Fu Chroo?*" *Really?*

"Yes," Moses confirmed. "Me see dim. De boat in da sea. Man with no leg and man in wheelchair."

"What aboot di uder mans?"

"Ah no see. He mus be heres."

"Gud." The man ended the call, and Moses closed his flip phone. He smiled as he stepped inside the house. He would have his reward money soon enough, and he would feed his whole family.

CHAPTER NINETEEN

G reg, Mango, and Ryan ate a late breakfast and went in search of Aaron Grose. He informed them of Jim and Karen's early morning departure on a dive charter. They would return in the late afternoon. Aaron handed the trio a laminated map of the local dive sites and suggested they visit some of them and come see him in the evening when he would introduce them to Jim.

The men used the rest of the morning to perform maintenance on *Dark Water*. Once they were done, they ate a quick lunch and loaded their dive gear into the RIB.

When they arrived at the first dive sight, Ryan helped Greg shrug into his BCD and attach the twin steel, eighty-cubic-foot dive tanks, one on each side of his torso. Greg dove sidemount, a configuration made popular by cave divers. Carrying one tank on each side of his body kept Greg from rolling side to side and allowed him to achieve neutral buoyance with ease. Ryan splashed right behind him and watched as his friend pulled himself through the water with swimmer's hand paddles and strong strokes of his arms. Greg wasn't a fast swimmer, and he enjoyed poking around under the coral and checking out the sea life.

They spent several hours exploring some of the shallower dive sites. It seemed the colors of the fish and coral were brighter and more vibrant nearer the equator. Sea turtles swam effortlessly beside them, barracudas lurked in the distance, grunts, parrotfish, and angelfish ducked in and out of the rocks. Lobsters waved their antennas and small crabs scuttled about on the sand.

"That was awesome," Mango exclaimed, climbing back in the RIB after the second dive.

"Wish it was a shipwreck," Ryan grumbled.

"What's the matter?" Greg asked. "You don't like nature?"

"I love nature," Ryan said. "As long as it's attached to a shipwreck."

All three laughed.

Ryan did enjoy looking at coral and sea life. He especially enjoyed it when a lobster was in a mesh bag on his hip, and a fish was on the tip of his spear. He'd spent many hours of his youth freediving, spearfishing, and lobstering as he sailed around the world on his old Sabre 36, *Sweet T*. He felt a touch of melancholy as he thought about the loose of the sailboat that had been his home since he'd left North Carolina at eighteen.

Mango ran the RIB back to *Dark Water* where the three showered before heading to dinner. While they saw Aaron Grose, he did not introduce them to either Darren Parsons or Jim Kilroy, even though they recognized both men from photographs provided by their DHS handler.

After dinner, Mango excused himself to get his bag and head out to *Dark Water*. They'd decided to have someone spend the night on the boat for security purposes. Ryan had lost the game of rock-paper-scissors last night, making tonight Mango's responsibility.

Ryan interrupted him, saying, "I'll do it. Stay in the hotel and enjoy the bed."

"You sure, bro? I don't mind."

"I'm good." Ryan stood and laid his napkin on the table. "I'm going for a walk before I go out."

"Be careful," Greg admonished. The background information they'd read about Caye Caulker indicated crime was low on the island. Still, gang activity existed and the sale of drugs to tourists provided a criminal underbelly to paradise.

At the north end of the island was a bar called The Lazy Lizard, drawing sunburned patrons like moths to a flame. Ryan ordered a Lighthouse beer from the bartender and walked out on the boardwalk overlooking a channel known as The Split. It separated the two islands which constituted Caye Caulker. The Split was popular with snorkelers, stand-up paddlers, kayakers, and bar bums.

Ryan watched the sunset with the other customers. There were oohs and ahhs, reminding him of the sunset watchers in Key West's Mallory Square. From the deck of the bar, cigarette smoke wafted down to Ryan. He was tempted to find the guy and bum a smoke from him.

Emily had asked him to quit. Not just for her, but for his health. After being a two-pack-a-day smoker on overseas deployments, he'd cut back to one pack or less after leaving the Navy. Quitting cold turkey was tough. He'd considered patches and gum but felt they were just another form of addiction. If he wanted to quit, he'd just quit. There was an unopened pack in his gear on *Dark Water*. He craved them.

He finished his beer and headed back to Caye Caulker Adventures to retrieve the RIB and go to *Dark Water*. He walked along the street, listening to music spilling out into the night from little bars and restaurants. Ryan wished Emily was with him.

His wandering mind snapped back to the present as he

sensed someone behind him. Occasionally, he heard the slap of a sandal. He could feel the man's eyes on him. Ryan focused on two men lounging against a small shack advertising high-speed Internet and prepaid cell phones. Alarm bells clashed in his head. Behind him, the man was closing in. Ryan wanted to look back.

Instead, he continued to walk at the same speed. He tensed his muscles. His ribs still ached, and his shoulders were sore. Ryan was ready for a fight and willing to bring it to the men waiting for him. He could almost taste the adrenaline as it surged through him. He walked on, rolling his left wrist in the tight bandage. The men stepped away from the shack. Ryan knew the drill. They wanted him to stop, so the man trailing him could give him a tap on the back of the skull with a pipe, or a sap, or a bullet.

"Bakra bwai, wee sen yu hoam." White boy, we send you home.

Ryan got the meaning, but not the exact interpretation. He stepped to his left, toward the man who'd spoken, wanting to gain distance from the lurker behind him. Ryan labeled the talker, Mouth. The one on the right became Muscle and the one behind him, Mystery. Muscle held a pipe in his right hand. Mouth had a shiny knife down by his leg. Ryan took two fast steps forward and punched Mouth in the mouth with the heel of his hand. The man's jaw unhinged, and his knees sagged under him. Ryan followed the first punch with a hard left, driving Mouth into his buddy, Muscle.

The movement threw Muscle off balance. Ryan turned to face Mystery. An iron pipe whistled past his head and slammed into his right shoulder. Pain exploded through his body and Ryan's arm went numb. Muscle staggered out from under his friend. Mystery took the time to bring the pipe back like a batter lining up for a home run swing.

CHAPTER TWENTY

J uan Comacho swung. Suddenly, the American ducked
under the pipe, stepped into Comacho's outstretched
arms, and punched him in the side of the neck.
Comacho dropped the pipe and clutched his throat, feeling
the muscles spasm and constrict from the blow. He gasped,
barely able to breathe, and fell to his knees. He watched the
world spin around him in slow motion.

Clutching his injured shoulder, the American turned and
lashed his foot out at Muscle's knee. Muscle, who Comacho
knew as Carlos Rios, screamed in pain as his knee twisted and
bent at an unnatural angle. Rios dropped his pipe and
grabbed his knee. Their big victim-turned-assailant landed a
sweeping left hook on Rios's chin. Rios's head snapped back,
and his body went limp.

Camacho knelt in the street looking at his two men
sprawled in the dirt. He made little wheezing sounds as he
struggled to breathe through his constricted windpipe. Both
of his hands were on his throat in a vain attempt to ease the
pain. His eyes tracked Ryan as Ryan attempted to rotate his

right arm where the pipe had struck him. He raised the arm above his head and winced.

Comacho staggered to his feet. People were crowding into the road to see what the commotion was about. He glanced at them and let his hands drop from his throat, even though it was the most painful thing he had ever experienced. He had to move, to get away from the man now advancing on him. He tried to swallow, but the swelling made it difficult. Panic rose in his chest as he started to hyperventilate.

The big man approached, and Juan thought about running, but he was in pain and his mind was slow to react. Even with a wounded wing, Comacho knew the American was more dangerous than most men he knew.

"Walk with me," Ryan ordered in a low, calm voice.

CHAPTER TWENTY-ONE

Ryan Weller clamped his hand on his attacker's shoulder and guided him away from the street. The man wheezed from the neck punch. The other two attackers were still on the ground. Ryan wanted to put as much distance between them and himself as possible. He also wanted answers. They came to the beach and Ryan stopped under some palms. He forced the smaller man to sit in an Adirondack chair.

Kneeling over him, Ryan carefully checked his attacker's neck and throat. A bruise was starting to form in the shape of Ryan's fist. "I hit you in the neck, probably did some damage to your trachea and larynx. You should be all right. The swelling will go down in a week, or so."

The man nodded, holding his throat. Ryan knew the unconscious clutching of the throat wouldn't help him breathe.

Ryan sat down on the arm of another chair. He worked his shoulder in a circle. It was painful, but the initial sting of the blow was going away. "What's your name?"

The man croaked, "Jua ... Juan Comacho."

"All right, Juan, why'd you attack me?"

"You ... you are ..." He swallowed before trying again, his throat visibly constricting. "You are *asesino de* Arturo Guerrero." Ryan watched the man's eyes drift to the sand and then up to lock onto his. "There is ... two-million-dollar ... bounty for ... you and ... Mango Hulsey."

With instant clarity, Ryan understood the attacks in both New York and Texas City were attempts to collect the bounty. "Who ordered the hit?"

"José Luis ... Orozco, new ... leader of Aztlán ... cartel."

"Did he send you after me?"

Comacho shook his head stiffly, trying desperately to keep his neck still but still move his head.

"Who do you work for?"

"Myself ..."

"You're trying to collect the bounty."

"Me and every ... body else in ... da world."

"What do you mean?" Ryan demanded. He needed to get a handle on this situation.

"Eduardo Sanchez ... Orozco's lieutenant, passed ... the word. You ... will ... will not get far. They will ... will find you, especially ... the Russian."

"What Russian, Juan?"

"Volk ... *El Lobo*."

"The Wolf?"

"*Sí*. He is hitman ... Orozco ... hired. I see his man." Comacho gasped in a wheezing breath. "At bar in Texas ... City where I got ... information about where you ... go. He's not far ... behind me. He may ... be ... here."

Comacho leaned forward in the chair. Snakelike, he whipped a knife from behind his back. He thrust it toward Ryan's belly. Ryan slapped the strike away with his left hand.

Excruciating pain tore up his arm and neck as he instinctually used his injured right arm to drive his fist through the little Mexican's jaw. The knife dropped soundlessly into the sand. Comacho slumped over.

Ryan jumped up and ran toward Caye Caulker Adventures.

CHAPTER TWENTY-TWO

Greg Olsen thanked the waitress for the beer and took a long swig. He relished the buzz the alcohol gave him. In the past hour, since Ryan had gone for a walk, he'd drunk six beers. A light night for him. He was finally coming to terms with his handicap. Becoming a paraplegic was a complication he hadn't handled well.

The day he'd gotten hurt, Afghanistan soldiers had found a collection of plastics explosives, artillery shells, grenades, AK-47s, and ammo. As a commanding officer of the imbedded Navy EOD unit, Greg had chosen to take what he thought was the easy job. Since the government didn't have facilities to store all the old ordnance—some of it gifts from the U.S. government to the Mujahideen to fight the Russians in the 1980s—the standard operating procedure was to blow the ammunition cache in place. Blowing the lot also prevented enemy forces from being able to use the munitions.

Greg had taken four of his EOD team and sent the rest to check out a possible IED at an Army vehicle checkpoint. Greg's convoy had been ambushed on the way to the ammo dump. His Humvee had been blasted open like a tin can by an IED. The blast sent shrapnel into his back, severing his spinal cord below the waist. Ryan had pulled him out of the Humvee and carried him to safety before charging off to counterattack.

He set the beer bottle down. The adventure of chasing Ryan across the Gulf of Mexico and driving the rescue boat had helped excise some of his demons. He was useful, not the way he had been, but he added value to the team, and that made him feel good. Better than sitting in an office.

There was no regret in his decision to wheel away from DWR's management team. He felt less pressure to live up to the legacy of this grandfather and his father. He hoped that with less pressure he would have less depression, but it was still there, lurking in the shadows of his mind. It was easy to feel sorry for himself and drinking often intensified those feelings until he had drowned them out. Unfortunately, he woke up every morning still afflicted with the same condition, and every day he tried to make his legs move as they had before. They always refused to answer his call.

Picking up the beer again, he took a long swig to drain it. Just as he was setting it down, a massive explosion rocked the building. The front window of the restaurant blasted inward, showering everyone in glass shrapnel. Gunfire poured through the opening. Greg shoved himself back, but the chair's rear wheels struck something hard. Momentum tipped the chair over backward. He tucked his chin to his chest and wrapped his arms around his body. His shoulder blades slammed hard into the tile floor, and he let out a groan. The wheelchair slid out from under his legs.

Bullets raked the wall above Greg. He tried to lie motionless on the floor. A spasm shook his leg. Behind him, bottles exploded, and dishes shattered. As the patrons stampeded from the building, they flipped over tables and cast aside chairs. Tourists were cut down in the gunfire. Someone stepped on Greg's hand, and he screamed. He crossed his arms over his chest and rolled his body under the bar to get out of the way.

Glancing to his right, he saw a woman lying face down on the floor. Her blonde hair splayed over her face and her brown eyes were blank. Blood oozed from slightly parted lips and pooled under her chest. Greg struggled to get away and his hand slipped on something sticky. He brought it up to his face. His palm was red with blood. Turning, he saw Darren Parsons staring glassy-eyed at the ceiling with three bullet holes in his chest.

Greg closed his eyes to shut out the carnage. At the same time, his body surged with adrenaline. His face, neck, and chest flushed with the powerful drug. Gunfire continued throughout the compound. Rolling onto his belly, he pulled himself along the floor toward his chair. Greg wished for a gun. Reaching his wheelchair, he jerked the footplate down, so the chair rested on all four wheels. Another explosion tore through the night.

"I don't want to die!" Greg's waitress sobbed.

Greg turned to see her lying spread eagle on the floor. "I think the last explosion was by the pool. If we keep down, we'll be fine," he lied to her. He manipulated his body into a seated position beside the wheelchair then levered himself up into it.

"What are you going to do?" she whispered.

"Get out of here. Come on." He motioned to the girl after getting his feet settled on the footplate. Her terrified brown eyes shone with tears and her chest heaved with her ragged gasps.

She crawled to Greg. "Do you want me to push you?"

"No." He shook his head. "Let's go."

CHAPTER TWENTY-THREE

Mango Hulsey sat on the bed in his hotel room with his back against the headboard. The muted television played a soccer match between Argentina and Brazil. "We're supposed to meet with Aaron's friends tonight, but we didn't," he said into the telephone to his wife Jennifer.

"Why not?" she asked.

"I'm not sure, Aaron said—" Mango was cut off by a loud explosion. The blast wave threw him from the bed and shattered the windows. He dropped the phone.

"Mango! Mango!" Jennifer screamed.

He scooped up the phone and brought it to his ear as an AK-47 spoke on full auto.

"What's going on, Mango?"

"Stay calm, Jennifer. I need to go."

"No, Mango. Don't go," she pleaded. "Stay with me! Stay on the line!"

Mango could hear the tears in her voice. The sobs of helplessness and fear. It stabbed at his gut, made him feel angry at the interruption, and desperate to return to his wife.

"I have to go, babe. I'll call you in a little bit." He pressed

END to silence her cries. It did nothing for the guilt that ate at his belly.

He moved to the window overlooking the balcony and pushed the curtain aside. A second bomb detonated in the pool courtyard, throwing him to the ground and raining broken glass across his body. Mango climbed back to his feet and looked out the gaping hole where the window had been. The curtains swayed in the ocean breeze, bringing in the stench of scorched wood and plastic. Leafless palm trees lay on their sides. Broken glass covered the sidewalks and grounds. The pool bar's thatch roof burned furiously on its twisted posts.

In the firelight, Mango counted seven AK-47-wielding men in black fatigues, combat boots, and balaclavas. He reached into his duffle bag, retrieved his Glock, and shoved two extra magazines into his back pants pocket while he assessed the room. The only way out was through the front door. A small window in the bathroom looked down on an alleyway. The rectangular frame was too narrow for him to climb through, and he loathed the jump from the second story. He feared his artificial limb would break, or worse, the fall would damage the stump of his leg.

He used his foot to sweep glass across the tile, so he had a clear place to lay down. Then he unlatched the door and dropped to the floor before letting it swing open all the way. He wiggled to the edge of the balcony. The shortest way down was the stairs by the two suites.

Screams tore the night air and Mango saw the invaders pull a woman from her room by her hair. Two more men kicked in the next room's door, systematically making their way down the length of the hotel, dragging people out.

"Why does this shit always happen?" Mango muttered as he crawled toward the stairwell. He had just passed the door to the suite and was almost to the steps when the door jerked open. Mango rolled onto his back, at the same time bringing his Glock up to point at the person in the doorway.

Jim Kilroy aimed a handgun at Mango.

Mango commanded, "Get back into your room."

"You're with them!" Kilroy's finger tightened on the trigger.

Karen Kilroy stepped out the room and looked at Mango. "Jim, put the gun down," she hissed. "He's not one of *them*. He's an undercover DHS agent."

"How do you know?"

"Because he's here with Ryan Weller." Her next words came through gritted teeth. "They're here for you, Jim."

CHAPTER TWENTY-FOUR

Ryan ducked under a low hanging palm frond. He paused at the vine-covered, bright pink concrete block wall running the length of the resort grounds from Front Street to the beach. As he prepared to climb around the wall, he saw an armed man standing on Caye Caulker Adventures' dock.

Fearing he might be seen and shot before he could get over the wall, he decided to go through the water and eliminate the guard. He stashed his wallet and cell phone under a nearby bush then ran back to a neighboring dock. He crawled into the warm water, using the low dock boards to pull himself to the end of the pier. The ache in his arm and shoulder were constant and the salt water burned his sliced wrist. He took several deep breaths and dove under the water. With strong kicks and pulls of his arms, he swam as fast as he could. When he came up for a breath, he tried to splash as little as possible and not draw the guard's attention. After another deep breath, he dove again, swimming hard.

Slipping under the Caye Caulker Adventures' dock, he moved closer to the beach. He wanted to see the action, count the forces he faced, and determine who they were. They could be anyone, he realized. A two-million-dollar bounty attracted a lot of attention. Getting out of Tampico, Mexico, without getting caught after killing Arturo Guerrero had taken some luck, and a lot of skill. He knew now he hadn't escaped as cleanly as he'd thought. The repercussions of killing the high priest of the Aztlán movement were coming back to haunt him. He feared for the lives of his friends and the innocent hotel guests he had endangered.

Peering up through the gaps in the dock boards, he saw the guard above him held an AK across his chest as he paced the length of the dock. A second man moved along the beach to prevent anyone from escaping or mounting a rescue. Ryan waited until the man walking the beach had his back turned before he moved out from under the dock.

The dock guard turned to walk toward the ocean. Ryan scrambled up between two boats and crept toward the guard. When the guard turned to make his way back to shore, he saw Ryan and brought his rifle up. Ryan blocked the rising muzzle and jammed his tactical folding knife into the man's chest, burying the blade to the hilt, the point slicing into the man's heart. Ryan purposely fell with the man into the water between two small boats. They made a loud splash and sank toward the bottom.

Ryan pulled his knife free and surfaced. Above him, the other guard, alerted by the splash, pounded down the dock. The guard he'd just killed had dropped his gun when they'd landed in the water and in the low light from the resort lights and fires, Ryan could just make it out. He dove back to the sandy bottom and retrieved the firearm. One of the things he loved about the AK was that it could be drowned or packed full of mud and the cheap Russian gun would still function.

In the darkness, he clung to a post under the dock. The guard turned in place, looking at the water on both sides of the dock for his lost companion. Knowing any gunfire coming from the marina would attract more attention, Ryan was loath to just shoot the man. His decision about what to do was made for him when gunfire erupted near the hotel. Ryan aimed the barrel of his rifle between the dock boards and sent a hail of 7.62-millimeter rounds into the man above.

He swung himself onto the dock, liberated the fallen man's extra magazines, and shoved them into the cargo pockets of his shorts before charging toward the resort.

CHAPTER TWENTY-FIVE

Greg fingered an eight-inch-long chef's knife he'd picked up from the bar on his way toward the busted hotel lobby doors. Even with the glass missing, he still had to pull them open. The corner of the door dragged on the floor, scraping an arc across the tile, and the waitress helped wrench it open. No one guarded the lobby, so they started toward to the hotel's main entrance. His wheels rolled smoothly across the polished floor.

Just outside the hotel's front door, Greg saw a man leaning against the wall, smoking a cigarette. His AK hung on a sling around his neck and he held the pistol grip loosely in his hand. Greg put the knife between his left leg and the wheelchair's plastic clothing guard and pushed through the door.

The guard turned and lifted his weapon. His casual demeanor indicated he was not expecting any resistance from the hotel guests. "Get back," he commanded.

Greg gave his wheels a hard shove. He whipped the knife up and across the gunman's arm, slicing deeply into the man's flesh. He felt the sharp edge of the knife skip on the rough surface of the man's ulna. The gunman dropped his weapon in shock. Greg brought the knife around and stabbed the blade deep into the man's ribcage. The guard dropped to his knees and then fell onto his face. With some effort, Greg rolled the man over and pilfered his cache of spare magazines before picking up the gun. He felt the waitress brush past him and glanced up to see her running across the street. She disappeared into the blackness between two buildings.

He checked to ensure there was a round in the AK's chamber before flicking the safety off. He moved through the lobby to its rear doors. They opened onto a small seating area and the pool deck beyond. He saw three men kicking in room doors and dragging out guests. They were holding their hostages under guard in an area close to the dive shop.

Greg angled his wheelchair, locked the brakes, shoved the butt of his rifle into his shoulder, and braced the gun barrel against the lobby door frame while he waited for the men to return from dropping off their prisoners. Just as they were about to kick in the next door, he pulled the trigger. His bullets blew the first man's brains across the lawn and hammered the second in the chest. The third dropped to the ground and returned fire.

The bolt locked open, indicating an empty magazine. He replenished the gun with a fresh load and laid it across his lap. He jerked away from the door as bullets chewed up the stucco, wood, and metal around his former position.

Retreat was not a word in his vocabulary. Rather, he was moving back to the next ambush site. The best place for him to make a stand was behind the twelve-foot-long reception counter. Black granite wrapped around the front, sides, and top of the counter. The hard stone was more effective at stopping bullets than the plaster and wood walls. However, protected he was, the enemy could come at him from both the front and rear entrances of the lobby.

Ensconced behind the granite, he waited for the end to

come. There was something about being shot at that sharpened one's focus. The adrenaline pumping through his system had wiped out the buzz of the alcohol. He hadn't felt this alive in years. He didn't enjoy shooting people, but they had pushed him, and he was ready to fight.

Let 'em come. This would be his last stand.

CHAPTER TWENTY-SIX

Mango Hulsey had followed Jim Kilroy into the Kilroy's top-floor suite and they listened to the full auto gunfight. He leaned out to find the source. He saw Greg blasting away from the lobby's rear entrance. Knowing Greg needed help, he turned to Jim Kilroy. "You got any more guns around here?"

"Just this one." Kilroy held up his Smith and Wesson M&P nine-millimeter pistol.

"We need to help my friend'" Mango said. "He's the one shooting at the terrorists."

"What do you suggest?"

"We go downstairs and start shooting those assholes."

"I got that part," Jim said. "Give. Me. A. Plan."

"Greg's probably trapped in the lobby. They'll try to flank him." Mango went to the big sliding doors overlooking the black ocean. "We go out the door and drop down into the alley. Then we'll go around the front of the building and start picking off bad guys."

"That's it?"

"What do you want, bro? You're supposed to be the international arms dealer, can't you come up with a plan?"

"You are DHS agent, aren't you?"

"I'm not, but I know a few," Mango replied.

"What the hell is going on?" Karen demanded.

"I'm just a one-legged man in an ass-kicking contest, and it's time to go win." Mango stripped the sheets off the bed, twisted them into a rope, and tied the two cream-colored, king size sheets together.

"What are you doing?" Karen asked incredulously.

"Honey," Jim said patiently. "We don't have time for that right now."

Jim took one end of the sheet rope and tied it to the balcony's railing. Mango dropped the other end of the makeshift rope into the alley. He climbed over the wrought-iron railing and rappelled down. Jim followed a moment later.

The two men ran to Front Street. Mango stopped at the corner, pressed himself against the wall, and then eased around it. He kept his gun up in his right hand, ready to kill any Tangos—military slang for terrorists—he might encounter. Flanking the hotel's front entrance were two walls protruding three feet out from the main wall which supported a faux balcony above. Mango ran to the stub wall and peered around it. The lobby doors were missing their glass, and a dead man lay face up with a kitchen knife sticking out of his ribs. Mango smiled, finally knowing how Greg must have gotten his hands on a gun.

He moved to the busted lobby doors and crouched down. "Greg?"

"In here." Greg waved from behind the counter.

Mango flashed an okay sign. Jim moved up beside Mango and stepped out to shoot at two terrorists flanking the hotel. A scream rewarded his efforts. The second terrorist brought his gun up and fired.

Mango dove to the ground. Not only was their flanker firing, but Greg had also resumed shooting.

CHAPTER TWENTY-SEVEN

R yan scurried up the dock into some bushes on the edge of the seawall. He watched as Mango and Jim Kilroy tied sheets to a railing and escaped into the alley. He hoped they were going around to the front of the hotel. Concentrating on the area around him, Ryan saw a group of hotel guests being held captive near the dive shop.

He sprinted the fifty yards to the back of the dive shop where he found a shack housing the air compressor used to fill the rows and rows of aluminum dive tanks. A small wagon sat beside them. Ryan had seen the dive instructors tow loads of tanks to and from the dive boats with it, and it was still stacked with a pyramid of tanks held in place with a ratchet strap.

An idea formed in Ryan's mind. He opened the door to the compressor shed. Hanging from a peg board, just inside the shack's entrance, was a five-pound sledgehammer, a large crescent wrench, and several screwdrivers.

He glanced out at the tanks. The standard procedure for most dive shops around the world was to use rubber caps to cover the tank valve to indicate a full tank. When the cap was off, the tank was empty. The tanks in the wagon had rubber caps on their valves. He grabbed the sledgehammer from the pegboard and set it in the cart. He then moved the wagon so the back of it faced the terrorists now approaching the lobby doors.

Picking up the hammer, he slammed it viciously into the valve on the top tank. Metal on metal rang across the courtyard. Ryan paid it no mind and struck a second blow to the valve. Again, he drove the hammer down. A fourth mighty blow broke the valve off. The tank, pressurized to three thousand pounds per square inch, shot off the pyramid like a missile as the air escaped through the tiny hole left by the broken valve. It skipped on the concrete just before the pool, took flight over the water, and smashed into a terrorist who happened to step into the tank's path. The impact killed the terrorist, and the scuba tank missile punched through the stucco and wood of the hotel wall.

Ryan shook his head in amazement at the missile's power, then bent to smack the next tank valve. The tank took off after three hits and swept across the pool deck. It collided with one of the few standing palm trees and ricocheted through a hotel room door. He knocked the valve off the third tank, which angled off to the left. The fourth cartwheeled across the water, dipped, and hit the concrete. It skipped and bounced, angling the nose into the air. The tank shot into the second story balcony.

This final tank drew the attention of the terrorists to Ryan's position. He made a break for the dive shop amid a hail of gunfire. At the front of the building, he found a man guarding the guests. Many of the guests were lying on the ground crying, bleeding, and distraught. Ryan brought his AK to his shoulder and fired a burst into the guard, who went down quickly. The guard fell beside a woman, who started screaming.

"Paradise ain't supposed to be like this," Ryan said wryly. He felt sorry for the woman, knowing that terrorism was probably something she only saw on the news.

Ryan stepped around the corner and saw a giant with long blond hair staring at him. He wasn't wearing a balaclava like his men. The giant raised his rifle and fired a burst as Ryan darted back behind the building. He tripped over the edge of the sidewalk and the barrel of his AK skidded across the concrete. Using the gun to catch himself in midstride, he stumbled to the door of the dive shop. He knocked the glass out of the locked door with the rifle's stock.

Inside, it was black. Only the dying fires provided flickering light, giving the interior a ghostly appearance. Ryan smelled rubber and neoprene laced with palm frond smoke. He crouched amongst the racks of dive equipment, trying to remember the layout from his previous visits.

The door on the far side of the shop shattered as the giant kicked it open. Ryan shouldered his rifle. Taking careful aim, he fired the remaining rounds in the mag. When the bolt locked open, the blond giant was still standing in the doorway. Ryan stared in amazement. The man should have been dead. Rapidly, he changed magazines and aimed at the man ducking into the store. He stroked the trigger again. The bullets stitched up the wall to the left of the giant.

"Damn!" Ryan looked at the barrel of his gun. It curved slightly to the left. "How in the hell?"

It was too late to do anything about the problem. The blond giant was diving at him. Ryan jammed the gun at the giant's chest to knock him off balance. The giant batted the gun from his hands as if it were a baby's play toy.

CHAPTER TWENTY-EIGHT

Volk screamed, "*YA nepobedim!*" *I'm invincible*, as he leapt through the air. Outstretched arms swatted away the American's rifle just before he landed on his opponent. They rolled across the floor, knocking over racks of clothing. Underneath him, Ryan flailed his arms and legs. The giant knew he was stronger and heavier, and kept his opponent pinned to the ground. He spun chest to chest, so his body and Ryan's were at right angles. Volk curled one arm around Ryan's neck and hooked the other through Ryan's crotch. In a display of strength, he picked his opponent up as he rose. Ryan repeatedly drove his elbow into Volk's back, but Volk only felt muted blows to his trapezius muscles.

The Russian laughed. Then he slammed Ryan to the ground. He stood over his opponent, looking at him as if he were a specimen he was about to crush. Volk raised a size-eighteen foot and aimed it at Ryan's throat.

The exasperating American devil rolled out of the way just as Volk slammed his foot down. He bellowed in pain as it crashed into the hard carpet-covered concrete. His scream became a roar of anger as he flexed his arms and advanced.

Ryan got a foot planted and heaved himself up. He clutched his back and fell back to the ground. Groaning, he tried to rise again.

CHAPTER TWENTY-NINE

Mango and Jim Kilroy dispatched the two terrorists at the front of the hotel. Mango stepped into the lobby and yelled to Greg, "You good?"

"I'm fine," Greg shouted back without taking his eyes off his gunsights. He hammered any terrorist who came near the rear lobby doors.

Mango stepped back to the door. "Jim, go around the front and see if you can flank them. I'll stay here with Greg and we'll try to advance."

Jim nodded and took off. Mango edged toward the restaurant entrance. He would provide crossfire if the tangos jumped to the other side of the lobby door to breach. Just as he reached the doors, a metal cylinder punched through the wall. The scuba tank skipped across the tile and hit the far wall, where it spun like a top on the floor.

Mango and Greg looked at each other in disbelief. A second tank slammed into the outside wall followed by a third hitting the balcony. Mango rushed to the rear lobby doors and shot one of the intruders and missed the other as the man sprinted away.

Out of the corner of his eye, Mango observed a guard topple over near the huddled hostages. Then, in the firelight, he saw a giant blond man fire his gun and run toward the dive shop door. Mango looked down at Greg, who had joined him. He pushed one of the glass and aluminum doors open for Greg to pass through.

Mango left him on the pool deck and sprinted to the dive shop. He ducked through the shattered door. Ryan was trying to rise as the giant advanced on him. Mango leveled his pistol on the blond's chest just as the big man saw him. Mango pulled the trigger twice. Volk spun on his heels and fled the dive shop.

Mango glanced at Ryan as he chased the giant out the door, amazed that his two 9-mm hollow points hadn't slowed him down. He speculated the man wore a bulletproof vest like many of his men. Staring out the door, Mango saw a group of men running toward the dock. Ragged bursts of gunfire rippled the air as they covered their retreat. Mango had his gun up and trained on the fleeing figures, but he didn't shoot, knowing they were too far away for him to hit with his pistol. The attackers gained the dock and hopped into a boat.

Mango didn't bother to chase after them as they roared away. Instead, he turned and knelt by his friend. Blood oozed from Ryan's right nostril and the corner of his mouth. His knuckles were skinned, bruised, and swollen from his fistfights. He had a cut on his hand, and the bandages around his left wrist were wet with water and blood.

"You look like shit, bro."

Ryan wrapped both arms around his midsection and lay back down. "I feel like shit, too."

CHAPTER THIRTY

A moment later Ryan Weller sat back up. Adrenaline hammered through him as he scrambled for the AK that he'd just crammed a fresh magazine into before Volk decided to play professional wrestling with him. Every bruise, cut, scrape, and torn fingernail on his body still throbbed and he'd feel it even more in the morning, but he forgot all about them as his eyes locked on the man coming through the shattered door of the dive shop. Jim Kilroy carried a pistol loosely in his right hand like it was a casual wear accessory of apparel. Mango turned and brought his own gun to play, trusting Ryan's instincts.

Ryan adjusted his aim to compensate for the warped barrel.

Kilroy jerked his pistol up, crouching into a combat stance as he aimed at Ryan.

Mango lowered his gun and said, "Relax, Ryan, it's Jim Kilroy." To Kilroy, Mango said, "It's cool, Jim."

Kilroy stood and let the gun dangle again. He stepped closer to the pair of ex-military men.

Ryan could barely make out Kilroy's shadowed face in the fading firelight.

"Be cool, bro," Mango warned.

"Be cool?" Ryan shot back. "What's stopping me from putting a bullet between his eyes and ending this right now?" His finger tightened on the trigger.

Kilroy said, "Because we need each other."

CHAPTER THIRTY-ONE

Aaron Grose stood on the second-floor balcony of the Caye Caulker Adventures hotel. In the harsh light of day, he could see the full extent of the carnage. Broken glass littered the ground, palm trees lay twisted and broken, fire had scorched the sides of the buildings and burned the roof of the tiki huts. Room doors lay twisted and broken from their frames where the terrorists had smashed them in. There were blood smears everywhere.

Even though he was grateful for the help of the three men who'd defended the resort, treated the wounded, and pitched in to put out fires, he was still furious with them. Before they'd arrived, Caye Caulker Adventures had been a peaceful, idyllic setting. His hard work had been destroyed in a matter of minutes, his reputation as a top-tier dive destination gone. Who would want to come to a place that had been attacked by terrorists? Why had this happened? He gripped the railing as a scream welled inside him.

His eyes lifted from the destroyed courtyard at the sound of two boats approaching the dock. Anger settled in his gut like burning coals, white hot and intense. His eye twitched and his lip curled in a snarl. Jim and Karen disembarked from their center console and the three Dark Water Research divers climbed from their RIB. Those men were the cause of his ruin. DHS agents were preying on him for back taxes, sending investigators after his friends, and, the man who called himself a friend was the worst.

"Jim Kilroy." The name rolled out of his mouth like burning acid. The man had infected his resort with low-life thugs, illicit money, and corruption. He owed Jim his life, his property, and his livelihood, but he couldn't see beyond the destruction Jim had caused. Unable to stand the sight of them, he stepped into his office and slammed the door. He'd never been this angry, not even with his father whom he'd purposely cut from his life. With a wicked kick, he sent the trash can flying across the room. Waste papers and trash flew into the air.

"Son of a bitch!" he screamed.

He stormed out of the office and downstairs. He saw the objects of his anger talking to members of the Belize Police Department's Criminal Investigations and Gang Suppression Units.

Over the course of the next several hours, Aaron watched as they reenacted the events of the previous evening, unsurprised when the police didn't arrest them. He knew both Jim and Ryan had ties to the U.S. government who had probably pressured the Belizean police to not arrest them. It rankled him. Where were his connections and support? Who was going to back him in rebuilding his life or aid the hotel guests and workers who had been killed or wounded in the night's actions?

Thankfully, his manager pulled him away to help clean out a freezer that had been damaged in the original bomb blast. Normally, the work would have been cathartic, but today, with every spoiled fish he tossed out, he seethed.

Aaron was tying a trash bag closed when one of his female dive guides, Missy, came into the kitchen and said, "You wanted me to keep an eye on those guys."

"Yeah." Aaron picked the bag up and carried it outside to throw on the growing pile of debris with the dive guide in tow.

Missy said, "They went into the bottom suite."

Aaron wheeled to face her. "When?"

"Just now."

"Thanks, Missy." Aaron headed for the back of the hotel. He had to force himself to walk slow to not draw the attention of the cops who stood around with M16s like the bad guys were going to spring out of the bushes and attack again.

Aaron shoved the door open and stepped into the hotel suite. Seated around a table were Jim and Karen Kilroy, Ryan Weller, Mango Hulsey, and Greg Olsen. They all had drinks in front of them. Karen got up from her chair.

Stalking across the room, he raised a finger and stabbed it at Jim Kilroy. "You ... you ..." Aaron fought for the words. "You're going to pay!"

"Aaron, not like this, please," Karen said softly, stepping between her husband and her friend. "Just sit down. We'll figure everything out."

"Figure what out, Karen? Figure out who's going to pay to fix my hotel, repair my business, and my reputation?"

"Easy, son," Jim said.

"Don't you son me. I was never your son. Hell, I was never your partner. You used me."

"Aaron, please, sit down," Karen pleaded. "We'll straighten everything out."

"And you—" Aaron wheeled on Ryan "—trying to get me to turn on Jim because I owe back taxes. Screw the government. They don't do a damn thing for me in Belize. I ain't paying a dime! Matter-of-fact, I'm going to become a

Belizean citizen, and the U.S. government can go screw itself."

Ryan stood and pointed at an empty chair at the round table. With a drill instructor voice, he commanded, "Sit down, Aaron."

Aaron stared blindly at Ryan, then followed the order.

"Can I get you something to drink?" Karen asked.

"Always the perfect hostess, huh, Karen? You knew all about Jim shoveling his guns and his money through my resort, but you couldn't bother to tell me."

Karen's bottom lip poked out, and her shoulders drooped.

"Listen to me, boy," Jim said, leveling a finger at Aaron. "You can scream at us all you want, but you leave my wife out of this. She didn't know anything about my business until a month ago. That's what our fight was about before she went to New York."

Aaron looked at the beautiful blonde. "I'm sorry, Karen. I'm just angry."

"And justifiably so," Jim said. "I, however, had nothing to do with the terrorists. You can thank these gentlemen, here, for bringing that ugliness to Caye Caulker. Ryan and Mango are wanted men."

Aaron looked over at them. "Wanted by whom?"

Ryan said, "We foiled a plan by Aztlán cartel leader, Arturo Guerrero. He wanted to start a war with the United States to take back the Southwest. I killed Guerrero, and now we have a two-million-dollar bounty on our heads. A Russian, named Volk, led those men last night. He's a bounty hunter and hitman who now works for José Luis Orozco, the new leader of the Aztlán cartel."

Mango pointed at Jim. "Guerrero was a customer of your buddy."

"You're leaving now, aren't you?" Aaron asked, before adding, "I don't need those men to come back."

"Yes, we're leaving," Jim replied. He looked at Ryan who nodded in agreement. "I want you to know I've arranged for crews and supplies to be shipped from the mainland to begin rebuilding the hotel. I've also deposited money into your account for the work. It's money you won't have to repay. In fact, I consider your debt to me paid in full. I've authorized my accountant and attorney to send you the required paperwork for your signature." Jim placed a hand on Aaron's shoulder. "Aaron, I'm sorry for what's happened. We'll make the best of it. Now, if you'll excuse us, these gentlemen and I have a few things to discuss."

Aaron stood and looked at Jim for a long moment. His eyes darted to Karen and lingered there. He took a deep breath to calm his jangled nerves. Even so, the adrenaline was still pumping. He'd worked up a good lather before coming into the suite. He'd wanted a fight but was plied with money instead. "You better have a damned good lawyer. I've got a feeling we're about to be sued."

Jim nodded.

"And I don't want guns, drugs, or whatever else you're dealing anywhere near here. As far as I'm concerned, you don't have to come back either."

Jim looked crestfallen and Karen wounded.

Aaron smiled at her. "You're welcome back anytime, Karen."

She did not return the smile.

He'd just lost his best friend. Now angry at himself for his harsh words, he turned to leave. Pausing to look at Ryan, he said, "In case you're wondering, I don't have any money left to pay my taxes."

"You kept your end of the bargain, Aaron," Ryan said. "The government will forgive your back taxes, but what you do from here on out is your business."

CHAPTER THIRTY-TWO

Ryan watched Aaron walk away. He was sorry for bringing death and destruction to the man's place of business. He felt for the victims who'd been wounded and scared during the attack. There wasn't much he could do about it now. Kilroy was making amends with Aaron for the damages. Greg could offer monetary and material support through DWR, but that was up to him.

Kilroy cleared his throat. "Let's get back to what we were discussing earlier."

Ryan turned to look at the arms dealer. "What's stopping me from shooting you right now? That would end your reign of terror and stop the shipment."

Kilroy laughed. "I've ordered Oso, the first mate on my ship, to make the delivery no matter what."

"Then what do you need us for?" Mango asked.

"You're mercenaries for the U.S. government but you have a conscience. You won't shoot me because I'm unarmed. You suffer from the cowboy syndrome. You believe you wear the white hat and every fight must be fair. Gentlemen, this world is more ruthless than that. There are children in Darfur who would kill you for less than the price of a Big Mac. Drug dealers have a less caring attitude than you do. So, I'm going to put your do-right attitude to work for me and your precious United States."

"What does that mean?" Ryan asked, pulling an unlit cigarette from his mouth.

Kilroy smirked. "I only sell weapons; I don't use them."

"That makes you a self-righteous prick," Greg muttered.

Kilroy ignored the barb and continued. "Have you heard of Toussaint Bajeux?"

Ryan, Mango, and Greg shook their heads.

"Bajeux is planning a coup to overthrow the government in Haiti. He'll use the weapons I am selling him to do so. He must be stopped, and you're the men to do it."

"Don't deliver the weapons," Ryan said dryly.

"It's a catch twenty-two," Kilroy said, leaning back in his chair, and crossing his legs. He folded his hands in his lap and stared at Ryan as he continued. "I'm a businessman. My reputation is at stake. I have to deliver the weapons as a show of good faith, and he's paying me a lot of money. Gold in fact."

"Where'd he get gold in the poorest country on Earth?" Mango demanded.

Kilroy shrugged. "That's not my concern. The shipment must be made, and you'll be my proxies. Oso is a brute. He doesn't have the finesse to work with the clientele."

"I'm here to stop you," Ryan said, letting a hint of anger raise his voice. "I don't give a damn about some third-world dictator asshole."

"You should. If he takes office, the balance of power in the Caribbean will shift. He has big plans to bring his country out of the stone age."

"Let him," Ryan said. "That place needs to be cleaned up."

"It's not about cleaning up Haiti." Kilroy shook his head sadly. "He talks a good game about clean water and food, but what he wants is power and control of the country's natural resources. If he gets them, everything will shut down."

Greg snorted. "Just another in a long line of hapless leaders to abuse their country."

"More than that," Kilroy said. "Do you know what's happening in Venezuela?"

Ryan let a look of exasperation cross his face as he rolled his eyes. He didn't come here for a lesson in current events. "Hugo Chavez forced socialism onto the population and now they're rioting in the streets because there isn't enough food, clean water, and electricity to meet the demand."

"Exactly!" Kilroy exclaimed. "If you allow Toussaint access to his weaponry that's what will happen. He wants to nationalize the oil fields, the gold mines, and the factories. Every economic resource you can think of will become property of the Haitian government. All the investments that private companies have made will go down the drain. Foreign capital and knowledge will flee, and there will be no one left who can coax the natural resources out of the ground. Sure, there may be a small portion of Haitians who know how to run a factory or keep an oil rig pumping at max capacity but not enough to keep everything at full strength.

"Once the flow of money is completely shut off and the population is starving, they'll flood across the border to the Dominican Republic and build more rafts to escape to the U.S. It will be a travesty of epic proportions. In short, we can't let Toussaint have his weapons and ammunition."

Ryan asked, "Why'd you agree to sell them to him?"

Kilroy chuckled. "For the gold."

They sat silently staring at each other. Ryan had yet to be convinced as to why he should even care about some wannabe dictator. He was still debating about just lunging across the table, shoving his knife into the man's eye socket, and rooting around in his brain pan. Once Kilroy was dead, he could call the Coast Guard and have them intercept the gunrunner's ship.

Kilroy broke the silence. "Parsons had a plan on how to deal with the matter, but he neglected to tell me the specifics. So, it falls to you to come up with a way to stop Toussaint from ruining Haiti with his ideology."

Ryan spoke for the group. "This isn't our concern."

"Actually, it is," Kilroy said. "You're wanted men and wanted men don't have a lot of choices. Killing Guerrero stopped his war, but it opened a whole new can of worms for you. Not only do you have a two-million-dollar bounty on your heads, you're being chased by every two-bit bounty hunter from here to Russia. Look at the guy who attacked us last night, Volk was it? Let me help you out, a little quid pro quo."

"Don't listen to this asshat, Ryan," Mango said.

Kilroy smiled. "Asshat, I like it. I'll have to use that one."

"Be my guest," Mango said sarcastically.

"But to the point, Ryan," Kilroy said. "You should listen to me. I'm helping you out. I'm offering protection. Go to Haiti and stop Toussaint Bajeux's coup and I'll get Orozco to lift the bounty."

"Damn, you're narcissistic," Mango muttered.

Kilroy held up a hand. "I know you think I'm full of myself, but I can make this work. I've dealt with Orozco before and he responds to money, coke, and guns. I can provide two out of three. He wants to expand his cartel's sphere of influence. I can help him achieve his goals, a little firepower, a little cash in the proper hands." Kilroy waggled his hand side to side.

Mango fidgeted in his chair and glanced at Ryan before asking, "You can really get the bounty erased?"

"Yes." Kilroy was emphatic.

"Why us?" Ryan asked. "Other than the bounty. Don't you have a bunch of interchangeable mercs?"

The arms dealer rolled his eyes. "Believe it or not, my operation is relatively small." His mouth took on a grim set. "Darren was a competent employee, and while I'm sorry he's dead, I find this an opportunity I can't pass up. You have connections to the DHS and the U.S. government, do you not?"

Mango glared at Jim. "Why don't you take it?"

Kilroy shook his head and gave Mango a half smile, a gesture that lifted only one side of his lips. "I don't handle the merchandise."

"What do you want with our contacts?" Greg asked.

Kilroy said, "I want you to tell the DHS about the shipment when it gets to Haiti."

"Let me get this straight." Ryan removed the unlit cigarette from his mouth. "You want us to collect payment, then call in the DHS, or whoever else, to seize the weapons?"

Kilroy smiled and spread his hands. "Exactly."

"This is nuts," Mango said. "Let's go and take our chances on the bounty." He started to get up from his chair.

Ignoring Mango, Kilroy stared across the table at Ryan. "Why did you go after Guerrero?"

Ryan tilted his head back in thought. When he looked back at Kilroy, he said, "I went after him because he was a disease that needed to be eliminated. He was a threat to the security of the United States and as long as he was allowed to walk around, he would continue his plans to destroy parts or all of the Southwest to achieve his objectives. I couldn't allow that to happen. Just like I can't allow you to keep delivering weapons. Some men just need killing."

Kilroy clutched his sides as he let out a loud belly laugh. After a moment, he took several deep breaths to calm himself and wipe a tear from his red face. "That's funny."

Ryan glared at Kilroy.

Mango and Greg stared at Ryan.

Kilroy took a drink and set his glass back on the table. His roving gaze covered all three men before stopping on Ryan. "I do the work of the Lord and the U.S. government. Some would say it's one and the same. Your personal vendetta doesn't bother me one bit. I've had men like you come after me, yet here I am." He spread his arms out wide. "I want you to use that same thinking when it comes to Toussaint Bajeux. He's an enemy of his people, a wolf in sheep's clothing, so he can become a ruthless dictator. He needs to be put down just like you put down Guerrero. Use your patriotic fervor and zeal and make it happen." Kilroy leaned onto the table. "Just make sure I get my gold first."

Undisguised animosity crawled across Ryan's face. His lips turned down and his brows furrowed, making his eyes narrow slits. Anger burned hot on his skin. Kilroy had read him like a book and was using his loyalties and his connections against him. Ryan knew the bounty wouldn't be rescinded. It was just a ploy to lull them into helping. Kilroy could collect his gold and cap it with a two-million-dollar bonus. *Screw this guy!* Ryan thought. *I'm going to sink his ship, kill him, and steal his gold.*

Kilroy stared impassively into Ryan's eyes. "What's it going to be, frogman?"

"This is stupid!" Mango exclaimed.

"I've given you the carrot. Now I'll give you the stick." Kilroy pulled his Smith and Wesson from his waistband and laid it on the table. "With one phone call I can become two million dollars richer."

Ryan looked at the gun. As soon as Kilroy had taken his hand off it, he'd lost the advantage. He could be over the table delivering strikes to Kilroy's face before the man could wrap his fingers around the grip again.

Kilroy looked up at Mango. "Your wife, Jennifer, lives on

your sailboat at DWR, and she works at Mainland Medical Center in Texas City." Jim pointed at Ryan. "Your girlfriend, Emily Hunt, works for Ward and Young in Tampa, Florida." To Greg, he said. "Shelly Hughes is not only the COO of your company, she's your girlfriend. To top it off, your sister, Anna, is a graphics design artist with her own company in Galveston."

Greg fixed his icy stare on the international arms dealer. "Are you threatening me?"

Kilroy came to his feet, placed his hands on the table, and rested his upper body on them. "Yes, I'm threatening you, Greg Olsen. I'm threatening your family, and I'm threatening your friends' families. There isn't a damned thing you can do about it. You're a cripple riding on your buddies' coattails."

Greg's gray eyes didn't move from Kilroy's, but his face flushed with anger. "You're a genuine, grade-A asshole, Kilroy."

Ryan sipped some water and watched Greg's red face. He knew Jim was pressing Greg's buttons, and he'd done an excellent job. Ryan didn't want to deliver the weapons either, but he had to keep his friends safe, and stop the shipment. Maybe he was just selfish, but he wanted to preserve his own life.

"What do we need to do?" Ryan asked.

Kilroy grinned. "I knew you were the smart one."

"Wait," Mango exclaimed. "You want to do this?"

"It's not my first choice." Ryan shrugged. If he could stop the shipment, end the bounty, and prevent a Haitian revolution, then he would be Kilroy's envoy.

"It's not a choice at all," Greg said. "No deal, Killer Roy, you said yourself you don't have many resources and I can get protection for the girls before you can act on your threats."

"Greg," Kilroy said condescendingly. "I know you want to ride along with your friends and be part of the action, but I'm telling you that you have no say in the matter. The decision is Ryan and Mango's."

"What do you think, Karen?" Greg asked. "Do you think your husband is capable of the violence he threatens?"

She shifted in her seat, glancing between her husband and the other men at the table.

"Do you think he can get to our families before I can get to your mother?" Greg asked her.

Karen's eyes widened, and her mouth formed a tight circle.

Kilroy reached for the gun. Ryan beat him to it, snatching it away by the barrel before Kilroy's hand was halfway there. He pressed the muzzle to Kilroy's forehead. Kilroy stood stock still, eyes riveted to Ryan's finger gently squeezing the trigger.

Karen shrieked and threw her hands over her mouth.

Kilroy held his hands up in surrender and started to laugh.

"What's so funny?" Mango asked.

The arms dealer said through a wide smile, "You think you have a choice."

"Everything's a choice," Ryan said. He dropped the magazine from the pistol, racked the slide, and ejected the bullet. He set the gun on the table in front of Kilroy. "Your threats are as empty as that gun."

Kilroy laughed again, picked up the pistol, and pulled a new magazine from his pocket. He slammed it home and depressed the lock to let the slide snap a fresh round into the chamber. "Alfred A. Montapert once said, 'Nobody ever did, or ever will, escape the consequences of his choices.'"

Mango said, "That includes you."

"Yes, you're correct. I will pay for my sins, but I'll be able to pay for them in gold when you finish this deal. This concludes the negotiations." Kilroy aimed the pistol at Ryan. "You have no choice."

Greg leaned forward, his voice was low and deep, "I said, no."

Jim looked over his shoulder and called loudly, "Comacho."

Ryan recognized the short man with a massive purple and yellow bruise on the side of his neck. His lower lip was puffy and the skin around his jaw shaded with blacks and blues. A second man in a black police uniform stepped into the room. Both held leveled M16s on their hips.

"These gentlemen are here to escort you to Mexico," Kilroy said.

Comacho rasped out, "*Vamonous, pendejos.*" *Let's go, assholes.*

"Seriously, this again," Mango moaned.

"Okay." Ryan held his hands up. "We'll deliver the shipment." He didn't want to be tortured or killed by a crazy Mexican drug lord. He'd promised Emily he'd come home safe. More important, he had to keep her safe.

Kilroy was offering to put him on the delivery vessel, a chore he believed he would have to do clandestinely. This was a means to an end; stop the shipment, stop Kilroy, keep their families safe. If he took down Kilroy, it would prevent him from putting more weapons into the hands of an already dangerous cartel, but it would also prevent him from negotiating an end to the bounty. Choices.

"Excellent." Turning to Comacho, Kilroy said, "Take these men to my ship."

CHAPTER THIRTY-THREE

On *Dark Water's* bridge, Greg Olsen watched *Northwest Passage* motor toward the horizon. He slammed his hand down on the fiberglass console and ripped off a string of curse words like he was revving a chainsaw.

After leaving the restaurant, Comacho and Kilroy had accompanied Greg, Ryan, and Mango to *Dark Water*. Ryan and Mango had collected clothes and dive gear. Comacho searched them thoroughly for weapons before allowing them to leave the vessel. They'd loaded the RIB onto the foredeck of the Hatteras and helped Greg retrieve the anchor.

Greg turned on the computer tablet mounted on *Dark Water's* dash and used the Internet browser to open marine-tracker.com. He keyed in the name of Jim Kilroy's ship. The website didn't find an icon for *Northwest Passage*. Greg slapped the console again and used his broad knowledge of curse words to utter several oaths.

He picked up his satellite phone and dialed Floyd Landis's number. While listening to the phone ring on the other end, he drummed his fingers on the console.

"Landis."

"It's Greg Olsen. Darren Parsons is dead, and Kilroy is forcing Ryan and Mango to make the weapons shipment for him."

"What do you mean by force?"

"Apparently, the new head of the Aztlán cartel has issued a two-million-dollar bounty for Ryan and Mango. Kilroy is threatening to turn them in if they don't comply. He's also threatened Jennifer, Emily, Shelly, and my sister."

"I've heard rumors about the bounty. I'll have security put on your sister, Jennifer, and Emily. I assume you can handle Shelly."

"Yes. Jennifer is at DWR headquarters. There's already security there, whatever good an unarmed guard is? I'll contact Anna and let her know what's going on."

"I'll have your security beefed up," Landis promised. "We tracked the men who attacked the three of you in Texas City to a Russian named Grigory Dmitri Morozov, otherwise known as Volk."

Greg cut him off. "He's the one who attacked the resort."

Landis said, "What do you mean attacked the resort? The resort you were staying at?"

"Yes," Greg said and went on to explain the night's events in detail.

"Okay. Do you know where Kilroy is taking Ryan and Mango?"

"Cap-Haïtien, Haiti," Greg said. "Some dude named Toussaint Bajeux is paying for guns with gold. Kilroy says he can get the bounty called off if they do the delivery. He wants them to load the gold first and then let you come raid the shipment and stop Bajeux from starting a coup."

"How did he expect us to stop the weapons shipment?"

With one hand pressing the phone to his ear, Greg held up an arm in an exaggerated shrug. "Call Larry Grove and have him bring his SEALs like last time."

"I don't think that'll fly," Landis said. "Not in Haitian waters with the UN contingency there."

"What should we do?"

"After Ryan's Mexican debut, I'm pretty sure he can handle himself."

"We're on our own?" asked Greg.

"I'll see what I can do," Landis said. "But I can't make any promises. Kilroy has protection inside the government. I told Ryan that when he started on this witch hunt. My hands might be tied."

"You're kidding me. You can't call the Coast Guard and have them intercept the shipment before it gets to Haiti?"

"I'll see what I can do. What about communications with Ryan?"

"He's *incommunicado*."

"Nothing? No sat phone?"

"No ... I'm an idiot," Greg exclaimed. "He has a tracker with him. If he turns it on, we can get a fix on his location."

"What kind of tracker, Greg?"

"He has something new hidden in a cigarette pack." Greg keyed the website into the tablet to pull up the tracker.

After a few minutes of silence, Greg said, "I'll send you the website and password, so you can keep track of what's going on for yourself."

"Are you on the site right now?"

"Yes," Greg replied. He studied the tracker website. "He doesn't have it on."

"You need to hightail it out of Caye Caulker. If Volk finds out you're still there, he'll come after you."

"We came to that conclusion as well."

"What're your plans?"

"I'm running to Jamaica. I'll get fuel and hang around until Ryan sends me a message."

"Take care, Greg, and let me know as soon as you hear something."

"Will do."

Greg shoved the throttles forward, feeling the big boat come up on plane, the bow slicing through the small waves as he ran from trouble.

CHAPTER THIRTY-FOUR

After leaving Caye Caulker onboard Jim Kilroy's vessel, they'd sailed for Nicaragua. Kilroy's operations went mostly unchecked in the Central American countries, which were the equivalent of the Wild West of arms trafficking. Kilroy was no stranger to Nicaragua, having started his career in the small country by providing weapons to the Contra rebels fighting the communist Sandinista government. He then partnered with the CIA to move guns from the United States to Nicaragua in exchange for ferrying cocaine into Los Angeles.

When the Iran-Contra scandal broke in Washington, the politicians had hunted for prominent scapegoats and settled on Oliver North, leaving the grunts on the ground to continue their work. The CIA kept Jim employed, moving guns around the Caribbean basin until the politics had again gotten too hot, and they dropped him. He became a wanted criminal while continuing to funnel weapons, explosives, bullets, rockets, and missiles to any rebel force or government willing to pay his fees.

The War on Terror changed the playing field and Jim was

back in the good graces of the CIA. He shipped guns to Iraq and Afghanistan to arm their bourgeoning armies and even bid on contracts to supply new weapons to U.S. troops. While most of his weapons contracts were now legitimate, he still sold guns under the table.

For these illegal shipments, he used an aged, rusty freighter named *Santo Domingo*. Captain Santiago Guzmán waited with the *Santo Domingo* in a small channel in the Escondido River estuary, near the town of Bluefields. The vessel was anonymous among the local shipping traffic and town made for a convenient rendezvous spot.

Kilroy left *Northwest Passage* at a commercial dock in Blue-fields for refueling. He, Mango, and Ryan piled into his center console fishing boat to make the run to the *Santo Domingo*. There, Kilroy introduced them to the captain before he had a private conversation with the first mate, a hulking Latino bruiser named, *Oso*—Spanish for *Bear*.

On his way off the *Domingo*, Kilroy lingered by the ladder with Ryan and Mango. "Oso is my eyes and ears on this ship. He'll make sure you stick to the straight and narrow. He has my number on speed dial. You make a wrong move and I'll know about it." He waggled his finger. "Remember, I know where your women sleep at night."

Then he dropped down the ladder to the waiting center console.

"Bastard," Ryan said as Kilroy roared off.

"What now?" Mango asked.

"We need to get a message to Greg. The transmitter only works with a clear view of the sky. It'll take a minute or two to align with the satellites."

"That means someone will have to distract our minder."

"Correct." Ryan glanced in the direction of the first mate, who watched them from the bridge wing. "Once we're underway, we can see what the schedule's like. Then we can look for a hole to exploit."

The two Americans spent the next few days observing the ship's company routine, but either Oso or one of his lackeys kept them under constant observation. To stave off boredom, Ryan and Mango did pushups, pull-ups, and jumping jacks. To substitute for running, they fashioned jump ropes from scraps of discarded line. In the corner of the galley, they picked through the thriller novels, smut magazines, and catalogs in what constituted the ship's library. Ryan began sunning himself on one of the cargo hatch covers.

Now, the *Santo Domingo* cruised toward Haiti over the vast depths of the Cayman Trench. They were passing Jamaica to the north. In another day, they would cruise through the Windward Passage, the strait between Cuba and Haiti, before circling the island of Tortuga off Haiti's northwest coast. Tortuga had been the original haunt of swashbuckling buccaneers, and still harbored modern-day pirates. Guzmán would rather spend an extra twelve hours circumnavigating the island than have a chance meeting with pirates while traversing La Tortue Channel.

When they arrived off Cap-Haïtien, Ryan would contact Toussaint Bajeux. He was unsure how he would do this. Kilroy had assured him Toussaint would know when the ship had arrived in the port city.

Ryan stood at the railing, watching the relentless waves. Winds off the African Coast pushed the swells across the Atlantic to wash onto the shores of North, Central, and South America, and all the islands in between. He gripped the rusty, pitted rail, feeling the flaking paint chips and corroded steel bite into his skin. He knew his hands would be stained orange from the rust, yet he continued to grip the pipe, tensing the muscles of his protesting forearms, triceps, and shoulders. His skinned knuckles turned white from the strain under his sun-reddened skin. His body still ached from the abuse of his fights.

He was forced labor on this unregistered, untraceable dark ship. Having been on the bridge numerous times, he knew there was no automatic identification system broadcasting the ship's name, GPS coordinates, speed, hull number, and course to the world via satellite uplinks to websites like marinetracker.com. The World War II era rust bucket had little more than an antiquated radar system from the same time period and a modern Furuno GPS and chart plotter.

"I wish I had a cigarette," he grumbled to himself, thinking about the unopened pack in his gear bag.

Ryan closed his eyes and filled his nostrils with the salt air and acrid diesel smoke. Kilroy had promised to bargain for their release from Orozco with more weapons. *Just what the world needed, more guns in the hands of outlaws*, Ryan thought grimly. Would Orozco be satisfied with his own load of weapons? If not, what was the answer to their dilemma? If Ryan got caught trying to sabotage the operation, he and Mango would be right back in the crosshairs. Jim Kilroy knew where they worked. He'd done his homework, and someone was feeding him information. This thought made Ryan worry about Emily.

He looked down at the water rushing off the bow of the ship and shook his head. He'd survived tours in Afghanistan and Iraq and other hazardous deployments around the world, but never tied himself down with a woman. He'd been a faceless cog in the wheel of the mighty military industrial complex. Retaliation for his actions in operations were taken out on other military units, or the bombmakers placed a bounty on his head like many other EOD technicians who routinely thwarted the enemies' plans of destruction. The whole military industrial complex was there to back him up and protect him. When he'd left the theater of operations, the threats to his life had stopped.

He was on his own now, and in a relationship. There was no hiding from bounty hunters and madmen bent on threatening family and friends. There would be no decamping for home, leaving the enemy on a foreign battlefield, and finding safety in America, no military might to ambush and blister the enemy. There was only one way to deal with these people, and that was head-on. He had to come up with a direct course of action because so far, he had winged it, and winging it had gotten him nowhere.

Unfortunately, he had no plan. Too many unknown variables were being thrown at him.

Before Ryan had just been the sharp end of the stick, thrust outside the wire to do battle with the evil forces lurking on America's doorstep. As he moved higher in rank, he had become more involved in the planning and leadership of the team and their missions.

Right now, he was racking his brain for all the skills he had learned. What kept coming to him was an often-repeated quote among military personnel, German strategist and Field Marshal Helmuth Karl von Moltke's, "No battle plan ever survives contact with the enemy."

What came next was the old axiom, "It never hurts to have contingencies."

But what contingencies? If he didn't know the players, or the playing field, how could he develop a plan, let alone contingencies? He smacked the railing with his palm and rust flakes fell as the rail vibrated. *Get it together, Weller, you're a highly skilled operator trained to act and think tactically. Connect the dots. There's no reason why you can't figure this out.*

"Whatcha thinking about, bro?" Mango asked, walking up beside him.

Ryan spit over the rail. "Trying to come up with a plan."

Mango shook his head and gave voice to what Ryan had been thinking all along. "Can't plan for what we don't know."

Captain Guzmán, an aged Dominican with skin like wrinkled parchment and deep-set black eyes, interrupted their conversation. Ryan wondered if the man was as old as the ship itself. He was undoubtedly frail and weathered enough to match the ship's exterior. The old man knew the currents and the winds better than most and could probably pilot the ship by just the stars and a sextant.

Guzmán asked if they would like coffee, holding out two cups filled with the black brew. Ryan gripped the rail tighter; afraid he would boil over at the captain who had treated him with nothing but kindness. His anger was at himself and at Jim Kilroy. Ryan let out a long breath and nodded. He let go of the railing and felt the pressure ease in his sore muscles. He took the chipped ceramic mug in his stained hands. Ryan smiled as he felt the hot liquid burn his lip, just the way he liked his coffee, black like his soul.

The captain handed Mango the other scarred cup before stepping back onto the bridge. A moment later he returned with his own mug. He looked up at Ryan and in Spanish said, "I know you're in trouble."

"I'll figure something out," Ryan said.

"The only true way out is death." Guzmán sipped his coffee.

"*La verdad.*" *The truth*.

Guzmán nodded thoughtfully and watched the sun setting on the western horizon. In the time he'd been aboard, Ryan had grown to like the old man. They sipped coffee and silently watched the day turn into night.

The captain pulled a pack of cigarettes from his pocket and shook one loose. He stuck it between his lips. He shook out another one and offered it to both men. Mango shook his head, but watched his friend closely, searching his face for weakness.

Ryan succumbed to temptation and relieved the man of the cigarette. Guzmán's leathery face cracked with a knowing smile. Mango shook his head as Ryan lit it.

"You promised Emily you'd quit."

Ryan checked the anger rising inside of him and managed a terse, "You've never broke a promise to your wife?"

"This is twice you promised her you'd quit, and you haven't."

Ryan turned away. There was no winning the argument. They were picking at each other because they were captives on a journey neither wanted to take, to a country neither wanted to go. Ryan thrust the cigarette into his mouth, lit it, and inhaled deeply. It felt good to breathe the pungent smoke and feel the rush of nicotine.

The trio stood in silence as the sun slipped below the horizon. Guzmán dumped the dregs of his coffee overboard and retreated to the bridge with all three coffee cups. Ryan and Mango walked down the stairwell to the main deck.

"I've got an idea for using the transmitter," Mango said.

Ryan stopped walking. He blew out some smoke. "Yeah?"

"Isn't it disguised as a pack of cigarettes?"

"Yeah." Ryan nodded.

"Next time you go sunbathing, lay it out beside you."

Ryan scratched the stubble on his cheek. "I'll do it tomorrow."

"Good, I'll see you later." Mango waved his hand in the air to dispel the smoke. "That thing stinks."

He turned away from Mango and leaned on the railing, knowing his forearms would be rust red to match his hands. The repetitive motion of bringing the cigarette to his mouth was soothing. When he'd drawn the last pull, he rose to his full six-foot height and stubbed the butt out on the railing.

He pocketed the filter instead of tossing it into the water. Salt water could break down many things, but cigarette butts were not one of them. He disliked seeing his fellow man pollute the oceans with their careless actions.

Ryan turned away from the rail and went to find the cigarettes in his kit. Maybe along the way, he'd figure out how to get out of this mess.

CHAPTER THIRTY-FIVE

Greg Olsen sat at the outside bar of the Royal Jamaica Yacht Club. With an ice-cold Red Stripe in his hand, he had a clear view of the turquoise pool surrounded by sun-bronzed beauties and splashing kids. Past the pool, a C-shaped breakwater protected a marina crowded with all manner of sail and motor vessels. Farther still were the dark blue waters of Kingston Harbor, framed by the verdant hills of Jamaica. His gaze traveled back to the sleek white-and-blue fiberglass of *Dark Water*.

After arriving at the yacht club, he had taken on a full load of fuel and fresh water. He wanted to be ready to go the moment he received a signal from Ryan. Greg monitored the tracker website, had a mechanic check over *Dark Water*'s engines, and paid two men to scrub down her hull before applying a new coat of wax.

The signal finally came. Greg was thankful because he had chewed his fingernails to the skin. He'd picked up the nervous habit of cleaning and cutting his nails with his teeth after his injury. For him, it was a calming action, and he noticed he was worrying his left thumbnail as he read the dispatch.

MANGO AND I ON CARGO VESSEL SANTO DOMINGO. PASSING JAMAICA TODAY.

GREG CALLED Floyd Landis who had also seen the burst transmission and initiated satellite coverage of the Caribbean to look for the *Santo Domingo*. Without the industry-wide AIS, the ship would be difficult to track. Fortunately, they knew the starting and ending points of the vessel's voyage. It wouldn't be difficult to gauge the vessel's speed and therefore its transition time.

The next call Greg made was to Shelly Hughes.

She answered on the third ring and sounded preoccupied.

"Want me to call back?" he asked.

"No, no," Shelly said. He could hear her moving around. "How are you?" Her voice changed to the sweet, soft notes he enjoyed.

"I can't be too bad, I'm in Kingston, Jamaica."

"Have you heard from Ryan?"

"Yeah, he sent me a message. I just got off the phone with Landis."

"Is everything okay?"

"All we know it that they're heading for Haiti. Do we have any assets there?"

Shelly moaned in disgust. "We had a few crews working on oil rigs for DINASA, but the Chinese ate us alive with contract prices. We ended up pulling everyone out. Right now, we're moving everything out of the way of Hurricane Irma. Speaking of which, you are aware you're in her projected track, right?"

"I know. I'm ready to run if I need to."

"Keep a close eye on this storm. She's one of the most powerful hurricanes ever registered."

"What about salvage vessels and crews?"

"Nothing close. We moved everyone, Greg," Shelly said in exasperation. Her voice steadied as she continued. "I'm prepared to send them in as soon as they're needed and let me tell you this: Admiral Chatel and I are preparing to do goodwill operations for some of the smaller islands. This storm is going to damage a lot of homes, infrastructure, and equipment."

"Okay, I'll keep an eye on it."

"Do you have something in mind for one of our teams?" she asked. "We're already stretched pretty thin."

"I don't know. I just thought I'd ask. Is everything else good?"

"I'd rather be in Jamaica with you." Shelly had gotten a taste of action when she'd helped Greg race across the Gulf of Mexico to rescue Ryan and Mango after their sailboat had been shot out from under them.

"I wish you were here, too," Greg said. He took a sip of beer and watched two kids jump off the edge of the pool, wrap their arms around their knees to form cannonballs, and splash half a dozen dozing bikini-clad women. The cool water against their sun-warmed skin made them sit bolt upright. Several screamed in surprise and Greg laughed.

"What's so funny?" Shelly demanded.

"Kids jumping into the pool. Can you call Jennifer and Emily and let them know what's going on?"

"Can't you do it? I've got work I need to get done, and you're not busy."

"Why don't you quit that stressful job and we can be Ryan's chauffeurs?"

"That sounds lovely, Greg ..." she trailed off.

Greg could hear another voice in the room.

Shelly said, "I have to go."

"Love you." Greg didn't know if she heard him.

Calling women to report on the progress of their men was not an activity he enjoyed. It felt too close to writing letters to the wives and families of sailors who had died under his command.

He set the phone down on the bar top and pointed at the empty shot glass. A minute later, the bikini-clad bartender brought a shot of Appleton Estate Jamaica Rum and a Red Stripe beer. Fortified, he picked up the phone.

CHAPTER THIRTY-SIX

Grigory Dmitri Morozov exited the plane, walked across the tarmac of Jamaica's Norman Manley International Airport, and climbed into a black Suzuki Grand Vitara. The massive man had to turn sideways to squeeze his shoulders in and to stuff his long legs into the front passenger seat footwell. He swore in Russian and ratcheted the seat all the way back. It was not enough to keep his knees from still being wedged into the dash.

The driver pulled away from the hanger, apologizing for the small vehicle. Volk ignored him and accepted a pistol from a man sitting behind the driver. He shook the Beretta 92F. The slide rattled. Volk shook his head in disgust at the lack of care the firearm had received and pulled the slide back. Next, he dropped the magazine and examined the full metal jacket rounds. He thumbed a cartridge out and looked at the name stamped into the brass. He held the bullet under the nose of his subordinate. In Russian, he said, "What is this shit? All the money I give you and you buy this junk?"

"We bought the best we could through our street gang

connections," Alexei Rodin answered. "We didn't have time to find decent weapons."

"What else did you get?"

"Twelve-gauge Mossberg 500 shotguns."

Volk nodded and crammed the bullet back into the magazine. Angrily, he slammed the mag into the butt of the pistol and rested the gun in his lap. He missed working for the SVR, Russia's external intelligence agency. There he had protection via diplomatic immunity and access to state secrets and resources. Pushed out by the petty politics and backstabbing created by the current czar for life, Vladimir Putin, Volk had become an outsider. He naturally fell into the lucrative wet work and bounty hunting offered by Chechen gangs and other organized criminal groups in the former Soviet satellite countries. After a stint as a lap dog for those *pidarasy—assholes*—he had stepped out on his own.

Absentmindedly, he rattled the pistol again, and again he missed the convenience of a diplomatic pouch. He could carry his favorite pistol, a customized nine-millimeter Yarygin Grach, the preferred pistol of the Russian police, through international customs without anyone being the wiser. How many unsolved crimes had he committed with that gun? He sighed and thought ruefully of it lying in the bottom of the murky River Seine. Stupid bourgeois French Gendarmerie and their dogs chasing him through the arrondissements like a common criminal.

Turning to Alexei, Volk asked, "How long until we arrive at the marina?"

"Ten minutes, Grigory Grigoryevich."

Volk shoved the pistol barrel against Alexei's head and roared, "Never call me that again."

Alexei, head jammed between the window and the gun, nodded.

Volk had told him several times that he did not like being

called by his first name, let alone being reminded he bore the last name of his father, a disloyal patriot.

Alexei recognized his mistake in the time it took him to speak the words, and he quickly moved on. "Using the tracker, we placed on Greg Olsen's Zodiac, we were able to follow him to the Royal Jamaican Yacht Club. We've been watching him since he arrived. He doesn't leave the club grounds. He acts like he's waiting for something."

"We'll find out soon enough," Volk said.

They drove along Buccaneer Beach, following the serpentine road past the Caribbean Maritime University to the yacht club. The driver parked the SUV under the shade of a tree just inside the yacht club grounds and shut off the engine.

The three beefy Russians exited the Suzuki. Two were dressed in pressed slacks with long-sleeved dress shirts under sport coats while Volk sported a pair of khaki cargo pants and a Columbia fishing shirt. They left the shotguns in the vehicle and walked to the clubhouse.

Volk bypassed the stairs, took a long ramp to the bar, and sat at the far end with his back to the breathtaking views of the harbor. He eyed the American in a wheelchair, who was eating a hamburger and washing it down with beer.

CHAPTER THIRTY-SEVEN

Greg Olsen watched the blond giant sit on a bar stool and order a beer. In the three days Greg had occupied a seat at the bar, he'd seen many people come and go and had made several interesting acquaintances, but Volk was the first Russian he'd seen. Greg recognized the man from a photo Landis had texted him after their phone conversation.

What the hell is he doing here? Greg wondered.

Trying to remain calm, Greg dragged a fry through a puddle of ketchup on his plate and shoved it into his mouth. *They must be here because they think Ryan and Mango are on* Dark Water. *How did they find me?*

The answer was logical. They had put a tracker on *Dark Water.* He castigated himself for not checking the boat for tracking devices. Then he cursed his useless legs for not allowing him full access to all the boat's spaces.

Greg dropped his hand to where he kept his cell phone clipped to his belt loop. With quick little glances at the screen, he pecked out a message one handed and sent it to Landis.

Greg looked up to find Volk taking a seat beside him.

"You know why I am here, *tovarishch*."

"I don't speak Russian, comrade," Greg said dryly.

Volk laughed and slapped a dinner plate-sized hand on Greg's back. "*Tovarishch* means comrade."

Greg smiled. "How ironic."

This time Volk looked puzzled.

"I was being sarcastic."

The Russian narrowed his brow.

"I was making fun of you, Wolfie."

Volk's eyebrows raised, and he laid his lips back over his teeth in what passed for his smile. "My reputation precedes me."

"*Da*." Greg sipped his beer.

Volk laughed again. "I like you, Greg Olsen."

"I'm guessing you're not here to make small talk."

"You are smart man. You will tell me where comrades are, da."

"I don't know."

"I'm sure you find out soon. By then we will be good friends." Volk looked out at the marina shadowed by the mountains blocking the setting sun. "I like your boat."

Greg had a decision to make. He knew where Ryan was going to be, and he wanted to get into position to help him if he could. With Volk here, Greg could not leave without either taking the Russian with him, or having Volk tail him. The third option was to do nothing and sit here until Ryan told him the weapons transfer was complete.

None of the options were appealing. The only way Volk could obtain the information he wanted was to either hack Greg's electronic devices, or to torture him. Greg knew a little about torture, having been through the military's Survival, Evasion, Resistance, and Escape school. The instructors had subjected him, and the other students, to torture and one thing always rang true. Everyone broke. It was just a matter of time before the pain became unbearable.

Volk put his hand on Greg's shoulder. "You will tell me." He began to squeeze.

Greg kept his face a mask even as the Russian dug his fingers deep into his muscles. Pain shot up through his neck and down his arm.

Again, he cursed the uselessness of his body and his lack of ability to fight off the bounty hunter. He would just have to outsmart them and to do that he would have to be on his guard.

CHAPTER THIRTY-EIGHT

Emily Hunt ran the shower as hot as she could stand. She had just finished a three-mile run and was ready to sit on the sofa, sip a glass of wine, and watch some television. She wanted to relax. Instead, she worried about her boyfriend. She let the water pound her back, feeling the heat loosen the muscles along her five-foot-ten frame.

"Damn you, Ryan," she muttered, wiping water from her cornflower-blue eyes and running her hands over her bra-length blonde hair, wringing the water from it. Darkened with water, it wasn't the normal color of harvest wheat. She pulled the thick mane over her shoulder and twisted it. Ryan had called it her Viking hair. The memory made her smile, but it didn't last long.

Once again, he was in trouble, and she was stuck at home worrying about him. The worry had been constant since Greg's phone call. Emily had once been involved with a fellow officer when she'd been a deputy in the Broward County Sheriff's Department. She understood what it was like to be the loved one of a deployed service member or police officer and to fear for his safety. It was something she never wanted to do again after she'd broken up with her former beau. Yet, she had chosen to get involved with Ryan.

Emily cocked her head to hear over the roar of the water. She thought she heard her cell phone chime. Shutting off the shower, she grabbed a towel and dried her hands before picking up the phone. A text message icon blinked on the screen. She tapped the icon, and a message from Greg appeared. She read it twice silently, then once out loud. "Russian is here. Has tracker on *Dark Water*. S.O.S."

After a moment of contemplating the meaning of the message, she said, "Why did you send this to me, Greg?"

She dried herself and pulled on pajamas pants and a T-shirt still pondering the mystery. On her way to the kitchen, she thumbed the phone icon, opened the favorites, and tapped the picture of Shelly Hughes. She waited for the phone to ring then put it to her ear. Shelly didn't answer.

Emily dialed the number again. This time Shelly picked up as Emily poured a glass of Moscato.

Without preamble, Emily blurted, "Have you heard from Greg?"

"He called me from Jamaica. He said he was waiting to hear from Ryan."

"He told me the same thing. But I just got a text from him that said some Russian was with him and they were tracking *Dark Water*."

"I don't know anything about it," Shelly admitted.

"Do you have the number for the DHS guy, Landis?"

"Yes. Didn't Ryan give it to you?"

"No," Emily said. "I didn't think I'd need it. I should have known better. Whenever Ryan's involved things go pear shape."

"This is true," Shelly said before reciting Landis's office and cell phone numbers. Emily wrote them down in a notebook she kept on the coffee table.

"Thanks, Shelly."

"Keep me in the loop."

Emily hung up and looked at the numbers scrawled across the paper. She fingered the phone and scrolled back to the text message. She composed a message, erased it, and wrote another one. "Do you need help?"

CHAPTER THIRTY-NINE

Greg's phone chimed, and he looked down at the screen. Volk had left the bar, leaving one of his men in his stead. He swatted a mosquito while he read the text from Emily, puzzled for a minute until he read the sender information above it and realized she had been the inadvertent recipient of his S.O.S.

He keyed a new message.

RUSSIAN BOUNTY HUNTER *Volk tracking Ryan and Mango. He's using me to find them. Get Ryan's tracker number from Ryan's office and send him message. Call Landis.*

"WHAT YOU DO?" the Russian minder asked in heavily accented English. He came around the bar and saw the phone in Greg's hand. Greg glanced around the bar, frantic to keep the man from reading his messages and knowing he was in contact with Landis and Ryan.

The man extended his hand. "You give me phone."

Greg stared up at the man. He could drop the phone into a glass of water, but that would cut off his communication with Ryan, and anyone else. He had thought about his next move for the past ten minutes. If he wanted to avoid torture, he could give Ryan's destination to Volk, but the bounty hunter could kill him just to tie up a loose end. If Emily passed on his message, Landis would know Volk was with him and might send help. She could also pass the word to Ryan. Sending Volk to Haiti would allow him to roam free and strike at any time. Taking Volk to Haiti on *Dark Water* would allow Greg to keep his enemies close and gain a chance to eliminate them.

Greg clipped the phone back into its holder. "I'll keep the phone. Let's go see Wolfie."

CHAPTER FORTY

Emily stared at the message. Ryan Weller had once again sucked her into the vortex surrounding him. She sent another text to Greg. No response came immediately, and she kept an eye on the clock as she waited.

After fifteen minutes, she dialed Floyd Landis's cell phone number.

A gruff voice answered, "Landis."

"Hi, you don't know me. My name is Emily Hunt and—"

"I am well aware of who you are, Ms. Hunt. What can I do for you?"

"I received a text message from Greg Olsen. He meant to send it to you but got me instead." She rushed on without waiting for a response. "It says there's a Russian bounty hunter named Volk following Ryan. He has a tracker on *Dark Water* and is going to use Greg to find Ryan. Greg said to get Ryan's tracker information from Ryan's office and send him a warning."

"Anything else?"

"Just that I'm worried. Why is a bounty hunter after Ryan?"

"I want you to know that Ryan is fine. I received a message from him this morning. He's on his way to Haiti."

"Haiti," she exclaimed. "Why is he going to Haiti and you didn't answer my first question."

Landis sighed. Emily listened to him move around, heard what she assumed were car keys rattling.

"What are you doing?" she asked.

"Going to Ryan's office to send him a message. I'm surprised you don't have his tracker information."

A car engine started.

Emily said, "I'm mad that I don't. Stop changing the subject and answer some questions."

"The new leader of the Aztlán cartel has placed a two-million-dollar bounty on Ryan and Mango's heads. Volk is one of several people trying to cash in on the bounty."

"What about Haiti?" she demanded.

"He's trying to escape the bounty."

"Why isn't Greg with him?"

"They had to separate. Look, I don't have time to explain it all to you right now. I hope I never have too. Ryan and Mango are going to be fine. We have plans to protect them."

"I hope they're more than plans," she muttered. A knock on the door interrupted her from continuing to give Landis a piece of her mind. She pulled on a robe as she walked to the door.

Emily slid the dead bolt back and opened the door until the chain caught. Through the gap she could see a man and a woman standing in the hallway. The woman's brown hair was in a bun and she wore jeans and DHS windbreaker. The man stood slightly behind her and moved into Emily's line of sight. He had on a wrinkled suit and his hair had been cut short to the scalp.

The woman flashed a badge, and said, "Sorry to bother

you, ma'am. I'm Agent Boyle. This is Agent Alzario. Floyd Landis, from Homeland, sent us."

Emily realized she was still clutching the phone to her ear. She hissed at Landis, "Did you send agents to my apartment?"

"Yes."

"Why?" She undid the chain and opened the door before walking back to the sofa.

"You, Shelly, Jennifer, and Greg's sister have been threatened by an international arms dealer named Jim Kilroy."

"Is this part of what Ryan's involved in?"

"Yes," Landis confirmed. "I also sent agents to stay with the others until this is over. Is there anything else, Ms. Hunt, I need to go?"

"How long until this is over?"

"Not long."

"I hope." She hung up the phone and turned to the two agents who were now standing in her living room. The front door was locked, bolted, and chained.

"Please sit down," Boyle said, motioning to the sofa.

Emily sat down wearily. She was unused to someone ordering her around in her own home. She cradled her phone in her lap, wishing Ryan would call and tell her this was all a bad dream. She looked up at the agents and disliked them immediately. Not because they were there to protect her, but because Ryan had placed her in a position which she needed protection.

Alzario walked through the apartment, checking doors and windows, while Boyle sat down uninvited. Her brown eyes were a little too far apart over a thin nose. She seemed to be examining Emily, and Emily pulled the front of her robe closed as Boyle gave her a condescending sneer. Emily self-consciously patted and smoothed her Viking hair.

She was a trained police officer and a professional insurance investigator, but Emily's heart raced. She closed her eyes and took several deep breaths. Finally, she asked, "Why are you here?"

"For your protection. I believe Mr. Landis explained it to you."

"You have no information other than a threat has been made?"

"Correct," Alzario said from the kitchen doorway.

"If you're staying here, I hope you brought your own blankets and food," Emily retorted. She disliked this inconvenience. This relationship with Ryan was becoming more trouble than it was worth.

CHAPTER FORTY-ONE

After his daily exercise regimen, Ryan had begun walking the ship, looking in the various rooms, holds, and lockers. The days at sea kept the crew busy and they didn't focus on the two passengers as much as they had when they'd first left Nicaragua. It gave him time to come up with a plan. So far, he'd found little inspiration.

Today, he knew they were making their way out of the Windward Passage and around Tortuga. He felt the time crunch. A saying of one of his old chiefs echoed in his ears, "If you don't believe there is a solution, then you won't find oned." Another day and they'd be off Cap-Haïtien. Having a deadline sharpened his thinking.

In the beginning of his Navy EOD career, he'd used checklists to help guide his decision making when he arrived at the game show—the bomb site. Then he also began to navigate by using his intuition gained through experience. One of the things he believed in was assessing the threat and effectively using what the enemy had given him. Now, he made his own checklist to identify what he'd been given and what he could use against the enemy. The two things that married his current foes were gold and guns. All he had to do was deny them both the opportunity to take possession of what they desired.

In a little-used compartment, he found the deck and shelves littered with odd sections of pipe, rusted pieces of metal, ropes, boards, and other assorted items cast off by the crew. He shook his head as he looked at the mess, thinking about the boot camp Recruit Division Commanders—the Navy's equivalent to drill instructors—screaming about gear adrift. They'd get right in your face and tell you what a worthless, lower-than-whale-poop, shipmate-endangering individual you were for leaving gear, equipment, or personal property unsecured.

Once, when Ryan and his fellow recruits were attending a class, the RDCs went into the barracks and knocked over lockers, scattered gear, toppled bunks, and stripped sheets in what was known as "a hurricane." The recruits knew it was coming, it was just a matter of when.

As they filed back into the barracks, they found everything askew. Amid the chaos, the RDCs made them drop into the push-up position. For the next two hours, they performed physical training with the windows and doors shut and the heat turned up. The floor became slick with sweat and the ceiling dripped condensation in what the RDCs referred to as "making it rain." The RDCs had marched up and down the room, screaming and yelling at the recruits, calling out exercise cadences, and harassing individuals they did not find worthy of joining their Navy. It was a lesson none of the recruits would ever forget, and forged in that fire was the deep-seated need to stow everything in its proper place.

Standing in the compartment, with a smile of remembrance on his face, an idea formed in Ryan's mind. He began to sort through the scrap, and set a few items aside, careful to make everything look as if it hadn't been disturbed. Which wasn't hard given the room's state of disarray.

He had another memory, this one from Iraq. They'd tracked a bombmaker to his factory and raided it. The bombmaker had been killed and the EOD team had taken a large number of explosively formed penetrators off the street. Capable of defeating the armor on Humvees and the Mine-Resistant Ambush Protected vehicles used to transport troops, the EFP was responsible for more deaths in combat than any other form of improvised explosive device.

The EFP was essentially a steel tube packed with explosives and capped with a concave piece of metal or copper to act as the projectile. Copper was preferred because it was more malleable. The force of the explosion turned the cap inside out, forming a bullet shaped projectile.

Ryan placed his foot on a small section of pipe as it rolled with the motion of the ship. While the *Santo Domingo* didn't have armor, she did have thick steel hull plates. There wasn't enough C-4 stashed in his cigarette packs for two shape charges large enough to cause the wounds he wished to inflict. He did have enough to build two EFPs. Detonating them on either side of the keel, at the bow of the ship, would ensure the ship went down quickly. The force of water rushing in through the damaged hull would tear out her bottom, and the ship would drive herself underwater.

As soon as the gold was onboard, he'd trigger the blast, and he and Mango would use one of the lifeboats to escape.

Ryan found two pieces of pipe with bolt flanges on one end then located two caps for them. He loosely secured the caps with bolts and found several thin sheets of metal. Using a hammer and a wooden stake, he formed the metal into cones.

Heading back to his bunk room, Ryan passed Oso, who glanced at his orange hands. Ryan held them up in a gesture of surrender and pointed into the hold. "I was helping to secure a few loose chains on the Humvees. We don't want them shifting around."

Oso regarded him with suspicion before turning away. Ryan breathed a sigh of relief and continued to their room.

Mango was lying on his bunk, reading a Clive Cussler novel.

"Which one is that?" Ryan asked, pointing to the book.

"*Mediterranean Caper*."

"The first Dirk Pitt. Man, I read every one of those. He and Travis McGee were the best when I was growing up. I wanted to be those guys. Always a cool adventure and always a good-looking woman."

Mango chuckled. "Now you're living the life."

Ryan grinned. "Yeah, something like that."

Mango swung his legs off the bunk and sat up. "Whatcha doin', bro?"

"Nothing to worry about," Ryan said, extracting seven packs of cigarettes from the carton. He stuffed the nearly empty carton back into his pack. He opened a pack and pulled a cigarette out. He stuck it in his mouth and arranged the rest of the packs in his cargo pockets.

"What do you think?" Ryan asked. "Do they make me look fat?"

"Actually, smoking *has* gone straight to your hips."

"Nice," Ryan chuckled.

"Seriously, if Oso sees you, he'll stop you for a spot inspection. What's going on?"

"I'll tell you about it later." Ryan slipped out the cabin door and made his way down to the storage compartment-turned-bomb factory.

He kept the unlit cigarette behind his ear while he worked. He'd disarmed more EFPs than he cared to think about, giving him firsthand knowledge of how to build them.

Ryan used a file he'd pilfered from the tool room and cut a groove into the pipe so the det wires wouldn't be crimped when he tightened down the bolts. Then he fished the wires through the gap between the pipe and cap and finished screwing the cap bolts down. Finally, he molded the C-4 into the pipe around the detonator, leaving room for the conical cap, which he inserted with the cone point facing into the pipe. After repeating the procedure, he had two homemade insurgency devices. He set the detonators to the frequency of the car remote he'd use to trigger the EFPs, and then removed the battery from the remote. He didn't want an accidental discharge.

Ryan hid his bombs in the room by covering them with a length of heavy, two-inch diameter rope. Satisfied with his handiwork, he exited the compartment and walked up onto the main deck.

He lit his cigarette which was now a bit soggy from sweat and saliva. It still tasted marvelous in the hot, afternoon sunshine. He made sure Oso saw him and when he finished his smoke, retreated to the bow of the ship.

The main cargo area had access to the forward hold, a smaller version of the main hold. It was empty on this voyage and as Ryan stepped cautiously through the cavernous room, he could hear water rushing past the hull and feel the pulse of machinery though the deck plates. It was dark and eerie. He hurried forward to a hatch that would access the bow of the ship. Clicking on a small flashlight he'd brought from his backpack, he shoved open the door. The narrow grate of a walkway extended through the ribs and stringers to the very prow.

Using the light, he inspected the hull to find a suitable location for his explosives. Not happy with the options he saw, Ryan got on his hands and knees, crawled under the decking of the forward hold, and shone the light around. He'd have to place the EFPs so they'd do maximum damage. If they didn't punch a big enough hole, and Guzmán backed off the ship's power and sent crews to secure watertight hatches and doors, the ship might have a chance of staying afloat. But Ryan knew they didn't have the manpower or the supplies to make the necessary repairs to save the old girl. He stopped moving and focused the light. He'd spotted the perfect place to secure his charges.

Ryan had to make two trips to the hold and enlisted Mango's help to keep Oso and the crew distracted while he carried the EFPs to their final resting place. He braced them on either side of the keel, ensuring the projectiles would hammer though the thick, metal plating. Then he secured them in place by jamming pieces of old metal and wooden strongbacks, which were stored in the forward compartment for damage control, between the EFPs and the ribs they rested beside. He ran the thin detonator wires under the decking to the access hatch and wired the hatch hinges and locking mechanism with C-4. He placed the receiver above the door where it wouldn't be seen.

When he pressed the detonator, the door would blow off its hinges and the penetrators would knock the bottom out of the old gal. The open door would allow the water to flow unimpeded into the forward hold.

He was hot and sweating when he finished with the job. His clothes were dirty and wet from the water sloshing under the hold, so he took a moment to change. Then he climbed to the bridge where he found Captain Guzmán carefully observing the weather. Bands of rain were pushing north ahead of the hurricane.

Guzmán said of the rainstorm, "It will pass to the east."

The *Santo Domingo* was well out to sea to avoid the Haitian fishing vessels, which sometimes tried to capture and ransom freighters and other sailing vessels much like the

Somali pirates had done. Ryan studied the charts laid out on the bridge's table, marked with their precise position and scheduled arrival time, but his eyes traced the water depths along the ship's course.

He joined Guzmán on the bridge wing and lit a cigarette. "How soon until we contact Toussaint Bajeux?"

"Not long, my friend," Guzmán replied.

CHAPTER FORTY-TWO

Greg Olsen powered the big Hatteras through the rolling waves of the Atlantic Ocean. His Russian passengers were still seasick from their transition of the Windward Passage. The fifty-mile-wide channel between Cuba and Haiti was the main shipping lane into the Caribbean Sea. It was also the entrance to the Cayman Trench. Confused seas were common in the restriction formed by the Nicaraguan Rise and the Cayman Ridge where the earth plunged to nearly seventeen hundred feet in depth and two oceans collided.

This was Greg's first passage through the strait. For him, navigating around the slower freighter traffic was more hectic than the actual waves themselves.

He had no compassion for his companions. He was just a boat-driving hostage at this point. When Greg had left the bar to find Volk, the Russian had been waiting for him on *Dark Water*. After Greg transferred to the boat, Volk had his men drag him inside the salon. The goons had set him on the settee. Volk rummaged through the small bag attached to the wheelchair's cushion where Greg kept his valuables. He'd taken the phone and scrolled through the contents until he found the message from Ryan and the conversations with Landis and Emily.

Greg was helpless without his chair, and Volk had all the evidence in his hands. The bounty hunter had then pocketed the phone and turned to leave.

"I'll take you to Haiti," Greg had said.

Volk turned back and gave him a hard stare. "We leave you here, take boat."

"Do you or your men know anything about running a boat like this?"

The blond giant had paused for a moment and then nodded as if he'd reached a decision. He had pointed at Greg. "You do nothing funny."

Now, only Volk kept him company on the bridge, his eyes on the instruments and chart plotter. The GPS's destination countdown timer was getting lower as the miles became fewer. Greg would be happy to get to Cap-Haïtien. There were few places on the Haitian coast where a private boat could take on diesel fuel because most Haitians still conducted their trades via sailing vessels and most cruisers avoided the island like the plague.

A long swath of bioluminescent phosphorescence bloomed in their wake. Above, the stars were intensely bright. Greg traced the shape of Ursa Major, aligning the two stars of the dipper, Merak and Dubhe, to point at Polaris, the North Star. They were not yet curtained by the clouds of the hurricane Greg knew were moving fast across the Atlantic. It was a race against time to locate Ryan and Mango and extract them before the storm hit.

He could feel the vibrations of the big diesels through the wheel. It comforted him to know they were running true. He had cut back on the speed, explaining to an irate Russian the relationship between fuel consumption and knots per hour.

"We are getting close. We find ship."

"We need fuel," Greg emphasized by pointing at the gauges.

Volk nodded. "I get drink?"

"Grab me a soda."

Greg smiled. One of the benefits of his guests being seasick was their lack of appetite. They hadn't taken advantage of the supplies he'd had loaded before leaving Jamaica.

After Volk disappeared down the ladder, Greg switched on the console-mounted tablet. It took several agonizingly long minutes to boot up and connect to the satellite internet system.

"What are you doing?" Volk demanded as he climbed back onto the bridge.

Greg looked over his shoulder at the big Russian. "Checking my email. You want to find Ryan? I need to know if he's communicated with me."

"You call him on phone."

Greg ignored Volk and focused on an email from Floyd Landis. He tapped it with his finger, and the screen changed to show the message. "I told you we'd find him. Look." He pointed to the email.

Volk set the can of soda on the console before leaning over Greg's shoulder. His breath stank of garlic and rotten food. Greg shifted his weight to lean farther away. Together, they read the brief email:

TOUSSAINT BAJEUX IS ONE OF THE MOST FEARED WARLORDS IN HAITI. HE CONTROLS MUCH OF THE NORTHEASTERN PORTION OF THE ISLAND WITH HIS BASE BEING SOMEWHERE NEAR CAP-HAÏTIEN. TOUSSAINT IS WANTED BY THE DEA FOR NARCOTICS TRAFFICKING AND BY IMMIGRATION FOR SMUGGLING HAITIANS INTO THE UNITED STATES. THE

HAITIAN NATIONAL POLICE HAVE LISTED HIM AS NUMBER TWO ON THEIR MOST WANTED LIST. HIS FINGERS ALSO EXTEND DEEP INTO THE DOMINICAN REPUBLIC AND INTO BOTH NATION'S POLICE FORCES. HE EVEN HAS UNITED NATIONS TROOPS WORKING FOR HIM IN EXCHANGE FOR DRUGS, SEX, AND MONEY.

TOUSSAINT HAS ESCAPED MULTIPLE HITS ON HIS LIFE, AT LEAST FIVE THAT U.S. INTELLIGENCE ARE AWARE OF. IF HE IS ACQUIRING MILITARY HARDWARE FROM JIM KILROY, IT'S A SAFE BET HE WILL ATTEMPT TO OVERTHROW THE SITTING GOVERNMENT IN HAITI AND DECLARE HIMSELF PRESIDENT.

I AM IN CONTACT WITH THE STATE DEPARTMENT AND THE CIA IN AN ATTEMPT TO STOP THE WEAPONS TRANSFER. AS YOU KNOW, HAITI IS EXTRAORDINARILY CORRUPT, AND WE CAN EXPECT NO HELP FROM THEM.

LANDIS

VOLK ASKED, "WHERE IS CAP-HAÏTIEN?"

"I thought you knew all the third-world shitholes?" Greg had told Volk they were going to Haiti, but not their specific port, hoping to dump him in either Port-au-Prince or another town on the western coast when they stopped to fuel *Dark Water*.

"Do not get smart with me." Volk slapped Greg across the back of the head.

"Ouch!" Greg cried and immediately rubbed his scalp.

"I warn you no more. Next time, you die."

Greg closed the email and used the internet to locate a marina in Cap-Haïtien. The port city on the north coast of Haiti operated a full-service container facility with petroleum storage areas alongside a massive concrete quay. He needed a smaller marina to fuel his sportfisher.

"What is taking long time?" Volk demanded after Greg had spent forty minutes looking for a marina.

"I think there's a marina in Cap-Haïtien."

"You think?" Volk asked incredulously.

"I see pictures of one but can't find a website. We have enough fuel to get there. It should take a few more hours to get around the northern peninsula and take the strait between Tortuga and the mainland. We can outrun any pirates or fishermen." Greg plotted the course on the GPS screen and hit *Go*. A new course extended across the blue screen. Turning to Volk, he said, "You can man the wheel. I need some sleep."

"Unacceptable." Volk crossed his arms.

"Look, I know you're used to living in a third-world mudhole—"

Volk shouted. "Do not insult Mother Russia!"

Greg waved a hand in dismissal. "We don't have time to argue. Follow the GPS plot and take us to Cap-Haïtien. We'll go in for fuel as soon as its daylight. We'll spot the *Santo Domingo* in the morning."

"And have no fuel to chase?"

Greg shrugged.

"We go into Port-au-Prince and get fuel," Volk demanded.

"How, at gunpoint? According to everything I've read, nothing is open at night. You and I both know nothing good would happen. I like my boat and have no desire to give it to the Haitian government, or some other warlord. Gunplay will get us all thrown in jail."

"You are right," Volk conceded.

"I'm going down to my room to take a nap. I set the autopilot to run us in close to Cap-Haïtien and then turn circles. As long as the seas don't blow up, we'll be good." He transferred from the captain's seat into his wheelchair and rolled to the lift. Going down would be a delicate balancing act as the boat pitched and rolled while plowing through the waves.

"You cannot leave."

"I need some sleep if we're going to find the *Santo Domingo*."

"What do I do?"

"Make sure we don't hit anything. When the autopilot begins the circle run, drop us back to five knots." He used the remote to lower the lift and, for the first time in three days, entered the main salon. Greg fixed a sandwich and drank a bottle of water before turning in. He sat on the edge of the bed, pulled a pistol from the false bottom in the nightstand and fastened it to the bottom of his chair.

CHAPTER FORTY-THREE

In 1670, Bertrand d'Ogeron founded Cap-Haïtien as a haven for French Calvinists. The tiny town grew exponentially as colonists, traders, slavers and farmers discovered the lush harbor. They transformed the city into the "Paris of the Antilles," known around the world for its architecture, culture, and artistic lifestyle. Sugar, coffee, cotton, and indigo fueled the boom on the backs of thousands of natives and imported slaves. The city suffered the growing pangs of the small country and through the years it had been raped by its citizens, burned by pillagers, and destroyed by earthquakes and hurricanes. Yet the resilient citizens rebuilt again, and again, forging Cap-Haïtien into the vacation destination for Haiti's upper class and tourists from around the globe.

Squalid huts and shacks rose on the hills above Cap-Haïtien's French architecture and thriving inner city. Slave rebellions, presidential coups, and revolutions had been hatched in this incubator; led by men who wanted nothing more than to bring food and water to their people, and to rise above the poverty that had stricken their country since the arrival of Columbus.

Toussaint Bajeux fancied himself one of those revolutionaries, refined in the pressure cooker of poverty and injustice to rage against his masters in Port-au-Prince. His escalation to power was due to equal parts of violence and charm. He'd started as a low-level errand boy for Cap-Haïtien's criminal patriarch, Stanley Joséph. He worked his way up through the ranks until he was a trusted member of Joséph's inner circle. The aged Creole ran things with an iron fist and tried desperately to control the rivalries within his syndicates.

These rivalries had cost Joséph his life, and Toussaint Bajeux, emerging from the man's room with a bloody knife in his hand, had united the factions. Those who stood against him were killed, along with their families.

Toussaint chose not to live in the inner city but in a modern home in the seaside resort of Rival Beach, an affluent suburb of Cap-Haïtien. From his front balcony, he had a commanding view of the harbor's shipping channel and easy access to a high-powered fishing boat he kept at the beach. He had utilized it to escape assassination attempts more than once.

Now, he stood braced against the deck railing, holding a pair of Leupold binoculars to his eyes. The noonday sun caused beads of sweat to form on his shaved head and roll down his temples. The red camp shirt clung to his body, and his white pants ballooned around his legs in the breeze. Removing the optics, he looked at his watch and then scanned the channel with his naked eye.

"They are coming," Jean Francois told his boss.

Toussaint put the binoculars to his eyes again without comment.

Francois lit a cigarette and watched the ocean. Long low waves rolled in and became clear, small breakers, lapping at the sand. Sunlight winked like diamonds on the water. A fresh wind carried the smell of brine with an undercurrent of raw sewage. Two massive cargo freighters steamed in from the Atlantic as a tanker exited the bay.

"They know to contact you on the private number?" Francois asked.

"Yes," Toussaint responded irritably; binoculars still glued to his eyes.

Francois nodded. "Would you like some shade, *patwon?*" —boss.

"*Non!*" Toussaint tried to keep the anger from his voice. "Go inside, Jean Francois, if you're hot. I can't stand your complaining."

Francois left the balcony and returned several minutes later.

"Phone call, *patwon.*"

"Who is it?"

"A Ryan Weller. He says he is Jim Kilroy's representative."

Toussaint handed the binoculars to Francois and strode to the telephone.

"Where are you?" Toussaint demanded.

"I'm on the *Santo Domingo*, two miles off Cap-Haïtien."

"You will go to the Sans-Souci Palace, purchase a ticket to La Citadelle Laferrière. Hike to the Citadel. Take the stairs to the top of the Batterie Coidavid. I will meet you there tomorrow afternoon at four."

CHAPTER FORTY-FOUR

The Citadelle Laferrière, simply known as the Citadel, was the mountaintop fortress built by Henri Christophe after Haiti gained independence from France in the early 1800s. Afraid the French would return, Christophe used slave labor to construct the fortification and equipped his redoubt with three hundred and sixty-five cannons.

The shape and angle of the massive stone and masonry structure appeared like the prow of a ship slicing out of the bedrock of the three-thousand-foot high peak of Bonnet a L'Eveque mountain. Christophe had designed the fort to be impenetrable from attack and equipped it with cisterns and storerooms to sustain five thousand men for up to a year. The fortress never saw action and fell into disrepair as Haitians concentrated on the basic needs of survival.

Ryan continued to fan through the pamphlet:

IN 1998, THE UN DECLARED THE CITADEL AND SANS-SOUCI PALACE AS WORLD HERITAGE SITES. THE ONCE-OPULENT STRUCTURE OF THE PALACE IS NOW ONE OF THE MOST

SIGNIFICANT TOURIST ATTRACTIONS ON THE ISLAND. BOTH THE UN AND THE LOCALS CATER TO THE VISITORS, PROVIDING TOURS, AND COLLECTING FUNDS TO AID IN THE RESTORATION OF THE TWO-HUNDRED-YEAR-OLD STRUCTURES.

RYAN QUIT READING and shoved the pamphlet back into the brochure stand. He glanced around to ensure his minder, Oso, had departed. They had ridden the ship's tender to Cap-Haïtien and caught a cab to the palace. Ryan had jumped from the taxi as soon as it pulled to a stop and admonished Oso not to hang around.

He crossed the stone veranda to where three teenaged boys laughed and chattered while sitting on a low stone wall outside the palace. Ryan found most Haitians spoke in Creole, a mixture of French, Spanish, English, and African dialect. He addressed the boys in the limited French he had gleaned while sailing through French Polynesia and the South Pacific. "*Parlez-vous Anglais?*" *Do you speak English?*

The boys continued to jabber amongst themselves until the boy Ryan had determined was the leader cut them off by saying, "For you, Cowboy."

"What's the fascination with calling every American *Cowboy?*"

"You are all John Wayne." He made pistols with his fingers and imitated pulling them from a holster and shooting. "Bang. Bang."

"I need to borrow a phone," Ryan said.

"Where's yours?"

"I dropped it on the bus on the way up here. I need to call my friend to let them know I'm here. I have some cash."

"American dollars?"

"*Oui.*" *Yes.*

"Ah, he speaks French so well." The boys began laughing.

"How much?" Ryan demanded, trying not to lose patience with the toughs.

"How much you got, American?"

"Ten dollars," Ryan replied.

"For one call."

"Fine."

The boy handed over a new Samsung smart phone. Ryan dialed Greg's number and got no answer. He began to dial another number, but the boy stopped him.

"One call, ten dollars. You make second call. It's also ten dollars."

Ryan handed over another ten bucks because he knew the boy would be pissed when he got the bill for an international call. Landis answered on the third ring.

"Landis, it's Ryan. Don't hang up."

"Where the hell are you?"

"Milot, Haiti." He stepped two paces away from the boys. "I'm meeting Toussaint this afternoon at the Citadelle Laferrière."

"Okay," Landis said. "I'm trying to line up some troops. We put protection on the girls."

Ryan asked, "Can we get Larry Grove and his crew down here?"

"No go as of now. I'm trying. State doesn't want to mess with anything happening in Haiti right now. They wouldn't care if a nuke went off there. It's up to you and Mango. Greg was in Jamaica, last I heard, and in the company of your bounty hunter, Volk."

"Shit," Ryan said with a roll of his eyes. *Why couldn't Greg stay out of this?*

"I imagine they're headed for Cap-Haïtien, or already there."

"I'll look for him."

"Be careful down there. Toussaint Bajeux and Volk are some bad *hombres*."

"Roger that. I'll call or send a signal when I have more information." Ryan hung up and erased the phone numbers from the phone's memory. He hit a number on the phone's favorites list to initiate a call to overwrite the data he'd just erased. Ryan knew getting the numbers was fairly easy if the user had a computer with recovery software. He wasn't sure if this kid was that sophisticated, but he could at least cover his tracks for a little while. He handed the phone back along with a twenty-dollar bill. "Thanks."

"No problem, Cowboy."

Ryan walked across the veranda and pretended to take in the view. From the corner of his eye, he watched the boy scroll through his phone. The boy looked up at Ryan before shoving the phone into his pocket. He and his companions hopped over the wall and disappeared into the jungle. Ryan figured Toussaint would know he made phone calls before he made it to the top of the Citadel.

He skipped the tour of the Sans-Souci Palace and searched out the four-wheel drive trucks designated to take tourists most of the way to the fortress. He paid the fee and climbed into the back with several other hikers. The ride was forty minutes over a rough road that jarred and jostled the passengers. At a small parking lot, the truck disgorged its commuters, and they set off up a paved path of rough cobblestones.

Ryan knew he was being watched. He could feel the eyes on his every move. He stopped at a small booth, what would pass for a rundown lemonade stand in the States, and purchased a coconut water. A stooped black woman used a machete to carve the top of a green coconut into a cone. She finished the job by lopping off the cone's point and inserting a straw.

Ryan took a sip and said, "Oh, that's good." He took another long drink. "I'm meeting Toussaint Bajeux at the Citadel. Have you seen him go by?"

If she recognized the name, her wrinkled face didn't show it. Her body was willow thin under a colorful dress and her hair streaked with silver. She shook her head. "*Non.*"

The worn athletic shoes he used for running and sightseeing were not the best choice of footwear for the long hike. They were better than the leather deck shoes he wore on the boat. His feet and ankles hurt, and he missed the support of his combat boots.

He continued to drink from the coconut while watching the trail. No one seemed to be paying attention to him. Even if the old woman had seen his party walk past, she probably wouldn't have told him because he was a stranger, and a *nèg blan*—white man. Or she was afraid of Toussaint.

Ryan suspected Toussaint had an alternative method for arriving at the Citadel. He pulled a cigarette out and lit it while relaxing in the shade of spreading mahogany and eucalyptus trees. Barefoot children played along the trail and chased each other with shrieks and shouts. He laughed at their merriment and thanked the woman for her kindness before moving up the path with long strides.

The fortress was incredible. Moss formed a tapestry of green on the ancient rock. Pyramidal stacks of cannonballs lined the fort's grounds, waiting for the return of the gunners to ram them home and send them flinging across the countryside. Ryan walked along the walls, climbing stairs toward the peak of the prow, Battery Croix-david. He estimated there were hundreds of stacks of cannonballs, some well over six feet high and at least a dozen feet long had been covered in wire mesh to hold them together.

He entered a courtyard with a roped-off set of stairs. A tall black man with a white skull painted on his face leaned against the stone block. He wore a top hat and had a boa constrictor draped across his shoulders. Sunlight made his muscular chest shine with perspiration under a long-tailed black coat.

"Welcome," he said, pushing off the wall. "I am Baron Samedi, giver of life and master of death. I am awaiting your body to ensure it rots in hell." He laughed diabolically, and half bowed as he swept a hand back and away toward the steps.

Ryan circled around him. His skin crawled when the snake lifted its head to watch him with beady black eyes. Its tongue flicked out. He couldn't take his eyes off the snake. He hated snakes, detested their slithering bodies, and hooded eyes. His whole body shuddered. His foot caught on the rope and he almost fell as he tried to climb over it.

The vodou man laughed as he straightened and adjusted the snake. With a leering grin, he swung the snake's head closer to Ryan. Ryan quickly retreated up the steps, his back against the cool stone to keep an eye on the snake and still see where he was going. Baron Samedi did not follow but pulled a wooden gate across the stairs to prevent other tourists from climbing to the top.

Small weeds grew through the cracks in the stone steps. Ryan marveled at the way nature reclaimed man's labors. At the top was a door flanked by two Haitians, holding AK-47s. One frisked Ryan thoroughly and efficiently, removing a folding knife before directing Ryan through the door. He had to duck under the low header to get into the room.

Standing just inside the door, he let his vision adjust to the dim light. Tables laden with candles provided the only illumination. The first thing he noticed was a woman clothed in a purple dress that fell to cover her feet. Purple lipstick offset her lustrous mahogany skin and her long jet-black hair had a slow curl to it. She stood behind a wiry black man, who sat in a chair with his legs crossed. He wore dark pants and an untucked white button-down shirt with the sleeves partially rolled up. Ryan's gaze moved to the man's face with its broad forehead, prominent cheekbones, almost square chin, and shaved head. The effect was not a handsome one.

"Welcome, Ryan Weller, ambassador of James Kilroy. I am Toussaint Bajeux."

Ryan nodded, staring at Toussaint's black eyes. It looked like the color had leaked from the irises and muddied the scleras into a strange brown.

"You have brought my merchandise, *non?*"

"It's on the *Santo Domingo.*"

"Very good."

"Where should we unload it?" Ryan asked.

"I will send barges to meet your ship."

Ryan pulled his cigarettes from his pocket, keeping his eyes closed to retain his night vision in the low light of the room as the lighter's flame flared. He offered the pack to Toussaint, the woman, and the armed man who stood in the shadows beyond the candle-covered tables. Ryan's eyes flicked back to the woman. She looked away, but when he focused on Toussaint, he felt her eyes on him.

Toussaint stood and walked behind the woman. When Toussaint draped an arm around her shoulders, Ryan saw her eyes flinch, but her face remained a stoic mask. He put his cigarette in his mouth, kept his thumb and forefinger on the filter, and took a long pull. He rolled his fingers to use his palm to shield his eyes from the flaring red cherry.

Toussaint leaned his face close to the woman's. To Ryan, it looked as if it took every nerve in her being to not pull away from his thick lips. She stood rock still and pleaded with Ryan with her blue eyes. He had seen women of African heritage with blue eyes before and knew it was a genetic anomaly. Her's were startlingly bright and clear. He was surprised he hadn't noticed them at first glance, but then he'd been distracted by her shapely figure.

He pulled the cigarette from his lips and let the smoke out through his nostrils.

"This," Toussaint said proudly, "is Joulie. She is a vodou *mambo*—a priestess. She is my good luck charm, and soon to be my wife. Together, we will rule over Haiti."

Her eyes closed as he used a finger to lightly brush a stray hair from her cheek.

"I was told to collect payment," Ryan said around his cigarette.

"Ah, yes, your payment." Toussaint stepped away from Joulie and clasped his hands behind his back. "It will be delivered when the cargo is unloaded."

Ryan looked Toussaint in the eyes. "That's not going to happen. I'll take delivery of payment first."

"You know why I am purchasing this cargo, *non?*"

Ryan stayed silent.

"Haiti has so much potential, yet we've squandered it for hundreds of years. Our labor has been exploited since the French first produced sugar here. We fought for our freedom only to be knocked down again and again. Even your United States government keeps us under its thumb by forcing us to quarter UN troops. Troops who will be remembered for bringing cholera to our country and sexually abusing our women." He held up a finger. "True, they have built schools and hospitals and brought peace after Aristide let his grip on our people slip, but they are a foreign occupier on our sovereign shores. Even with these peacekeepers, gangs run our nation. We, the warlords, have split the country into our own provinces, each policing our own territory, caring for our own people. Still, it is not easy. The government gives away our natural resources. Haiti has more oil than any other Caribbean nation, yet we see little money from the drilling contracts."

Ryan listened to the man's tirade, swiveling his gaze between Toussaint and Joulie. The guard lurked in the darkness.

"Come, let's go outside." Toussaint motioned for Ryan to follow. Joulie fell in step, and the guards trailed after them.

They climbed a set of stairs to the ramparts of the old fort. In the distant haze, Ryan could see Cap-Haïtien.

Toussaint walked to the angled prow and stood on the narrow point. He spread his arms to encompass the whole of the jungle. "Look at this beautiful country. We have killed our land by chopping down trees to cook and heat our homes. We have depleted the soil with poor farming practices and our rivers run with sewage and chemicals from factories and mining. Only bandits grow fat and rich in this godforsaken nation." He dropped his arms to his sides and turned to face Ryan.

Ryan said, "Some say you made a deal with the Devil to escape French rule and he still rules your country with an iron fist. A fist made stronger by vodou."

"Ah, the Devil," Toussaint said with a mirthless chuckle. "He is present on this island. The vodou came with our ancestors from Africa. We look upon our vodou spirits as God's helpers, much like your Catholic saints."

Ryan, again, remained silent. He had exhausted his thoughts on the matter. The gangster was charismatic, as were most leaders who rose to power. Toussaint's muddied gaze roamed over Ryan and he felt a chill course through his body. In the light, Toussaint's hooded eyelids reminded him of those of a cobra.

"Haiti has two of the world's most powerful commodities, gold and oil. My people go hungry in their shanty towns while foreign corporations grow rich extracting our wealth. It's time to bring the money home, to us."

"By us, you mean you when you've conquered the other gangs and set up shop in Port-au-Prince."

"You have a lot of sass for an arms dealer."

"I'm just the delivery man."

"Even more reason for you to fear and respect me. Your boss does. Why do you think he's not here? Why does he send a middleman to do his dirty work?"

"To keep his hands clean," Ryan replied.

Toussaint smiled. "Exactly. I will deliver payment when I have the equipment onshore."

"You can inspect and test all the weapons and equipment on the ship. The gold will be loaded before we hand over a single bullet. I speak for my employer on this term. It's non-negotiable."

Toussaint wagged a finger at Ryan. "You drive a hard bargain, Mr. Weller. I like you. You will come work for me, lead troops for me."

"I'm not a mercenary."

"Were you a solider?"

Ryan grunted in disapproval. "I was a sailor."

"Regardless, you took pay from your government to be a fighter. Is that not the definition of a mercenary?"

"A patriot."

"Ah, a mercenary wrapped in the flag of his country."

Ryan looked over at Joulie, who stood on the edge of the parapet gazing at the jungle floor, thousands of feet below. The wind ruffled the fabric of her dress and tousled her glossy hair.

"She is beautiful, *non?*"

"She is," Ryan agreed. It was more than beauty, it was an inner strength, a magnetism that made him want to confide in her, to make love to her.

"You must come work for me when we complete this transaction."

"I have a job," Ryan retorted.

"I'll make you a rich man. We'll restore the glory of my country and take our rightful place among the island nations. Once again we'll be the crown jewel of the Antilles."

"I'm not looking for a war, Toussaint."

"Yet, you are a merchant of death."

Toussaint had made his point. Ryan was a fool to think he was anything but a mercenary and a death dealer by default, whether coerced or by choice. The original mission to find Guerrero's pirates seemed innocuous at first glance, a self-righteous mission sanctioned by the DHS to clear hazards from the sea lanes. Taking out Arturo Guerrero had been a bonus to keep him from destroying any more of the American Southwest.

Breaking it down to bare bones, he was a mercenary paid by the U.S. government.

"Truth in my words, *non?*"

Ryan looked back at Toussaint. With a shrug, he said, "I'm like you. I work for what's best for my country."

"Yes," Toussaint said with a rueful smile. "What the government asks us to do and what is best for the country are not always the same thing."

"You said a mouthful there."

Toussaint turned to a guard and motioned with his hand. The guard pulled out a cell phone and made a call.

The warlord gazed out over the landscape. "We will bring a new era to Haiti. You have a hand in that, Mr. Weller. Tomorrow, we'll unload your ship."

From across the valley, the sound of rotor blades reached them. A dark green Bell 212, a civilian version of the Vietnam-Era UH-1 Iroquois, came charging toward them.

"Our ride to my home. Tonight, you'll be my guest, and we'll laugh and drink and scheme."

"Can I have my knife back?" Ryan asked. "I'm here to sell you guns, not stab you to death."

Toussaint gestured to the guards. One stepped forward to hand over the knife and Ryan slipped it into his pocket.

The helicopter settled on the moss-covered rocks. Its copilot hopped out and slid open the cargo door. Toussaint, Joulie, Ryan, and a guard climbed into the plush leather seats and settled headsets over their ears. Soundproof padding hung on the helicopter's walls, but it did little to deaden the thunderous roar of the aircraft's jet engine and rotor blades. Ryan had ridden in enough helicopters to know it was virtually impossible to communicate without the headsets.

The familiar lurch of his stomach rising into his chest accompanied the aircraft lifting off the deck. The fortress faded away as the helicopter turned north.

They flew over rugged mountains then sprawling farmland before sweeping along the outskirts of Cap-Haïtien. Toussaint pointed out sights of interest, including the massive shipping quays and the Coast Guard base.

"What's floating in the water?" Ryan asked.

"Trash," Toussaint replied. "The ocean washes plastic bottles, aluminum cans, and all manner of debris from across the Atlantic. The locals pick through it to see if there is anything of value. Most of it is left to float."

Ryan nodded. He'd seen similar rafts of junk polluting the waters and beaches of many countries. On every beach, a searcher could find cigarette butts, plastic containers, rope, fishing line, and various other litter throw away by passing ships, fisherman, and tourists. Most did not care about the litter, or if they did, there were few places to dispose of, or recycle, the garbage. It saddened him to see the apathy for the oceans.

The helicopter swept over shacks and shanties, stacked one atop the other, and painted garish shades of blue, yellow, and green, intermingled with the browns and whites of poorer hovels. A towering cathedral slid past, and they followed a long strand of beach.

Toussaint sat forward and pressed his face to the glass. He reminded Ryan of a little kid on his first flight. Ryan glanced at the Joulie. She sat with her hands folded in her lap, staring straight ahead. She hadn't said a word, but when she caught him looking at her, she gave him a small, soft smile. The simple act lit up her entire face.

There was no pleading in her eyes, just a beautiful woman with a charming smile, and he understood why Toussaint was in love with her, even if she didn't love him.

Tearing his gaze away from Joulie, he leaned forward to see out a window. When the helicopter turned into the breeze coming off the ocean, Ryan saw the landing pad. A shimmering pool occupied the space between the modern white stucco, steel, and glass house and the landing pad. Lush foliage and blooming flowers covered the terraced property. A small public road separated the home from the beach.

Just after landing, the pilot slowed the rotor speed and asked his passengers to disembark. The group exited the aircraft, and the pilot took off as soon as they were clear.

"Welcome to my home," Toussaint said. He swung his arms wide to encompass the grandeur of the grounds.

"A nice place," Ryan said. "We have a saying in America, 'The rich get richer, and the poor get poorer.'"

Ryan's host gave him a hard look, then laughed. "A mercenary who speaks his mind. Are you afraid of spoiling your bargain?"

"Not my bargain. You've already agreed to the terms."

"Your honesty and hostility can sabotage your employer's deal."

"It wouldn't break my heart."

"But it will break your bones, your spirit, and your life."

"I'm already a wanted man. You'll have to pick a number."

Toussaint led the way into his home through sliding glass doors. He walked to a small bar and began to pour a drink. He suddenly turned and looked at Ryan. With the rum bottle in his left hand, Toussaint stroked his block of a chin with his right.

"That's right." He smiled gleefully as he resumed pouring. "Joulie, this is the man who shot Arturo Guerrero." Toussaint picked up his drink and turned to face Ryan. "You have a bounty on your head, *non?*"

"Yes."

"Two million dollars, *non?*"

Ryan nodded. "Correct."

Toussaint handed Ryan a glass of dark-colored liquor. "Fifteen-year-old Rhum Barbancourt, from Haiti's oldest distillery."

Ryan tasted the rum. It was strong and smooth. His stomach growled at the scent of food coming from the kitchen. The last time he'd eaten was just after leaving the *Santo Domingo* when he and Oso had stopped for a traditional Haitian breakfast of spaghetti with diced hot dogs topped with ketchup.

Toussaint led the way to a dining room. Ten chrome framed chairs, each with a different colored cushion, were pushed under a long chrome-and-glass table set with white China. Polished silver utensils nestled in white napkins.

"Sit," Toussaint commanded, taking his place at the head of the table.

Ryan took a chair to Toussaint's left. Joulie sat across from him on her fiancé's right.

A waiter began to pour wine and fill water glasses. A

second man brought plates of food piled with chunks of roasted meat covered in slices of vegetables.

"This is a Haitian specialty, my mercenary friend," Toussaint said. "*Griot*, or fried pork, and *pikliz*, a combination of cabbage, onions, bell peppers, carrots, and my favorite Scotch bonnet peppers. The vegetables are pickled in white vinegar, salt, and garlic. It is *magnifique*." He kissed his fingertips.

Before Toussaint dug in, he motioned over his shoulder. A man stepped forward and bent down beside him. He cut a bite-size piece of pork then stabbed a chunk of meat with a fork along with a healthy portion of vegetables. He shoved the large bite into his mouth and chewed. The warlord and the chef watched the man expectantly. The poison tester swallowed and smiled.

The chef beamed.

Ryan watched the curious scene with interest. The taste tester was the bodyguard who had accompanied them in the helicopter. Ryan first noticed him lurking in the darkness just beyond the glow of the candlelight in the small meeting room at the Citadel.

Toussaint smiled at the chef, held his hand out, palm down, and used his fingers to wave the man away. The chef scurried back to the kitchen and Toussaint began to eat.

Between bites, Ryan asked, "I saw quays in Cap-Haïtien, will we unload there?"

Toussaint waved his fork in the air. Around a mouth full of food, he said, "No business while we eat."

Ryan glanced at Joulie. She smiled at the waiters and received beaming grins in return. She gave softly spoken directions to them and thanked them for serving the food. While they showed deference to Toussaint, they doted on Joulie.

He went back to his meal. He had to admit the food was excellent.

When Toussaint finished, the waiter collected the plates and brought steaming cups of hot chocolate. The drink was not like the hot chocolate Ryan's mother made for him as a child, or the powdered version found onboard ships and in their MREs. This drink had hints of cinnamon and spices with a citrus bite, combining to make one of the best after-dinner beverages he'd ever drunk. He said as much to his host.

"Ah, this is one of Joulie's favorites." Toussaint put his cup to his lips while watching her. She looked at him for the first time since they'd sat down at the table. When she gave Toussaint a smile, before sipping carefully from the steaming cup, Ryan saw it was different from the smile she'd given him.

"Your fiancée doesn't seem very happy to be in our company."

Toussaint laughed. "I assure you, she is most pleasant. Say something to our guest, *mon amour*."

Joulie smiled at Ryan. Again, the genuine emotion lit up her face. Her blue eyes sparkled. In a warm voice, tinged in her native patois, she said, "Welcome to our home, Mr. Weller. I am pleased you have enjoyed our food."

"I'm pleased to be here." Ryan smiled back at her, wondering if Toussaint could hear the disconnect between the way Joulie spoke to him and the way she spoke to everyone else.

"Come, Mr. Weller," Toussaint said as he stood. He smiled. "We're old friends now, we have dined together, a great ... *joie de vivre*, how do you say ..." For the first time he seemed at a loss for words, and he twirled a finger in the air as if trying to jumpstart his mind. Suddenly, he snapped his fingers. "A happiness derived from life."

Ryan snorted. "I wouldn't say we're thick as thieves."

Toussaint laughed again. "I really do like you, Ryan. May I call you Ryan?"

"Sure." Ryan shrugged and stood. He carried his glass of rum with him as he followed Toussaint into a study. The Haitian opened a box of cigars and withdrew two. He picked up his refilled glass of rum along with a lighter. They walked through a set of sliding glass doors and onto the pool deck. Small lights illuminated walkways, and the pool was lit with underwater bulbs which cast an eerie glow through the translucent water.

When Toussaint offered Ryan a cigar, he passed.

Toussaint lit his cigar before saying, "You asked about the quays in Cap-Haïtien?"

"Yes, can we unload there?"

"*Non*. We'll unload at sea onto barges. There are too many eyes watching us at the port. Many work for me, but some for my competition. I want them to be surprised by my newly acquired military hardware."

"I assume you have the payment handy."

"Of course."

"I'd like to be done with this tomorrow."

"As you say, 'the sooner, the better.'"

Ryan nodded. "May I make a phone call?"

"Why? You are my guest. You are perfectly safe here."

"I want to make arrangements with the crew."

Toussaint waved his hand to dismiss the statement.

Ryan fingered the two cigarette packages in his pocket. Cigars were good, but he preferred his Camels. One pack contained his burst transmitter. He would use it to send a message to Greg, but he had no way of contacting Mango. He pulled out a cigarette from the regular pack and lit it. He asked, "Are you concerned about Hurricane Irma?"

"*Non*. It is well to the south of us and will hit the Lesser Antilles first. They'll reduce the force of the storm and it'll be of little consequence by the time it reaches us."

"I'm cautious about unloading at sea with the weather

approaching. It could mean heavy swells, which will make handling the cargo a royal pain."

Toussaint conceded the point with a nod. "Then we'll need to unload quickly."

Ryan sipped his rum. The long hike to the Citadel had worn him out. Dinner and the rum made him sleepy. He took a final draw on his cigarette and crushed it out. "I hate to spoil the party, but I'm tired and ready to hit the sack."

Toussaint nodded. "I understand."

"Please excuse me, *Mesye* Bajeux."

"You speak Creole?" Toussaint asked, surprised his guest had used the Creole term for mister.

"I heard it enough on the walk up to the Citadel. Every one of them beggar kids were so damned polite." He shook his head.

Toussaint laughed. "Let me show you to your room, *Mesye* Weller."

Ryan followed him through the house to a room with a view of the ocean.

"Make yourself at home. But first, empty your pockets onto the table."

Ryan looked past the warlord at the guard shadowing their every movement before dropping his cigarette packs, lighter, and folding knife onto the steel and glass table. He stepped into the room, and his host closed the door behind him. The door locked with a click.

CHAPTER FORTY-FIVE

Jesula Duvermond finished storing the clean dishes in the cabinets of Toussaint Bajeux's spacious kitchen. She wiped down the countertops and the center island before switching off the lights. Her work finished; she was thankful to be going home. She pulled off her apron as she walked down the road to her small home.

Under the starlit sky, salt air mingled with the scent of hibiscus and wild impatiens. She turned off the road onto a path which would lead her cross country to the house she shared with her husband and three children, as well as her mother and father. Her weathered hands gripped small trees to steady her descent. It was a journey she had made count-less times since beginning her job at Bajeux's home.

A large man stepped out of the shadow of a tree. She let out a gasp and clutched a hand to her chest. "You startled me, Simon," she said in Haitian Creole.

"*Mwen regret sa, Manman.*" *I am sorry, Mother.* "Do you have news about Bajeux? He took her arm in his to help guide her down the path.

"*Wi,* he has a visitor." She continued in her native tongue,

"His name is Ryan Weller and he's delivering a load of weapons."

"Toussaint confirmed this?"

"He said he was acquiring new military hardware."

"Where? When?" Simon asked.

"Tomorrow. Toussaint will unload at sea. Onto barges."

At the door to their home, he kissed his mother's cheek and disappeared into the darkness.

Jesula said a prayer to the vodou gods and to the Holy Mother for the protection of her son. She made the sign of the cross over her breasts.

CHAPTER FORTY-SIX

Unable to sleep, Joulie Lafitte slid from her bed. The glowing clock on the nightstand read two a.m. She pulled a black silk robe around her shoulders as she walked to the window. She gazed out at the darkened landscape lit by a half-moon. Her mind wasn't on the beauty of the foliage or the barely audible murmur of waves on the beach. She was thinking of the handsome stranger two doors down.

He had no fear of Toussaint and spoke to him without regard to his authority. She knew of no one who dared to speak to the warlord with such irreverence. It thrilled her to be in his presence. His commanding authority and his handsomeness aroused feelings she had forced into dormancy. But it was something more, she'd seen him before and had stood in his presence.

Her thoughts trailed off as she closed her eyes and leaned her forehead against the cool window pane. She had grown up in a small mountain village near the Dominican Republic border. Her parents had eked out a living by farming the barren, rocky soil, and herding goats. She remembered a happy childhood, playing in the small stream, chasing the other children, and snuggling with Mother at night near the charcoal fire while she cooked their meal.

Then, when Joulie was five, her world had changed without warning. An earthquake savaged the country and a landslide had killed her parents. She could still see their mangled corpses through teary eyes. She had called their names and patted their cheeks, but they wouldn't answer her. Her hands became stained with the blood oozing from Mother's nose and mouth, and Joulie's lips tasted of copper from kissing Mother's face.

Joulie had been dragged away by a village elder and watched as they buried her parents in shallow graves with the rest of the dead. Several days later, an elderly woman arrived at the village. She walked with a strange stiffness and leaned on a staff to aid her movements. She'd explained that she was Joulie's grandmother, Farah, the mother of her mother.

Farah took Joulie back to her home. Joulie disliked the new town and deeply missed her parents. Farah sent her to a local school run by one of the many nongovernmental organizations operating in Haiti. She'd never seen a white woman before, and suddenly there was one teaching her about math and science, reading and writing. Dana told her class about going to college and traveling. The children all clamored to know about America and dreamed about living in a land where food and water were plentiful. Joulie wanted to go to America with Dana.

At the same time, Farah tried to draw Joulie into her world. She was a *mambo*—a vodou priestess—and saw enormous potential in the young girl. She began to teach Joulie the spells, chants, and traditions of a priestess. Joulie didn't want to learn the old ways. She wanted to go to the United States, and such practices were frowned upon there. Farah prepared a ceremony for her granddaughter and invoked the spirit of her mother, whom Farah had also taught to be a priestess. Mother's spirit came into Joulie's body, and she began to sway back and forth on her knees. Joulie could feel her mother inside of her, all around her, the love and affection Mother had shown her completely enveloped her. Mother whispered a message into her ear. "Help your people. A man will rise to power. You will be the thorn in his side."

When the trance broke, Joulie was left sweating, shaking, and gasping for breath on her hands and knees. It was almost terrifying to hear Mother's voice. Yet, Joulie knew the message was real, and that she must prepare.

She enveloped herself in vodou culture, learning to be a priestess and serving her people and the many gods they called upon. It wasn't long before she developed a reputation for being able to speak to the spirits and deliver messages from the dead. She was able to see glimpses of the future and when she wanted to expound on them, Farah explained to her that as mambos they allowed the future to happen normally unless it revealed itself as it had in Joulie's dream. People from surrounding villages began to seek her advice, asking her to cast spells, and to intervene with the dead.

Just after Joulie's seventeenth birthday, Farah came to her with a man whom she instantly recognized as the man Mother had whispered about. Her belly turned cold with fear. Farah introduced him as Toussaint Bajeux. He had come to seek her advice. By the time he left, Farah had arranged a marriage between the beautiful priestess and the warlord.

Joulie turned away from the window. Her body shook as if she were cold. Even her teeth clattered. She couldn't stop the shaking, no matter how tightly she clenched her muscles. She threw herself onto the bed and pulled the covers over her body. The shivering did not stop. Squeezing her eyes shut, she called to Mother.

The image of a cell phone came into her mind.

A present.

For the man.

Joulie sat bolt upright. The shivering stopped. She tossed back the covers and raced to the giant armoire. She pulled back the door and knelt on the terracotta tile. Reaching through the hems of dresses and coats, she found an old shoe she'd shoved into the back. Her hands closed around the rough leather and she drew it out. An old flip phone she'd secreted away several years ago slid out of the shoe. She didn't know if the battery still had a charge. She prayed that it would work.

As it dropped into her palm, she felt a jolt of electricity. Her eyes closed as she remembered a vision she'd had years ago, just after the announcement of her arranged marriage. It came to her now in startling clarity. In the vision, she was a leaf on an oak tree in a hurricane. As the leaf tore free of the tree, she felt the action inside of her body, a twisting, tearing, strain in every muscle, causing her to lay spread eagle on the ground and scream as if her limbs were being painfully stretched. Fluttered away from the tree, her body collapsed into a ball. She was floating on the breeze yet falling. The ground came up fast. She knew the impact would hurt and her body tensed in anticipation.

Plummeting toward the earth, she saw a giant hand reach out. *Curious*, she thought. *Why is it white?*

She landed in the palm. The fingers closed slightly to allow her to nestle into the flesh. She felt safe, warm, and content. The hand released her, and she stood on the ground, gazing up at a man with brown hair. She ran a hand along the man's cheek and stared into his green eyes. She felt a deep longing to be with him, to satisfy and please him. She knew she must present him with a gift. As her fingertips left the man's face, he smiled and instantly vanished.

Joulie had closed her eyes, reveling in the soft warmth of the man's presence. She drifted in darkness. A cargo ship floated out of the gloom. She realized she was standing on the ocean, watching it pass. Looking up at the vessel's stern, she saw a name. She blinked but could not make it out. Then the ship disintegrated in a massive explosion.

When she awoke, she was lying in her bed, Farah wiping her head with a damp rag. The older woman smiled. "I was worried about you, my child."

"I had the most terrifying dream."

"You screamed several times while you were in your trance. I didn't want to interrupt an important vision."

"Vision?" Joulie sat up.

"Yes, you have seen the future." Farah dabbed the rag against Joulie's cheek.

"How do you know?" the young woman asked, pushing aside Farrah's hand as she sat up. She drew her knees to her chest and hugged them.

"I, too, had a vision," Farrah explained. "That vision was of you, beside your dead parents. The *loa* showed me the path I must take. They have shown you the path you must take."

Joulie's blue eyes narrowed, and her brow furrowed. "I can't remember much of the vision." She wondered how she could follow the gods' path when she couldn't remember what it was.

"It will come to you at the right time."

"How long will I have to wait?"

Farah shrugged. "I waited thirty-two years for my vision to come true."

"Thirty-two years!" Joulie exclaimed. She didn't want to wait that long. She wanted to go to America. Somehow, she knew she would escape Haiti. She also knew she must marry Toussaint to be the thorn in his side as Mother had told her to be. That didn't mean she was happy about it. Only by defeating him, could she earn her freedom.

. . .

JOULIE JOLTED BACK to the present. Every vivid detail of the vision was fresh in her mind. She couldn't believe she'd forgotten something so powerful, so real. Even the feelings of desire for the man had returned to intensify her lustful thoughts.

The phone was the present.

She was the present.

Quickly, she slid the phone into the pocket of her robe and adjusted the fabric to compensate for its weight. She tied the belt around her waist and crept to her bedroom door.

She had willingly come to live with Toussaint and thought of him as her master, not a fiancé, for he used her status as a *mambo* to hold sway over the people and used her insights to help guide him. Still she dared not break his trust and sneaking out to see Ryan Weller would fracture their relationship. She had seen Toussaint beat, shoot, and starve people to death who betrayed him.

She made her way along the dark hallway on her tiptoes, careful to not trip on the rugs or bump into the small tables. Her bare feet were silent on the cool tile floor. She paused outside Ryan's room to look at the items he'd left on the table. Then she carefully eased off the door lock, craning her neck to see if anyone had heard the snick of metal on metal as the lock slid opened. She stepped inside. Before she let the door swing closed, she placed a small piece of cardboard she'd torn from a tissue box between the latch and the striker plate to prevent the door from locking.

A thrill coursed through her body when she saw the man lying in bed. He sat up as she approached. She stopped at the edge of the mattress, conscious of his bare chest and the corded muscles of his arms. Slipping a hand into her robe pocket, she retrieved the phone. In the process of holding it out to him, her hand tugged the robe's belt loose. Joulie wanted him to see her in her short, blue, satin nightgown.

Ryan stared up at her. She felt self-conscious under his gaze. She wanted to reach for the belt and retie it to cover herself but left it open. If she was to be his present, then she should use all her charms to make him understand that he was to help her escape.

She moved the phone closer to him, hyperextending her palm and fingers to allow him to see her offering. Without taking his eyes off hers, he took the phone. Shivers tickled her spine as his fingers brushed her palm.

He flipped off the covers and stood to face the window. He was clad only in boxer briefs and she tried not to concentrate too hard on his muscular body as he walked to the window. He examined the phone in the low moon light and hit the button to power it up. He delighted her with a smile when it turned on, the screen's glow reflecting on his face.

Joulie watched as he dialed a number. He held the phone to his ear. The call went to voicemail. He dialed again. The call went to voicemail. This time he left a hurried message. "Greg, it's me. Toussaint is offloading the cargo tomorrow."

Joulie moved to stand by the window. From here, she could see the moonlight on the waves. Absently, she played with a small gold pendant, sliding it back and forth along a gold chain. Farah had given it to her before she'd left with Toussaint. She heard Ryan dial another number. *I like this view more than the one from my room. I'll ask Toussaint if I can move. No! He'll know I've been here.*

"Landis, it's me, Ryan."

"Did you get yourself a phone?"

"No, it's a gift."

Joulie looked up sharply, eyes wide.

He grinned at her. "I'm at Toussaint Bajeux's house. We're offloading the cargo from the *Santo Domingo* tomorrow morning."

Every hair on Joulie's body seemed to stand on end when

she heard the name of the ship. She tuned out the rest of the conversation as she saw the ship float through her vision and explode.

Ryan snapped the phone shut and handed it to Joulie. The action broke her trance. She placed it in her pocket. The robe shifted, exposing more of her dark skin. She wanted to let it slide from her body and step into his arms, yet she sensed it was the wrong thing to do. He was preoccupied and seemed not to notice her nearly naked figure. She shrugged the robe back on and tied the belt.

"Thank you," he whispered.

She nodded.

"Why are you engaged to him?"

"It's my duty," she whispered, her voice resigned.

"Why?"

Joulie faced him, her blue eyes searching his face. "I am a symbol of the vodou goddess of love and the warrior mother. He wants me to use my gifts to convince men to follow him into battle and reunite the clans and families into one nation. We will use our natural resources to bring electricity, water, and food to our starving nation."

"That sounds like a memorized speech."

She shrugged and turned back to the window. She'd given the prepared speech many times.

"Can vodou really help?" Ryan asked.

"It's deeply rooted in our heritage. Our spirituality comes from our African ancestors and vodou is a uniting part of our society. The Spanish and French forced us to accept Catholicism. They tried to wipe out our beliefs. But, our *loa* —our spirits—are still with us. We serve them, not worship them."

"You're a vodou goddess?"

"No." She shook her head and smiled. "I am a mambo, a priestess."

After a long moment, Ryan asked, "You don't want to help your country?"

"I do, but not this way. Not by war. We've suffered enough." She paused, drawing in a ragged breath. She placed her hand on his cheek and traced her fingertips along his skin. "You are in great danger."

"Yeah, so are you for being in here."

She felt him tilt his head into her hand. "No, the ship will blow up. I saw it in a vision."

"You can see the future?"

"Only what the loa reveal to me."

"Can you see what Toussaint has planned?"

"I am not a *bokor*—a sorcerer. I do not practice the dark magic. There are some things he keeps from me. I do not know, and I will not ask, either him or the gods." A shiver racked her body.

"What happens if we stop the shipment?"

"Toussaint will try again. That's why I brought you the phone. You need to kill him. For me and for my country."

CHAPTER FORTY-SEVEN

Daylight found *Dark Water* circling outside Cap-Haïtien. Greg drove the Hatteras into the harbor and cruised the waterfront. Small fishing boats with ancient outboards littered the beaches, and rusty steel work vessels were rafted together in the middle of the anchorage.

On the west side of Port de Cap-Haïtien was a long concrete quay. Near the shore end of the quay was a collection of power and sailboats. Greg made for them, keeping careful watch on the depth sounder and the sonar.

"Hey, Volk," Greg said.

The Russian was standing at the front of the bridge, one hand gripping the bridge's hardtop cover for support. "*Da?*"

"I think we should post a guard. We have the nicest boat in the place, and I don't want anyone getting sticky fingers."

"What is this, sticky fingers?"

"It means to steal. A person who steals has sticky fingers."

"Makes no sense."

Greg shrugged. Easing the boat toward the concrete pier, he instructed the Russians to hang fenders over the boat's rail. He shook his head in disgust while he watched their clumsy attempts to knot the fender ropes to the boat rails.

As they came alongside the pier, a man hustled out of a long, brown building. He smiled as he caught the bow line.

Greg shouted to him, "Do you have any diesel?"

"*Non!*"

"Where can I get some?"

The man pointed across the water. Greg glanced over his shoulder at a large power plant on a small peninsula. At the very end of the peninsula sat a squat building with a gray roof beside a dock occupied by four boats. Two more boats were tied to posts sticking out of the water.

"Thanks," Greg yelled.

The man waved as Greg backed the boat away.

"Shipwreck." Volk pointed at a sunken boat lying on its side between the two docks.

Greg had also seen the rusted hulks of at least two other wrecks lurking just below the waves. He spun the Hatteras and angled it toward the far dock. Beyond the rickety wooden pier Greg could see a massive, round above-ground fuel tank, longer than the crew cab pickup truck parked beside it.

There was no space at the dock, so Greg had the men rig several more fenders. He came alongside the largest vessel and slowed just enough to kiss the steel fishing boat with *Dark Water*'s fenders. Immediately, one of the Russians jumped to the other boat and tied off the bow and stern lines.

An older white man, with a shock of white hair and a white beard, came out of the marina building and jogged down the dock. He climbed on the boat where the Russian was tying off the lines and looked up at Greg.

"Hell of a nice boat you got here."

"Thanks. We need some diesel."

The man shaded his brow with his hand. "Where ya headed?"

"Trying to link up with a friend of ours."

"Right, right." The man nodded. "I'm Billy Parker. I got your diesel. Gonna cost ya, and I don't know if I can fill ya all the way up. Diesel can be scarce in these parts."

"I'll take what I can get. Should get us down to Luperon." Greg had done the calculations before they came into port and knew they could make the port city just across the Dominican border without taking on fuel, but every drop would help.

"I know they got plenty of diesel down there. The Dominican Republic is a hell of a lot nicer than here." He glanced down at the mess the Russian had made with the ropes. "These boys sure don't know how to tie off a line. You got any experienced crew with ya?"

"Just what I got," Greg told him. "We ran over from Jamaica."

"A far piece. That will make seamen out of ya, crossing the Windward." He bent, untied the line, and rewrapped it around the cleat. He straightened and watched Greg ride down on the lift. "Sure am sorry we can't get you off the boat. I can move this one if you need to get somewhere. Course we'd have to raft 'er off you."

"No worries," Greg said. "I'm all right. Anywhere close we can get some supplies?"

"Got a few little stores down the road. You'll be lucky if you find much. Damn hurricane preparation about wiped them out."

"I'd like to be gone before it hits."

"When's your friend comin' by?"

"Should be any day now."

"I'd say if he don't make it in the next day or two, you ought to light out for Luperon, get you a tank of diesel, and get the hell out of here."

"Sound advice." Greg rolled over to the edge of the

gunwale and leaned closer in a conspiratorial manner. "Should we post a guard? I don't want any trouble."

"I'd say you'd be pretty safe here. Course them Haitians get a look at a boat fine as this one and, well, you never know what might happen. If you got a gun on there, I'd keep it hidden, like. Don't want them government people down here takin' you off to the hoosegow. Say, before I go and forget, I'm gonna need to see your papers, and take the fee. Gotta make sure the government gets its take."

Greg went into the salon and came back with the boat's papers and their passports. He paid the entrance fee, and Billy Parker took their documents to the building where he could copy them. Volk sent one of his minions to keep an eye on him.

Ten minutes later, he was back. "We done took care of the paperwork. Everything is in order." He handed back the packet of papers. "About that diesel?"

Greg handed him a credit card which Billy took to the office. He came back carrying a long hose and plugged it into the fuel tank filler neck.

"What's the capacity of the tanks?"

"Nineteen hundred gallons."

Billy Parker let out a whistle. "Ain't no way I can put that much in. I can give you half."

"I'll take whatever you can give me," Greg said. The tanks were more than half empty from the long run. Ideally, he'd liked to fill them completely.

"I'll go watch the counter. You have one of them boys make sure the hose don't come out."

"Roger that." Greg pointed at the Russian who had tied off the boat and indicated he should watch the hose. The man nodded.

Twenty minutes later, the tanks had all the fuel Billy

Parker was willing to give them. He had Greg sign the credit card receipt.

"Want a beer?" Greg asked.

"Don't mind if I do."

"Come on aboard."

Billy Parker stepped over the gunwale of the Hatteras. The soles of his bare feet were black with ingrained grime. He accepted the cold Stella Artois from Greg and took a took a long swig.

"That sure is good. All we got is Prestige. Been a long time since I've had a Stateside beer."

"Why are you in Haiti?" Greg asked.

Billy swirled his beer. "I came down here to help out after the earthquake in 2010. I kinda fell in love with the place. I mean, this place is kind of a paradise all its own, and the U.S. government sends my checks down here regular as clockwork. Helps to be retired."

"I appreciate the help," Greg said.

"Glad to be of service. This place keeps me busy, and I like it. Locals leave me alone, and I got me a Haitian woman to cook and clean. She does other stuff too, if you know what I mean." He gave Greg a wink before draining his beer. "I gotta get back to work. You holler if you need anything."

"Will do," Greg said. "Oh, hey, you know a guy by the name of Toussaint Bajeux?"

Billy's face clouded. "That the friend ya's meetin'?"

"No, just a guy I'm supposed to stay away from."

"You best stay away. That man is dangerous."

Billy Parker stepped off the boat and went back to his building.

Volk, who had been leaning against the counter while listening to the exchange, said, "I'm going to send Alexei and Gregor to store. You check new messages."

Greg pulled out a tablet and connected to the internet. A new message from Floyd Landis appeared in his inbox:

TOUSSAINT BAJEUX UNLOADING *SANTO DOMINGO* OFFSHORE OF CAP-HAÏTIEN TODAY.

CHAPTER FORTY-EIGHT

Simon Duvermond sat in in the middle of the beat-up pickup truck's bench seat, sandwiched between Wilky Ador and Evens Cotin. In the bed of the truck, three other men sat with their backs to the cab and tightly gripped the bedsides as the pickup bounced and swayed along a rutted sand road.

Wilky stopped the truck at the head of a rough wooden dock and the men climbed out. Some lit cigarettes while they waited in the shade of a thatched-roof hut. Simon accidentally kicked a rotten fish carcass, and the men swore at him as the stench drove them from the shelter.

They scanned Acul Bay, looking over the sun-drenched waters and green hills. The mouth of the bay was challenging to navigate due to the ever-changing shoals. It took a skilled pilot to maneuver through the small islets and sandbars. The navigational hazards had fooled more than one captain, and their shipwrecks now littered the ocean floor.

Evens Cotin pointed at a small boat cutting a white wake through the blue water. In Creole, he said, "He's here."

The men watched as the battered fishing vessel

approached. A rickety white cabin hunched over the helm. Extending from the cabin to the stern of the boat was a metal frame covered by a frayed canvas top, bleached white from the sun. There was one man behind the wheel and another in the bow, holding a rope.

Simon stamped out his cigarette and walked to the back of the truck. He opened the tailgate and pulled a heavy, wooden box to the rear of the bed. One of the men who'd ridden in the truck bed walked over and grabbed the other end of the wooden crate containing AK-47s and two RPG-7V2 reloadable rocket-propelled grenade launchers, spare magazines, and five grenades for the RPG launchers. They carried it onto the dock and set it down as the boat coasted to a stop. The bowman sprang out, tied a line to a dock post, and ran to the back to tie off the stern line.

Simon and his mate loaded the box into the boat after Wilky, Evens, and two others stepped aboard. The bowman untied the bow line and pushed the boat away from the dock. The boat pivoted on the stern line. When the boat was perpendicular to the dock, the man unwrapped the stern line and leaped aboard. The driver bumped the drive into gear with a grinding thunk and they sped away.

Holding onto the metal frame for balance, Simon watched as the small archipelago at the mouth of the bay slid by. The knot in his stomach tightened. They were going to war.

He recognized Rat Island, made famous by Christopher Columbus's meeting with several indigenous Taíno there. Since Columbus's invasion—the Haitians thought of it as such—many men had vied for control of the island nation. Toussaint Bajeux was another tyrant who believed he was in line for the throne.

The men in the boat belonged to a rival gang, one that wanted to see the current administration remain in place. For years, the government had pitted the gangs against one another, using them to control neighborhoods, and implement political warfare for the power elites who provided weapons, cash, and protection.

In 2006, the UN Stabilization Mission in Haiti began a crackdown on the gangs, raiding their bases, arresting leaders and their followers. These raids resulted in civilian casualties and extensive collateral damage. The UN deemed it a success. However, the families under the protection of the gangs saw increases in violence, rapes, and murders, some at the hands of the UN troops themselves.

Many of the gang members were driven undercover. Leaders such as Toussaint Bajeux and Wilky Ador continued to run their businesses, protect their people, and advocate for clean water, food, and adequate housing despite the pressure from the government.

Simon glanced over at the man he considered a friend and a mentor. Wilky stood beside the old captain, one hand braced on the back of the captain's seat. He wore a gray T-shirt, dirty white pants with the cuffs rolled up past his ankles, and like his men, his feet were bare. Wilky had a quiet disposition, yet he commanded a large group of men on the Northwestern Peninsula. To allow their rival Toussaint Bajeux to take delivery of the weapons would mean death to many Haitians and cause even more strife in one of the poorest nations in the world.

Simon moved closer to hear the captain and Wilky speak.

The captain said, "The freighter is further away than we thought. Toussaint is unloading off the coast near Fort Liberte Bay. It will take us about an hour to get there."

Wilky nodded. "We must hurry to beat the storm."

CHAPTER FORTY-NINE

Ryan Weller and Mango Hulsey stood at the rail of the ancient freighter, *Santo Domingo*. They stared down at the tugboat holding a barge in place alongside the cargo vessel. On the barge was a single pallet. Its twin swung from *Santo Domingo*'s crane.

The pallet's cargo was a steel box. By Ryan's rough calculations, the gold in the two boxes was worth just north of twenty-five-million dollars. A steep price for guns and ammo.

The crane swung the pallet inboard and lowered it into the freighter's cargo hold. Oso took charge of moving it deeper into the ship while the crane retracted its cable and swung outboard again. The crewmen on the barge attached the crane hook to the second pallet and the crane operator hoisted it aboard.

"Well, the man got paid, bro," Mango said. "I sure would like to get my hands on some of that gold."

"You and me both," Ryan said. He fingered the EFP detonator remote in his pocket.

Along the southern horizon, dark clouds were forming. The flat sea conditions they'd enjoyed yesterday and early this morning were diminishing. The long, rolling swells, pushed ahead of the storm, would make transferring cargo hazardous.

The two men tracked the progress of the gold strong box as it disappeared into the *Santo Domingo*'s hold. Once it was unhooked and moved out of the way, the ship's crew attached the crane hook to an MRAP. The tan truck with a boat-shaped bow frontend was capable of transporting six troops plus a driver and passenger. Mounted on top was an armor shielded M2 fifty-caliber machine gun.

Ryan was about to press the EFP detonator when he saw a pallet with a large cardboard box on it. The top flaps had been peeled back and Ryan paused as he saw what was inside.

"I'm going down there. I'll be back in a few minutes," Ryan told Mango. "Stay right here." He turned and jogged across the deck to the stairs and leaped down them two at a time. He stopped by Oso, who was acting as loadmaster.

"This is going to take forever," Ryan said to the first mate.

"*Si*. We can feel the swells down here. How close is the storm?"

"According to the radar, it's still two days away, but it looks like it could be here any second."

Oso said with confidence, "We will finish in time."

Ryan looked at the long rows of Humvees and MRAPs sitting beside more crates of ammunition, rifles, tactical gear, load-bearing assault vests, RPGs, pistols, and a host of other items Toussaint Bajeux had ordered.

Ryan walked over to the open cardboard box and lifted out two rEvo III rebreathers. Standard scuba diving gear consists of a tank mounted on the diver's back. The diver breathes air from the tank and exhausts it into the water in what is known as open circuit operation. A rebreather func-tioned as a closed system, recycling and scrubbing the diver's breath of carbon dioxide and injecting oxygen into the breathing loop. This allowed the diver to stay underwater longer and remain undetected.

Pressing the button on each of the rebreather's electronic consoles gave him the percentage of diluent and oxygen in their respective tanks and he was glad to see they were all full. He glanced up to motion for Mango to join him in their stateroom, but Mango wasn't standing by the hold. Hefting the two rebreathers, Ryan began to walk away.

"Where are you going with those?" Oso asked.

"Toussaint won't mind me taking a little payment for services rendered." He wanted them as compensation for putting his ass on the line. If he was going to act like a mercenary, he should get paid like a mercenary. And he had formulated a new plan to escape from the ship and from the bounty. He and Mango would strap the rebreathers on, blow the EFP, and swim out of the sunken ship.

"Bring those back," Oso demanded.

"I'm putting them in my cabin. I'll take it up with Toussaint when I see him."

"They're on the manifest. He's paid for them and will want them."

"Like I said, I'll take it up with him when I see him."

Oso pulled out a pistol and aimed it at Ryan. "Put them back."

"No, Oso. Put the pistol away."

"I will when you return the diving gear."

"I'll be in my room if you need me." Ryan kept walking. He paused at the top of a ladderwell and looked down at the stout Nicaraguan. The man had holstered his weapon and was checking items off a list on a clipboard.

Ryan continued to his stateroom and set the rebreathers down on his bunk. He ran the automated function tests on both and double-checked tank pressures. Next, he strapped one on his back, opened the breathing loop, and breathed through it while watching the computer. There were no issues or leaks he could detect. He did the same for the second rebreather and found no problems with it.

Ryan stowed the rebreathers and walked up to the bridge. He wanted to spend a minute with Guzmán. He felt bad for what he was about to do, and he wanted to warn the man, but, he couldn't. Guzmán had a pair of binoculars to his eyes, focusing on the Haitian coast.

"Anything interesting out there?" Ryan asked.

"Some small boats."

"What about the weather?"

Taking down the binos, Guzmán said, "It should hold long enough for us to unload."

Ryan looked down at the barge where crewmen were strapping down a Humvee.

"What do you think about all of this?"

The old man shrugged and pulled out a cigarette. He offered the pack to Ryan, who took one. Guzmán got his lit and looked back at the water. "It is not for me to say. I am only a ship captain."

"You ever want a job working for someone other than Kilroy, my boss would hire you."

"Who is your boss?"

"Greg Olsen. He owns Dark Water Research."

Guzmán nodded. "I know of this company. They are quite large." He shrugged. "I have my ship, and I'm my own man."

Ryan shrugged. "The offer stands."

"Thank you."

Ryan went down the ladder to the main deck and joined Mango, who was staring into the ship's hold.

Mango said, "I don't think we'll make it. These guys are going too slow."

Ryan snubbed out his cigarette. "Don't worry about it. Toussaint's not going to get everything anyways."

CHAPTER FIFTY

Toussaint Bajeux stood on the beach several miles west of the entrance to Fort Liberte Bay. A mobile crane sat in the soft sand with its wheels and external legs on pads to keep the heavy machine from sinking into the ground. The operator was busy slinging the large military vehicles from barges run in through the surf by the tugboats. Between the MRAP's weight maxing out the crane's lifting capacity and the worsening weather, Toussaint employed groups of men to wade in and out of the water, dragging boxes and crates from the barges to stack them in the back of the off-loaded MRAPs and Hummers.

Bajeux watched as the weather continued to worsen. The surf had built into three-foot swells which forced the tug captains to continually manipulate the boats to keep them from being forced onto the beach. The tug pushing twin barges struggled valiantly in the waves. At each link, where the three vessels connected, they surged and plunged when the waves passed under them.

As quickly as possible, the men unloaded the trucks,

stacked them with weapons, and then drove them to a rendezvous point further inland.

Toussaint made a running leap and landed on the bow of a barge. He ran back to the tugboat and climbed onto the vessel's bridge.

"Hurry, we must unload as much as we can."

The tugboat captain was too busy jockeying his craft to object. He backed away from the beach, and the ride smoothed out as they passed the breakers.

"The storm, she is worse," the tug operator fretted.

"Drive," Toussaint commanded. He patted the holstered pistol on his hip.

"Sir, my barges are not designed to be in the large swells."

"I'm paying you, *non?*"

"*Wi*, but—"

"*Non*! You will take us to the ship."

The captain turned his vessel toward the *Santo Domingo*. Waves battered the barges as they labored through seas.

CHAPTER FIFTY-ONE

The Hatteras GT63 sliced through the building waves. Spray cascaded off the wide Carolina bow flares. Greg steered them in a downwind leg of a search block that ran east into the Atlantic, north to Tortuga, and south to the Dominican Republic border. Greg reasoned the *Santo Domingo* would be close inshore to limit the amount of distance the tugs had to travel, which meant less than a mile out. These parameters made their search box smaller, but it still covered hundreds of square miles of open ocean.

He heard the salon door open and slam shut before a Russian puked over the gunwale, joining his partner at the stern.

Greg flipped open the console cover and pressed the button to zoom out the weather radar. Bands of rain were spread across the islands, pushed ahead of Hurricane Irma. The storm had already devastated the Lesser Antilles as she tracked along the ribbon of green jewels forming the Caribbean's necklace.

"This is going to get bad!" Greg yelled.

"We hunt prey," Volk said. "We have power to run away from storm."

"We should be running right now."

"You will not run."

The man was right. Greg wasn't going to run. Not with Ryan and Mango so close. Their mission was almost over, and they would need a ride back to Texas City. Unfortunately, he'd brought the bad guys to the party. This was a coalescence of forces: Mother Nature, Volk, Toussaint Bajeux, Jim Kilroy, and who knows who else was lurking out there.

Greg glanced down at the radar again. The hurricane had lessened to a Category 4, but was building again, bringing dangerous waves, deluges of rain, and winds strong enough to blow over the Hatteras. He closed the clear instrument cover and woke up the tablet. The current screen showed engine performance numbers. He opened an Internet browser and began to scroll through hurricane news to gauge how fast the storm was moving and how much time they had to vacate the island.

"Tugboats going out," Volk reported.

Greg looked up, surprised to see them steaming through building seas. He picked up a pair of binoculars and studied their path. They motored straight for an ancient freighter. He could see men milling about the freighter's deck. Using the zoom, he concentrated on two men near the starboard rail. Greg recognized Ryan's posture, the easy swing of his step as he moved, like a big, shambling, beach bum. Mango walked with a more mechanized gait, a slight sway to compensate for his prosthesis.

"You see your comrades, *da?*"

"*Da, da,*" Greg said in annoyance. He itched to grab his pistol from its a custom-made holster under the seat of his wheelchair. He'd placed it there when he'd gone down to take a nap before arriving in Cap-Haïtien. Right now was the perfect opportunity to grab the gun and dispatch the three goons. Except he would need to transfer from the high captain's seat into his chair to grab it, and if he did, Volk was sure to turn around before he could draw and fire.

He set the autopilot and swiveled in his seat.

Volk sensed his movements and turned.

"Just getting more comfortable." Greg lifted himself up by the seat's armrests to allow for a pressure relief to keep the blood circulating in his legs. He wanted to avoid getting a pressure sore on his bottom. It was a move Volk had seen him make thousands of times.

"Don't get cute," Volk said.

"I'm already cute enough."

Volk frowned. "Such lip from Americans. You are a sarcastic brood."

Greg laughed as Volk turned back to his binoculars. He waited a minute more and glanced over his shoulder at the two men in the cockpit. They were still bent over the rail, praying to Neptune.

Waiting a moment longer, he shifted again, and made the transfer down to the wheelchair.

Volk swung around. "What are you doing?" he demanded again.

"Just want to adjust the spray curtains." Greg wheeled to the side of the bridge and pulled down the heavy plastic drapes hanging from the roof. He finished zipping the starboard side closed and went to the port side. He got the curtain down and secured before turning to see where his minder stood. Volk watched the freighter through his binoculars.

Slowly, Greg reached between his legs and pulled the Sig Sauer .380 from its holster. The boat rolled heavily to starboard. He had to grab onto a rail to keep from tipping backward. His right hand brought the gun up.

From ten feet away, Volk was impossible to miss. He braced his hand against the console and aimed the muzzle at Volk's back. The man's sheer mass alone meant Greg would have to hit him at least twice and maybe three times in the Mozambique Drill, two to the chest, one to the head.

"Hey!" a Russian voice yelled from the cockpit.

Volk spun as Greg fired. The shot went wide as the boat rolled. Greg pulled the trigger again.

The big Russian dove at the man in the wheelchair. He slapped away the firearm before Greg could get off the third shot. The gun spun out of Greg's hand and landed on the deck. It slid off the back of the bridge and into the cockpit. Greg's hand stung from the blow. His eyes were tracking the gun, and he didn't see the heavy hand smack him across the face. He reeled in the chair and fell over. His arms lurched out to catch himself.

Before Greg could right himself, Volk shoved him all the way over. Greg tumbled onto the heaving deck and slammed into the settee. He winced as pain shot through his back and elbows. He looked up at the Russian looming over him.

"I told you, no tricks!" Volk flipped the wheelchair upside down and ripped the gun holster off. He tossed it into the ocean. The chair slid across the deck and came to rest against one of the padded benches.

Greg levered himself into a seated position and used his arms to take the weight off his butt.

Alexei, one of the seasick Russians climbed onto the bridge. He pulled a gun from his waistband. "I kill?"

"He's not worth killing. A cripple who cannot even die properly." Volk spat on the deck. "Get him into captain's seat, so he can drive boat, unless one of you useless fools can do it."

They seized Greg roughly under the armpits and lifted him onto the settee.

"Get his feet," Alexei said.

Volk grabbed Greg's feet while Alexei lifted from behind and they transferred him into the seat.

"Do not try stupid trick again," Volk warned.

"I had to try," Greg said sullenly.

"You will die next time."

"Stop telling me and just shoot me already! You think I like being a cripple?" Greg stared boldly into Volk's face. Throwing his arms wide, Greg screamed, "Just do it!"

Volk laughed so hard he had to grip his stomach. Between breaths, he said, "I kill you ... ho, ho ... after I kill your friend."

CHAPTER FIFTY-TWO

The spray coming off the bow of the fishing vessel had soaked Simon Duvermond to the skin. Except for the captain, and Wilky Ador, who stood under the small cabin roof, the rest were just as wet. Several of the men leaned over the rail, vomiting in time with the rolls of the boat. Simon had thrown a tarp over the crate to keep the guns dry.

Simon felt the lurching of his stomach with each rise of the bow before it smacked hard into the next wave. He looked up from his misery when the captain shouted. On the horizon was a freighter that had seen better days. Rust streaked the sides where the faded, black paint had peeled off. A cloud of black smoke hung over the stern as the craft labored the stay in place. A tugboat and a barge were just coming alongside the freighter and a second tug pushing two barges was rapidly approaching.

Simon stared at the name on the ship's stern. In block white letters, it read *Santo Domingo*. As he watched, the ship's crane began to hoist a desert tan American Humvee from its hold. There was no machine gun mounted in the armor-protected turret above the cabin.

Evens Cotin jerked the tarp away from the weapons box. The men pushed through their seasickness and grabbed rifles. Simon found an RPG shoved into hands. Wilky Ador shouldered the second rocker launcher.

Without orders, the captain increased the speed of his vessel, angling for the massive freighter. They closed the distance quickly.

Wilky turned to Simon. "We shoot on my command. You will aim for the tugboat. I will aim for the ship. Fire and reload as fast as you can."

"Which tugboat?"

Wilky grinned a gap-toothed smile. "Take your pick."

Simon was no stranger to the RPG-7. He had practiced with it on another boat. He and Wilky had each fired a rocket a piece.

"You know what to do," Wilky yelled and gave him a thumbs-up.

Simon nodded and turned to his RPG. He checked it over quickly and loaded a rocket.

"Run us in close," Wilky yelled to the captain.

The captain fed more fuel to the engine.

Simon steadied himself against the starboard gunwale of the small craft which would pass the freighter on the starboard side, allowing Wilky the most advantageous shot. Simon lined up his rocket with the approaching tugboat.

Ahead, the freighter loomed large over the smaller boat. People were now visible on the upper decks. Simon was oblivious to this as he waited for the command to fire. The waves made it hard to sight the rocket accurately. He prayed it would hit its intended target. He braced his head against the RPG's round, wooden cover and stared down the iron sights.

At two hundred meters, the rocket had a fifty percent chance of hitting its target. Every meter farther away decreased its accuracy even more so. A crosswind could blow the warhead off its path. These were things Wilky Ador had told his pupil when they'd test fired their rockets. Simon didn't doubt Wilky's statements, and concentrated harder on adjusting for the roll and pitch of the two vessels.

"Fire!" Wilky shouted an instant before he triggered his rocket.

The RPG's backblast ripped the tarp from its metal frame and ignited it in flames. Simon's backblast scorched the wooden boat's stern.

Simon watched as his high-explosive anti-tank round screamed across the water. It missed the barges by mere inches and slammed into the bow of the tug. Simon bent to grab the second round as Wilky pulled the trigger on the fresh rocket he'd just loaded. The hot gases peeled off Simon's skin as easily as it did his clothes. The blast's concussive force flung his lifeless body over the side of the boat.

Wilky's first rocket had struck the water near the ship's bow. The force of the explosion had stove-in the riveted plates of the freighter's bow. He was too busy watching the second warhead, designed to penetrate armored steel, slice through the skin of the *Santo Domingo* and explode inside the freighter's bow, to realize he had killed his friend.

"Shoot!" Wilky commanded. His men began to fire wildly at the freighter and the tugboats.

The gang leader turned to share a joyous moment with Simon. To his dismay, he couldn't find his friend. Wilky shrugged and loaded the next warhead; the one Simon had been bending down to pick up.

He aimed it at the tugboat tied alongside the listing freighter. With a grin on his face, he stroked the trigger and sent the rocket down range.

CHAPTER FIFTY-THREE

Greg's head pounded from the smack Volk had given him. His ear rang, and he felt dizzy. He'd never been seasick, but if his equilibrium didn't return soon, he might join the Russians as they chummed for fish.

"Tiny boat is going to ram freighter," Volk said.

Greg, busy navigating some traffic as they circled off the coast, angled the Hatteras toward *Santo Domingo* for a better view.

Light flared under the canopy of the tiny boat and the canvas top erupted in flames as it blew into the air. Then a second streak blazed away from the boat. Greg managed to see the first impact near the bow of the freighter. It hit just in front from the hull and sent up a geyser of water. The freighter's bow plunged into the frothing sea. When it reemerged, Greg saw the hull plates had been knocked inward.

He turned in the direction of a boom rolling across the water. A massive ball of fire erupted from the ragged hole torn in the tugboat's skin.

"Ho, ho, ho, ho!" Volk laughed, his deep baritone carrying over the wind.

"What's so funny?" Greg asked.

"The man was blown off tiny boat by RPG." Volk laughed again.

Another explosion roiled the air when a warhead smacked into the bow of the *Santo Domingo*. A gaping hole appeared just above the water line and the freighter began listing to starboard as she continued to plunge through the seas.

A fourth RPG round struck the tugboat alongside the freighter. The tugboat's bridge exploded into flames. Shattered window glass shredded the air.

Immediately following the RPG strikes, the men on the fishing boat opened fire with machine guns. Bullets pinged off sinking steel.

"Get us out of here!" Volk shouted.

Greg spun the wheel while shoving the throttles forward. He hated to run away from Ryan, but at the same time, he couldn't help him if the Haitians damaged the Hatteras.

CHAPTER FIFTY-FOUR

Ryan found himself face down on the deck of the freighter. His hands and knees ached from slamming into the unyielding steel. He shook his head and rose to his knees and then to his feet. Under him, the ship's starboard list increased by the second.

He saw Mango farther forward, near the massive cargo hold opening. He, too, was climbing back to his feet. Both men ducked behind structure to avoid the incoming gunfire.

Ryan ran hunched over toward Mango.

"Get the lifeboats in the water!" Captain Guzmán shouted from the bridge. "Get the guns into action!"

The machine guns Guzmán was screaming about were near the sinking bow of the *Santo Domingo* and covered by old oil drums to keep them clean and dry.

"I'm going for the gun," Ryan shouted to Mango.

Together, they sprinted to the port side barrel and levered it off the gun. Ryan wasn't surprised to find a well-oiled, professionally maintained, M2 fifty-caliber "Ma Deuce" with a bandolier of bullets already fed into the chamber.

The ex-Navy EOD technician jerked the gun's charging

handle back, grasped the double grips, and depressed the thumb trigger.

"What are you doing?" Mango screamed over the roar of the gun. "Shoot those guys!" He pointed at the fishing boat.

Ryan ignored him and continued to send burst after burst through the shattered windows of the second tugboat. The one he'd seen Toussaint Bajeux on. He aimed the gun low, allowing the thumb-sized bullets to blast through the tin skin of the tug and punch down through the bridge deck. He hoped he hit everyone taking cover there.

The men in the fishing boat realized Ryan was manning the Ma Deuce and began concentrating their fire on his position. He swiveled the gun to aim at the smaller boat and rained fire down on them. It was like watching the hand of God strike. Green tracers formed a solid, visible rope of bullets. Wood splinters flew into the air and body parts exploded as Ryan walked the bullets down one side of the boat and back up the other. His machine gun clicked empty just before he could shoot the last man. They didn't need to worry about him, because he threw away his rifle and dove into the water. The boat's gasoline tank erupted in fire.

"What do we do now?" Mango shouted. His ears still rang from the intense pounding of the fifty cal.

"Come on," Ryan yelled back, and he ran toward the bridge. The detonator in his pocket had been forgotten.

Passing the crane at the base of the bridge, they saw Guzmán lying on his back in a pool of blood, legs twisted underneath him.

Ryan kept moving and opened the port bridge castle hatch. The weight of the hatch and the angle of the ship caused the door to slam open and bounce against the bridge bulkhead. Ryan was thankful he'd jerked his fingers off the edge of the door—they would have been cut off. He needed to be more careful.

Santo Domingo was a ship who knew she was dying. She groaned in resignation as the ocean swirled in through the holes blasted through her skin. Unlike the new ships, she didn't have a double-walled hull and watertight bulkheads to seal out the intruding water. Even if she did, there wasn't any crew left to provide the damage control desperately needed to save her.

Ryan and Mango ran half on the deck and half on the starboard bulkhead as they maneuvered deeper into the ship.

CHAPTER FIFTY-FIVE

Toussaint Bajeux lay huddled in a corner of the tugboat with his hands over his head. The bullets had punched ragged, fist-sized holes through the tug's aluminum skin. They'd ripped and tore at everything around him. Shattered window glass was strewn about the cabin and some had found its way into his clothes. Smoke poured from the hole in the bow where the rocket had detonated and ripped away a chunk of metal large enough to drive a car through, but it hadn't done enough damage to sink the tug.

"Cut away the barges! Cut away the barges!" the captain shouted as soon as the hailstorm of bullets stopped raining down. Both had taken refuge behind the large control console. It had sustained hits but was still relatively intact.

"Get up, *Mesye* Bajeux. I must cut away the barges. I may be able to save the tug."

Toussaint looked up at the brilliant sunlight streaming through the bullet holes. He scrambled to his feet. Once again, he'd come through the fire unscathed. The loa were smiling on him, giving him a sign that he would conquer Haiti and rule forever.

His elation was gone the instant he looked out the broken window. The *Santo Domingo,* along with its load of weapons and armament, was sinking. Of little consolation was the fact that the small fishing boat, which had initiated the attack, was being torn to shreds by automatic fire. He entreated Baron Samedi to deliver their souls to the Devil.

Anger seethed though Bajeux when he caught sight of the two men manning the machine gun on the freighter. "Damned mercenaries." Then he laughed when he thought of Ryan Weller's defiance at being labeled as such.

"*Mesye* Bajeux," the captain shouted as he leaped back onto the tug and climbed to the bridge. "We must prepare to abandon ship."

"What?" Toussaint spun around.

"The ship, she is sinking." The captain ran off the bridge and scrambled up a ladder to the top of the tugboat.

Toussaint followed. Together they stood on the roof, watching as the *Santo Domingo* succumbed to the sea, dragging the other tugboat and barge with her into the deep.

Toussaint thought about the cargo on the sinking ship. They'd only unloaded a small portion of what he'd ordered from Jim Kilroy. While he could cause considerable damage, he didn't believe he had enough to take over the government and hold it while he transformed the country. Sadness crept over him, not for the equipment, or the gold, or for himself, but for the people of his country.

A horn sounded behind them. Toussaint turned to see his thirty-seven-foot Carver Voyager come alongside the floundering tug, Joulie at the wheel. She gave him a brief smile before he and the tugboat captain scrambled aboard the pleasure craft.

CHAPTER FIFTY-SIX

"Hey, bro," Mango shouted. "We're supposed to be getting off this tub."

"We are," Ryan yelled back.

"Want to explain that to me?"

To keep from falling, they were clinging tightly to the port handrail as they descended a ladderwell.

Ryan said, "If we go down with the ship, everyone'll think we're dead, right?"

"Yeah, and we will be."

Ryan jerked open the door to their stateroom and leaped back to let the hatch swing through its arc. They clawed their way into the stateroom on the port side of the ship. The deck was almost at a forty-five-degree angle.

"You ever dive with a rebreather?" Ryan asked.

"A few times, we had the old Draeger units."

"These are a little more sophisticated, and a lot easier to use. I already checked them out. They're good to go."

"We're going to swim out of here?"

"Yep." He grabbed his gear bag and pulled it out from under his bunk. "We're going to sit down in the hold and wait for the ship to sink. Then we'll swim to shore. Everyone will think we're dead. End of bounty. End of story."

"What about Jennifer? I can't die without telling my wife."

"We'll hide out on Haiti until the hurricane passes. After that, we'll cross over to the Dominican Republic and find a ride home."

"This sounds complicated, bro."

Ryan pulled mask, fins, and boots out of his gear bag. He stepped out of his worn Top-Siders and shoved his feet into neoprene dive boots. Mango followed suit with his own gear.

"So, were you planning this all along, or what?"

"I had no idea we were going to get attacked," Ryan replied.

"Then why steal the rebreathers? I watched that little showdown you had with Oso."

"Because I decided I was a mercenary and I wanted to get paid. These babies are like eight grand a piece." He held up the car remote. "And I rigged the ship with explosives."

"That's what you were doing?"

Ryan chuckled as he helped Mango shoulder the rebreather.

Mango asked, "How were we going to get off the ship before you stole the rebreathers?"

"Lifeboat."

When he had Mango adjusted, he slung the second rebreather onto his back and explained the rEvo's procedures as he buckled and tightened the straps.

"So, the fishing boat was just a coincidence?"

"Pretty much. Must be one of Toussaint's rivals."

"Think you hit him when you were spraying the tugboat?"

"Let's hope so." Ryan strapped a dive knife to his calf.

Holding his fins in his hands, Ryan led the way deeper into the ship's bowels. He wanted to be in *Santo Domingo*'s hold as it went down. If the ship rolled further to the starboard, or over completely, the hold would be the easiest place to navigate out from. Even though they'd spent the last several weeks on the *Santo Domingo* and were intimately familiar with her layout, those same ladders, passageways, and decks would look distinctly different upside down.

The lower they went, the more water they encountered. Two decks above the main hold, water boiled out of the hatches.

"Good time to test our gear."

"Good luck, bro," Mango said.

Ryan turned and clasped the hand Mango held out. They chest-bumped in a bro hug and set about donning their fins and masks. Ryan opened the breathing loop and took a deep breath. He watched Mango do the same, and Mango signaled he was ready to dive.

Holding the railing, Ryan pulled himself down through the restriction. Once past the hatch, the force of the water flow lessened, although not completely. He realized they didn't have any weights to compensate for their buoyancy. He hoped the dive lockers containing the lead weights hadn't been craned over to the barges yet. Otherwise, they would need to find something else to help hold them down.

Glancing over his shoulder, he saw Mango right behind him. They descended through the next ladderwell, following the light coming in through the cargo hold. Once past the last hatch, they swam through the flooded cargo bay and dropped down to a row of Humvees still chained to the deck.

Ryan found the pallet with the diving gear on it and helped Mango stuff lead weights into his pockets. Mango did the same for his dive buddy. On the pallet were several tanks of one-hundred-percent oxygen and others marked with partial blends. Ryan grabbed two bottles of oxygen and two bottles of compressed air.

They put the spare bottles in the front footwell of a Humvee and climbed into the rear seats to wait for the ship to finish sinking.

All around them the ship moaned with exertion. Items tumbled and rolled as the list became more pronounced. Chains holding one of the MRAPs gave way. The heavy vehicle plunged in slow motion into the Humvee in front of Ryan and Mango's refuge. The chains on the driver's side of the Humvee broke, and the weight of the MRAP shoved it onto its side. The MRAP flipped over onto its top, coming to rest with its nose on the Humvee and the rear bumper jammed against the ship's hull.

Ryan glanced at his dive computer. They'd passed one hundred feet in depth and were still dropping like a stone. When he'd last glanced at the depth sounder on the *Santo Domingo*'s bridge, while offering Guzmán a job, it had read four hundred feet. According to the charts, the ship was steaming along the continental shelf where the island's ancient volcanic sides dropped deep into the ocean. The ship had angled inshore to gain a respite from the waves and the depth chart said the seabed rose up quickly.

He prayed he was correct, and the inertia of the ship would guide them into shallower water, closer to the fifty-fathom mark—three hundred feet. That depth was well beyond the recreational limit for scuba divers and would limit salvage operations on the vessel. The gold was there, and it would draw Kilroy and anyone else who knew about it like a Siren. And like the mythical Greek creatures, Ryan had no doubts that the search for *Santo Domingo*'s treasure would lure men to their deaths.

Terrible screeching sounds ripped through the water as the increasing water pressure slowly crushed the ship's hull. In the fading light, Ryan could see Mango's face. He couldn't read his expression. Mango must have sensed him looking and glanced over. Ryan flashed an okay sign with each hand. The gesture of reassurance did little to help the panic in Mango's eyes.

From inside the Humvee, they felt the whole ship shift and shudder as the ship's bow buried itself into the seafloor. It quivered like an arrow stuck in the dirt. Slowly, the stern began to settle to the ground.

Dirt and sand blossomed up as the ship slammed down. Particulate blocked out what little light that came through the cargo opening, turning Ryan and Mango's world dark as night. The current quickly carried away the particulate and allowed light to stream through the cargo hatch again.

The Humvee was now on its right side, suspended by its chains. Any items that hadn't fallen during the ship's plummet to the seafloor began raining down. A four-foot-long pipe wrench plunged head down to slam into the side of their Humvee.

Ryan felt the chain on the front driver's side snap, sending a shudder through the vehicle. He grasped the back of the seat in front of him and the handle screwed to the frame above his door.

Mango frantically motioned for them to exit the vehicle. Ryan signaled with an okay sign. He reached for his door handle.

The rear driver's side chain gave way and the Humvee slid down the vertical deck on its tires, hit the limits of the passenger side chains, and flipped over onto its roof. The Humvee's momentum snapped the two remaining chains. It rolled again and crashed into the ship's hull, coming to rest on its wheels.

"Holy shit!" Ryan yelled into his mouthpiece. Mango lay in a tangle. Ryan pointed at him and flashed the okay sign.

Mango held up his middle finger.

Ryan leaned his shoulder into the Humvee's door and

tried to force it open. The door wouldn't budge. He gestured for Mango to try his door. Mango did, and found his door jammed shut as well. Mango's eyes were wide and round. He held up both hands with extended middle fingers.

Yeah, I know. Screwed the pooch, Ryan thought. He was glad he couldn't hear Mango berating him for trapping them inside the Humvee in three hundred feet of water. He looked up at the hole in the roof where the gunner normally stood. It wasn't large enough for them to exit while wearing the rebreathers.

They took turns leaning forward and trying the front doors of the Humvee. Neither would budge. Ryan crawled into the back under the slanting fiberglass cover. He braced his shoulder against the bed of the truck and shoved up with his feet. Nothing gave. He tried again with the same result.

Physical exertion at three hundred feet underwater was not a good thing. Ryan tried to control his breathing and closed his eyes to focus and calm himself. In his mind, he chanted the mantra he'd always lived by when scuba diving. *As long as you're breathing, you have time to figure things out. Don't panic. Panic kills.*

He thought of every exit out of the Humvee. The only one open was the gunner's turret. During the Humvee's tumble down the deck, the frame had twisted just enough to keep the doors from opening. He'd seen it happen before after IEDs had detonated under the machines.

There was also a lot of weight on the outside of the machine. At three hundred feet, they were at more than ten atmospheres below sea level. This meant there were more than one hundred and forty-eight pounds of pressure per square inch squeezing everything together. The massive water pressure caused the *Santo Domingo* to continue to creak and groan. More parts and pieces fell.

In the near darkness of the Humvee cab, Ryan Weller

realized the only way to live was to take off his rebreather, exit the gun hatch, pull the rebreather through, and put it back on before opening the truck's door for Mango. It was an excessive task load at depth.

He loosened and unbuckled the rebreather's straps before sliding the whole contraption over his head. As he did so, he had an epiphany. He glanced at Mango, who scowled with narrowed eyes and shook his head.

Instead of holding his breath and dragging the rEvo after him, Ryan pushed the rebreather out the hole and kept his teeth clamped tight on the mouth piece. The rEvo barely fit through the turret. Mango helped him snake the straps and buckles through. Then he levered himself out of the gun turret and pulled the rebreather back on. He took a minute to relax and regulate his breathing. They still had a long swim ahead of them. He couldn't afford to burn through all his gas by working hard.

Mango pounded on the cargo hatch door. Ryan swam around to the latch. The handle twisted freely. Mango shoved the door open and floated out. Ryan reentered the Humvee and removed the four tanks he'd stowed in the driver's side footwell. He helped Mango strap two to his rebreather harness and Mango strapped the other two to Ryan.

Ryan pointed toward the ship's cargo hold opening with his right hand. Then he extended his left forefinger and brought it beside his right forefinger, indicating Mango should stay with him. They swam out of the cargo hatch into the open ocean.

Mango pointed at the upside-down tugboat and they both stared at the carnage. The ship's twisted crane boom draped over the barge. A Humvee lay on its side, still attached to the crane's cable.

Mango tapped Ryan on the shoulder and held up his hand

in a fist with his thumb extended to the right. He rapidly rotated his wrist it back and forth to ask, "Which way?"

Ryan knew the ship had gone down paralleling the coast of Haiti. It had listed to the starboard side as it sank, which meant the cargo hold was facing land. How far they would need to swim was another story. He checked the compass built into his dive computer and tapped the large S. Mango nodded, consulted his own compass, and flashed okay.

Ryan straightened his left arm out, locked his right wrist on the left elbow, and allowed the compass to swing. It spun wildly. He'd forgotten that the ship's metal hull would confuse the reading of a compass correcting to magnetic north. They'd need to swim away from the ship before he could establish a true reading. He aimed his left hand at a small mound in the seabed and they began to swim.

CHAPTER FIFTY-SEVEN

G reg Olsen stared forlornly at the air bubbles roiling and bursting on the water's surface as they escaped from inside the two sunken vessels. The stiffening breeze quickly whisked away the burning fishing boat's black smoke. Toussaint Bajeux stood on the top of a tugboat's bridge roof.

Greg had seen ambushes before, and the speed and fury of this one matched the best. Not only had they no warning the boat was attacking, there was also no time to save the sinking vessel. The daring ferocity of Ryan and Mango's counterattack was a testament to their training and bravery. *Or stupidity*, Greg thought.

He feared Ryan and Mango's retaliation had prevented them from escaping the doomed ship. He spun the wheel to take *Dark Water* closer to the wreck site. He wanted to look for survivors and, with any luck, pick up his friends. Although having them safe from a sinking ship and on the Hatteras was, Greg thought, *like hopping from the skillet into the frying pan. Terrible news all around.*

An older model cruiser sped up to the slowly sinking

tugboat and took Toussaint and another man onboard before accelerating away.

Greg heard Volk cursing in his native tongue even though he was at the top of the tuna tower. He had lost his payday, and that put Greg in a bind. He wished he'd saved his pistol for a better opportunity if Volk decided to summarily execute him because Ryan and Mango had gone down with the *Santo Domingo*. He'd dared Volk to kill him, begged him in a moment of self-pity, but now he wanted nothing more than to kill all the Russian bastards.

Volk dropped down the aluminum ladder and stood on the bridge with his fists on his hips, his brow furrowed, and his lips pursed as he squinted into the distance.

Greg wanted to poke fun at the Wolf but kept silent in fear of retribution. He ran his tongue over the inside of his mouth, feeling the broken skin from Volk's last punishment.

"They dead?" Volk asked.

"If they didn't get off the ship."

"This is magic man," Volk said as he turned to look at Greg. "José Luis Orozco told me of Weller's exploits in killing Arturo Guerrero. Your friend has nine lives, *da*?" He relaxed his posture and wagged a finger at Greg. "I think he is alive."

"Man, I hope so," Greg muttered.

"We wait here for him."

"Not gonna happen, Chief. As much as I want to find my friend, we have a storm heading our way."

Volk braced himself on the bridge console as Greg turned the boat into the waves to circle the continuous stream of bubbles erupting from the sunken ships.

"You take us to marina. Your friend will call."

"And if he doesn't?"

Volk's lips peeled back in his trademark grin. He made a fist with his thumb sticking out, then drew the thumb slowly across his throat as he stared at Greg.

CHAPTER FIFTY-EIGHT

Ryan and Mango worked their way along the sea floor, kicking slowly to conserve energy. Ryan constantly monitored his direction, speed, and gas consumption. Once they were a good distance from the ship, the compass had given them a true reading and they corrected course. Now, they were fighting a current, which was running west, parallel the coast. To control their speed, he counted the number of kicks he made per minute. These were skills he'd learned in the Navy. He knew Mango had learned them as well. Every member of the U.S. military who qualified as a diver, regardless of branch, went through the Navy's dive school in Panama City, Florida. During his time in EOD, Ryan had plotted and swum more tracks than he could count, most in strong currents or near blackout conditions.

The conditions they were swimming in now were more than favorable. They had at least forty feet of visibility, the water was eighty-five degrees, and the current was moderate. His concerns centered on their time at depth, which would be minimal as the sea floor gradually sloped upward, acting as a natural ascent line, gas consumption, and backup contingencies if their rebreathers failed.

If one of the rEvo's quit completely, the diver would switch to the air tank strapped to their side. He would make a slow ascent to the surface, and swim like hell for the beach, if he didn't get the bends during the rapid ascent, but most likely they would.

Ryan rechecked his computer and twisted to look up at the surface, two hundred and fifty feet above them. He could hear buzzing propellers signifying smaller pleasure craft and the deep *whomp, whomp, whomp* of a commercial vessel. It sounded like the massive boat was going to run them over.

Could we have drifted into the channel for Cap-Haïtien? Ryan asked himself. He'd kept a steady compass bearing and tried to use reference points underwater as natural navigation aids. It was possible they'd drifted west. Anything was possible. He thought he'd stayed in a straight line.

Doubt fogged his brain. He stared at the computer and then at the compass. Was he getting them lost? He glanced over at Mango, swimming beside him. *He would have noticed if we were off course, right?*

Ryan tried to clear his mind and focus on the facts. Air pressures were right. He felt good. Their ascent was steady. He took a deep breath and leveled off in the water column again. He extended his left arm out straight and clamped his right hand on his left elbow. The compass was rock solid on the same line they'd begun when they'd left *Santo Domingo*'s cargo hold. Things were fine, Ryan told himself. *You've done this a million times. This is just one more training scenario.*

He nestled down into a rhythm, counting kicks as he watched the timer on his computer, and scanning ahead for visual cues. At this depth, those cues were just small marks in the sand and mud. His worry eased as he remembered that the ripples in the sand ran parallel to the coast. They were following the ripples in.

Gradually, their depth lessened, and they came upon a reef system. Ryan could see the vibrance of the coral and marine life even though it was muted by the depth. Past twenty feet, reds disappeared, then oranges at fifty. He knew they were in less than one hundred feet of water because the yellows were still vibrant against the wash of blues. Tiny fish darted in and out of the coral heads and around the purple sea fans. Ryan knew few divers had explored this section of paradise.

A dark shadow materialized out of the gloom. It was a wreck of an ancient steel-hulled boat heavily encrusted with coral and entangled with fishing line and fouled anchor ropes. Some of the largest fish they'd seen on their journey lurked near the artificial reef structure. Several long barracudas eyeballed them, and a pair of amber jacks chased each other through the wreck. A hogfish with its elongated snout rooted in the sand at the base of the hull. Mango pointed at it with a finger gun and jerked his thumb to mime shooting it. Ryan waggled his hands in a surfer's "hang loose" sign.

Forty minutes later, the two men lay in the sand, eighteen feet beneath the surface, watching a pink-and-green bicolor parrotfish comb the coral for dinner. With its hard beak, the parrotfish pecked off algae. Parts of this reef were bleached white. Silt from the barren hills had washed into the ocean where it clogged the reefs and killed the coral.

The motion of the waves rolled, lifted, and nudged them forward. Both men were ready to be out of the water. Ryan felt a shiver course through him. His body was trying to make up the temperature difference between it and the water, which sapped heat twenty-four times faster than air. He glanced at the computer, only five more minutes before they could surface. The rebreather was pumping out almost pure oxygen to help eliminate any residual nitrogen in his system.

Ryan held up five fingers on his right hand under the flat palm of his left, indicating they had five minutes at their final safety stop then flashed Mango the okay sign. Mango shot him the bird. Ryan shook his head. Mango had given him the bird every time Ryan had asked if he was okay. As far as Ryan knew, this was Mango's longest and deepest dive.

He closed his eyes and let his body ride the ocean swells while he maintained a grip on a chunk of dead coral. For the first time in the last hour and a half, he let his mind drift from the dive. His thoughts found their way to Emily Hunt. He wondered what she would think of all of this. Did she even know where he was, or about his troubles with Kilroy and Toussaint? He missed her and wished he was home with her right now. He felt sentimental and sappy.

The beeping of his dive computer saved him from dropping further into introspection. Their safety stop was complete. Mango pointed his finger at the beach and made a *let's get out of here* motion.

The two men swam into waist-deep water and stood up. A three-foot-high wave nearly knocked them over. Each placed a hand on the other's shoulder for stability, pulled off their fins, and waded up to the beach. When they hit the sand, they shed the rebreathers and spare tanks.

"Well, Google Maps, where are we?" Mango asked.

"I have a general idea, but you're not going to like it."

"Let's hear it, bro."

Ryan pointed west. "Cap-Haïtien is probably twenty miles that way." He pointed east. "That way is Fort Liberte Bay and the Dominican Republic."

"Where's the closest place to grab a beer?"

"That, I don't know."

"Well, I'd kill for one right now." Mango dropped to his knees in the sand.

"You and me both."

"What're we doing with this gear?"

"I'm going to carry the rebreather and leave the tanks."

"Bro, you're seriously crazy."

"I'm getting something out of this deal."

Mango shook his head in disgust. "You're going to hike twenty miles with a rebreather on your back? Might as well have a target that says shoot me."

"You're probably right," Ryan agreed.

"Of course, I'm right."

"I wouldn't let your wife hear you say that."

Mango rolled his eyes. "You did get something out of the deal. You're alive. Well, you're dead, but you're alive."

Ryan chuckled as he dragged the spare tanks and rebreathers into the brush. He crawled out from under an acacia tree, brushed his hands together to knock off the sand, and said, "Let's go out for some Haitian food."

"What's that, like beans and rice?"

"You know, like Mexican and Chinese."

"Get outta here." Mango waved his hand and started up the beach.

They came to a dirt road running south. A yellow Grove crane sat buried to its axles in the loose sand. Someone had attempted to dig it out, and from the deep ruts, in front of the crane, they had also tried to tow it out with another vehicle.

"This reminds me," Mango said as he kicked the crane's tire with his prosthetic foot. "I think I saw *Dark Water* milling around before we got blown up."

"Greg knew where we were coming here."

"Let's find a phone and give him a call," Mango said. "I'd like to get out of here before the hurricane hits."

"Sounds like a plan."

"How far will we have to walk?"

Ryan shrugged. "Couple of miles."

"I'm getting too old for this shit." Mango gave his leg a little extra muscle and his prosthetic rattled as it sprang forward.

"You want to hang out here? I'll go find us a ride?"

"I think I've got a couple of miles in me."

"It'll be like old times," Ryan said. "Want to jog and sing chants?"

"Hell, no."

They fell into silence as they marched along, automatically falling into step as they kept a brisk pace. Both were used to long swims and runs as part of their military service, but neither had been at operational tempo for several years. Their physical stamina was not what it had once been.

"Sure could use that beer right about now."

"I know what you mean, bro," Mango agreed. "I'm dry as a bone."

Ryan estimated they'd walked about two miles when the road made an abrupt right. A smaller track continued straight.

"What do you think, Robert Frost, the road less traveled?" Mango asked.

"When did you become the poetry scholar?"

"Every wanderer knows that rhyme."

"True," Ryan agreed. "But I think we should stick to the path well-traveled. This thing should lead us to civilization, and we want to get there sooner, rather than later."

"Lead on." Mango swept an open hand in the direction the road headed.

They continued walking, eventually coming to a small crossroad. A pickup truck with three different colored fenders was half on the road and half in the ditch. From the tracks, it appeared the man had attempted a U-turn and the truck's rear wheel had dropped into a small hole. When the gray-haired Haitian man gunned the motor, only the wheel over the hole spun.

"Can you give us a ride to town?" Ryan asked.

The man looked at him blankly then started speaking in Creole while gesturing at the back of the truck.

Ryan held up an okay sign. He and Mango went to the back of the truck and leaned on the rusty tailgate. When they had their feet set, Ryan shouted for the man to go and Mango gestured forward with his hand. The old man trounced on the gas, and his two pushers leaned in hard. The truck eased forward with the back tire slipping and spitting sand as it tried to grab traction.

Suddenly, the truck shot forward. Ryan and Mango lost their balance and fell to the ground. They were showered with sand as both tires bit and accelerated.

"Great," Ryan muttered as the truck rocketed away.

He climbed slowly to his feet then helped Mango up. In the distance, the truck stopped on the side of the sandy road. The right backup light came on as the driver shifted the transmission into reverse. The truck barreled backward, and the driver slammed on the brakes to bring the truck to a stop beside them.

The old man hopped out of the cab. He pointed at his saviors and motioned for them to get into the truck bed. "Hello. Hello," he repeated with a broad smile. "Hello." He smacked the truck bed with his hands and motioned again for them to get in.

Mango was first to climb in. Ryan followed as the old man got back in his truck cab. He mashed the accelerator. The tires spit dirt, and the truck bounced and swayed and lurched down the rutted road. Ryan felt like his teeth were going to rattle out of his head. He kept a death grip on the sides of the truck bed and braced himself with his feet.

Ten minutes later, the truck slewed sideways as the driver turned onto another road. This one was at least smooth, and the passengers were able to relax their white-knuckled fingers.

The truck stopped in front of a squat cement block building with a steeply sloped roof and a cross hanging from the peak. A small cluster of homes and shops circled the church. From the driver's seat, the Haitian motioned for them to exit the truck bed. Ryan and Mango dismounted and stood in front of the block building while the truck sped away.

Mango spun in a slow circle. "This is one of those 'blink-and-you-miss-it' places."

The door to the block building opened. A middle-aged black man with close-cropped hair stepped out. He was thin to the point of emaciation, yet his clothes appeared tailored to his slim figure. He smiled with stained brown teeth, and said, "Welcome to Paulette."

"Who are you?" Mango asked.

"I'm Marco Vilmar. I'm the pastor of this church." He hooked a thumb over his shoulder at the building.

Both men shook hands with the pastor and introduced themselves.

Marco invited them inside and they followed him through the door.

"Is there a place to get something to eat and drink around here?" Mango asked.

"I was just sitting down to supper," Marco said. "Please join me, I would love company."

"Thank you," Mango accepted for both men.

Ryan asked, "Do you have a cell phone?"

"I do." Marco patted his pants pocket.

"May I use it? I'll pay for the calls, Pastor."

"Certainly." Marco pulled a worn Nokia flip phone from his pocket and handed it to Ryan.

"If you'll excuse me for a moment?" Ryan asked.

"Certainly." Marco motioned for Mango to follow and they continued to the front of the church and through a side door.

Ryan sat down in a pew and dialed Greg Olsen's number.

"*Da?*"

The thick, rough voice caught Ryan off guard.

"Hello?" the voice said.

"Who is this?" Ryan demanded.

"This is the Ryan Weller?"

Ryan felt his skin prickle and his throat constricted to force down rising bile. The word came out low and menacing. "Volk."

"*Da*, my reputation precedes me?"

"Where's Greg?"

"He is fine for now, but he is not who I want. I want you, Ryan Weller. I want the two million dollars your life is worth." He laughed a deep throaty roar. "I told him; you were *kot*. You are running out of lives."

"Let me talk to Greg."

Greg came on the line. "Ryan?"

"Hey, buddy. You doing okay?"

"Yeah, I'm fine. Volk took my gun and knocked a few teeth loose."

"I'm coming for you," Ryan promised.

"Don't," Greg said. "That's what he wants."

"Enough!" Ryan heard Volk scream. Wind blew over the phone's speaker before Greg's phone bounced on the Hatteras's fiberglass deck. He heard more rustling, and then the Russian accent returned. "I have your Greg. You want him to live? You come to me."

"Where?"

"Cap-Haïtien. The dock beside the power plant. We'll be on *Dark Water*."

The phone went dead.

Ryan shouted, "Hello," several times.

Mango approached holding two bottles of water. He handed one to Ryan and took a sip out of the other.

Ryan explained the phone call.

"What're we going to do?" Mango asked.

The big man put his face in his hands. "I don't know."

CHAPTER FIFTY-NINE

"I'm telling you, I don't like it," Mango said.

Ryan hunched over the wheel of the Honda Pilot they'd rented in Cap-Haïtien after Pastor Marco had driven them to the port city. "I don't either, man, but we need help."

Mango slouched in the passenger seat. Ryan gripped the steering wheel so tightly that the knuckles of both hands were white. He relaxed one hand and buzzed the window down. A guard, with a polished Sam Browne gun belt and holster over a dark blue uniform, leaned in the window.

"I'm here to see Toussaint Bajeux," Ryan said.

The guard looked suspiciously at Ryan and Mango before saying, "No one is here."

"Tell Toussaint that Ryan Weller is here to see him. Tell him I can get his gold back."

The guard eyed them suspiciously and stepped into a booth beside the driveway gate. He stared at Ryan as he lifted a phone from its cradle and spoke into it. A moment later, the guard hung up the receiver and ordered them out of the car.

"Guess that answers that question," Mango said as he

leaned spread eagle over the hood of the car while the guard patted him down.

"I told you he wasn't dead," Ryan said.

The guard frisked Ryan before pointing at a gate behind the guard shack. The two Dark Water Research employees stepped through the gate and walked up the driveway.

Looking up, Ryan saw Toussaint standing on a balcony beside Joulie. He had on dark slacks and a white button-down shirt with the sleeves unbuttoned. She wore a simple blue dress with a multicolored headscarf.

Toussaint called down, "You're a brave man to walk into my home after trying to kill me."

Ryan stopped walking. "I came to broker a deal."

"A deal." Toussaint burst out laughing.

Joulie said something to her fiancé which neither Ryan or Mango could hear.

Toussaint stopped laughing. "Come inside, gentlemen." He turned and disappeared through a glass door.

Ryan and Mango continued to follow the driveway as it wrapped around the back of the home. Jean Francois met them beside the garage. He led them through another gate onto the pool patio. Toussaint stood in the shade created by the upper balcony with a cigar in one hand.

The warlord motioned them to stop when they were several feet from him. He ordered Francois to step aside. Francois moved behind the two visitors but kept his hand on his holstered pistol. Toussaint took a long draw on his cigar, then he let the smoke out in a stream and said, "The only reason I entertain you is for Joulie. She has vouched for you and says you will not attempt to kill me."

"She's right," Ryan said. "I'm not here to kill you. I'm here to make a deal."

"My guard said you can recover the gold, *non?*"

"Yes. I know exactly where the ship is, and I have the equipment to recover it."

"Interesting, and what do you want in exchange for this service, besides your lives?"

"My employer is being held hostage by a Russian bounty hunter named Volk. I need your help freeing him."

Toussaint ordered the men to sit and Joulie brought out two tumblers filled with dark liquid. She set them on a table between Ryan and Mango. She disappeared inside again and returned with a third glass, which she handed to Toussaint.

"Anything else, gentlemen?" Toussaint asked before sipping from his glass.

"A cigarette."

Mango rolled his eyes.

"Even your friend knows you shouldn't smoke," Toussaint goaded.

"I shouldn't do a lot of things, but smoking is the least of my worries right now. Remember, Toussaint, I'm just a mercenary. I work for the highest bidder. Right now, I'm selling myself to you."

Toussaint laughed, holding his gut with his left arm while he leaned forward.

Joulie gave Toussaint a questioning look as she handed a pack of Marlboro Golds to Ryan. He shook one loose and lit it while Toussaint wiped tears from his cheeks.

Between gasps, Toussaint said, "You ... You are a mercenary."

Mango stretched out his right leg to take the weight off his prosthesis. "What's in the glass?"

"Rhum Barbancourt," Toussaint replied. He took a seat and motioned Ryan to sit. Joulie moved to stand behind her fiancé.

Ryan took a sip of his rum. He smashed out his cigarette and lit a second one, earning him a glare from Mango.

"Is this your mother?" Toussaint asked, motioning to Mango.

"He's my work wife," Ryan said.

Toussaint laughed again. "Work wife! You Americans and your slang."

"Look, we're not here to discuss colloquialisms. I need your help killing Volk."

"What's your plan?" Toussaint asked.

Ryan glanced up at Joulie's cool blue eyes then back to Toussaint's black beads. He leaned forward and sketched out a rough draft.

CHAPTER SIXTY

Mango watched *Dark Water* and her Russian guards through the scope of a Russian-made Dragunov sniper rifle. An hour ago, Joulie had dropped him off along the commercial docks. He'd boarded the neglected hull of a one-hundred-and-forty-foot fishing vessel, the only boat left along the commercial docks. Inside the bridge, the crew had helped him set up a table to lie on, so he was level with the windows. He was far enough back in the structure that he would remain undetected and so light would not glint off his scope although the clouds were now blocking most of the sun. They had twenty-four hours before the hurricane would hit. Right now, Irma's leading edge was demolishing the island of Puerto Rico. Everyone was keeping tabs on the storm's movements and praying it would bend to the east and avoid Hispaniola all together. Mango knew the storm trackers predicted it would cross the island before hitting Cuba and striking the Florida Keys.

The big fishing boat he was on made for a steady shooting platform. The long concrete quay blocked the incoming waves, and the vessel's crew had snugged her tight to the jetty.

After helping Mango arrange his overwatch position, they'd disappeared. Mango suspected they were trying to make a dent in the large donation Toussaint had made to their drinking fund, and in an hour or so, they'd be so drunk that they may not care whether they even got underway to avoid the storm.

Through the forward bridge windows, Mango could see Toussaint's Carver Voyager. The boat was coasting to a stop, its bow angled toward *Dark Water*.

He took a moment to look away from the scope and surveyed the scene. Across five hundred feet of open water, an old two-masted yawl and a trawler fishing vessel were moored to a T-shaped dock. Both boats' noses pointed toward open water. *Dark Water* had been snugged against the steel hull of the fishing trawler with her bow toward land. It would have made more sense for her bow to be facing out for a rapid getaway, and so it took the seas better, especially with the rollers starting to build in the bay. Some of the larger waves lifted and jerked the big boats.

When they'd reconned the area yesterday, Ryan had mentioned the Hatteras's orientation and they'd observed only two Russian guards besides Volk. To get to the T-dock required them to drive down the single access road on the tiny peninsula. The whole thing was a choke point, and Volk would see them coming as soon as they turned down the road leading to the marina. The easiest way to approach the dock unseen was underwater. Putting the boat stern out was logical for Greg because he knew Ryan would be coming from that direction, and Ryan could observe what was happening in the cockpit before he made his approach.

Mango settled his eye back to the scope when he saw the Honda Pilot come to a stop in the marina's dirt parking lot. Joulie exited the passenger side, and a man matching Ryan's physical height and weight climbed from the driver's seat. He wore a black ball cap pulled low over his brown hair and sunglasses to mask his features.

The small team was confident the man would pass the distance test. Volk had only seen Ryan one time, and in low light conditions during a fist fight. Toussaint had called a Belgian who worked for the UN and offered a substantial bribe for the man to assume the role of Ryan Weller. They had explained the risks to him, and he expected that he might be involved in a gunfight, though his only job was to divert the guard's attention.

Joulie's hips swung like a runway model's in her tiny jean shorts and an orange bikini top as she strutted down the dock ahead of Fake Ryan. The Russians were instantly distracted. The gunman on *Dark Water*'s bridge turned away from the water and ogled the woman. A second gunman stepped out from behind the hull of the sailboat and moved up the dock to meet Fake Ryan.

The two people not in Mango's sight picture were Greg and Volk. Mango believed they were in *Dark Water*'s salon, and the boat's tinted windows made it impossible to verify his assumption.

Mango had been dubious when he heard Ryan's promise to help Joulie escape from Toussaint, but he had to admit Ryan's plan to get her onto *Dark Water* was working well. It was time for Ryan to make his appearance.

CHAPTER SIXTY-ONE

Ryan stepped into the water as soon as Toussaint dropped the engine into neutral. The Carver coasted forward, pointing like an arrow at *Dark Water*. Ryan took a compass bearing off the boat's keel, extended his arm, locked his wrist in place, and began the swim toward the Hatteras. The rebreather he'd recovered from the beach was functioning flawlessly. No bubbles marked his progress, and the bay's choppy waves hid him from view in the shallow water.

It took him less than ten minutes to cover the distance to the Hatteras. He swam beneath *Dark Water*'s hull and came up under the bow. Looking across the bay at the commercial docks, he hoped Mango was ready to rock and roll. He ducked below the surface again and swam under the dock where he shed the rebreather, mask, and fins. He bundled the gear together using a short piece of rope and left it tied to the piling, the counter lung inflated enough to allow the gear to bob just below the surface.

A moment later, he pulled himself up on the dock. The guard was talking to Fake Ryan and Joulie, who had her hands in her back pockets and rocked back and forth on the balls of her feet. She gazed up at the unshaven Russian with what Ryan could only describe as fondness. He realized it was the same doe-eyed look she'd given Toussaint; a look that would melt any man's heart. Only Ryan now knew it lacked sincerity.

The board beneath Ryan's foot creaked. The Russian spun, reaching for the pistol behind his back. Ryan advanced with lightning speed and reflexes honed through hours of training. His knife came up in his right hand and he drove it deep into the man's sternum.

Ryan eased the dead man to the dock, liberated the pistol from the Russian's holster, and brought it up to cover the Hatteras. Joulie had squatted behind the hull of the fishing boat. Fake Ryan dove off the dock as the guard on *Dark Water*'s bridge fired the first shot.

The roaring bellow of a shotgun's discharge echoed off the boat hulls. Buckshot splintered the decking right where Fake Ryan had been standing. The shot was immediately followed by the chunk-thunk of the Russian working the shotgun's action before more buckshot peppered the docks, boats, and water.

Ryan dropped to the weathered dock boards and rolled behind the trawler. When he looked up, he saw Joulie staring at him. Their eyes met, and she looked unafraid.

He dropped the Russian's pistol on the deck in front of her and pulled his own from the small of his back.

The guard stopped firing.

Ryan sprang into a crouch and ran forward.

CHAPTER SIXTY-TWO

Mango Hulsey saw his partner's head pop out of the water just forward of the Hatteras's bow and then disappear again.

"Showtime, bro," Mango muttered.

He tracked Ryan's movements as he reappeared on the dock. As soon as Ryan was within five feet of the Russian guard speaking to Joulie, Mango refocused his scope on the second Russian on *Dark Water*'s bridge. He had yet to see the bounty hunter.

Mango's sole purpose was to take out Volk. He had to be patient. They wanted Volk to think he was safe to expose himself and when he did, Mango would put him down like the dog he was. The Wolf had led his last pack into battle.

Mango watched the guard on the bridge expend his last round then thread more twelve-gauge shells into the Mossberg 500's magazine tube. The man's movements were clumsy as he fumbled the rounds out of his pocket and jammed them home. The Russian dropped more than one in his haste.

Mango whispered, "Slow is smooth, smooth is fast, bro. Take all the time you need."

He had a glimpse of Ryan leaping up and firing. The bridge guard's head snapped back, blood and gray brain matter splattered across pristine, white fiberglass. The shotgun dropped from the man's hands.

"Greg's gonna be pissed," Mango said while scanning for the final target.

Then Mango saw Ryan creeping up on the cockpit of the Hatteras, arms extended, pistol locked in both hands. Ryan paused on the deck of the fishing boat and appeared to be speaking with someone before raising his hands in surrender.

CHAPTER SIXTY-THREE

The bounty hunter crouched in the doorway behind Greg Olsen. He had a pistol pressed against Greg's temple. The only visible part of Volk's head was his brown right eye, framed in the triangle formed by Greg's head, shoulder, and Volk's arm holding the gun. Through that triangle, he focused solely on his prey, the bounty worth two million dollars. His ticket to riches.

"Throw your gun down," Volk yelled.

Ryan released his left hand from the pistol and held his hands apart and up in the universal sign of surrender.

"Put the gun down," Volk said again. He felt Greg move, and he tightened his grip on his hair. Greg let out a barely audible groan. Anger surged through Volk's body. He twisted Greg's hair out of spite. He wanted to hear the man cry out in pain, needed Ryan Weller to know how high the stakes were. Greg Olsen was an expendable pawn.

"Bleat for friend," Volk's whispered voice rasped in Greg's ear. "Tell him you hurt. I know you want to die. Let me help you. Do something to save friend."

Volk's fist twisted the hair, wrenching Greg's head to the left. He shoved the pistol barrel harder into his skin.

"Don't do it, Ryan," Greg pleaded. "Shoot him. Shoot the bastard! SHOOT. ME."

They both watched as Ryan squatted and set the gun on the fishing boat's rail. He straightened up.

"Your friend is pussy," Volk said to Greg. "He is weak for wanting to save you. He should shoot you to kill me." To Ryan, he yelled, "Push it overboard."

Slowly, Ryan brought his leg up and used his foot to knock the gun over the rail. It made a quiet splash, the sound of a rock sinking into deep water.

Volk felt his hostage slump in defeat. He ordered Ryan to step into the cockpit.

CHAPTER SIXTY-FOUR

J oulie's fingers curled around the barrel of the pistol Ryan had dropped in front of her. She cautiously pulled it across the rough planks of the dock. Blood speckled the gun's slide and grip. She had little desire to touch the pistol, let alone fire it, but she was desperate to escape the clutches of Toussaint Bajeux. To do so, she would need to muster all her nerve, and help Ryan Weller kill Volk.

She squatted behind the trawler's hull with the gun laid across her palms. Tears fell to mix with the blood on the pistol. When she was a little girl, her grandmother had taught her that life was sacred. Those who murdered practiced the dark arts. Her life's purpose was love and light and life.

Joulie closed her small hand around the grip, feeling the cold steel of the gun fuse with her determination. She remembered the basic tutorial Mango had given her in the Honda Pilot and what she had learned by watching Toussaint and his men. Her thumb forced the safety off. Metal ground against metal, setting her teeth on edge. And she felt something else, something that stilled the quivering inside her. For many years she had known she carried the name of her ancestor, the pirate Jean Lafitte, and Joulie felt his presence calming her nerves.

Still she trembled as she rose just enough to see through the railing around the fishing boat's hull. Ryan was in *Dark Water*'s cockpit cuffing his hands in front of him. To cross to the Hatteras, she would need to climb onto the fishing boat and traverse a deck littered with ropes and nets. If Volk could see Ryan, he would plainly see her.

Joulie focused on the next boat along the dock. To get a better shot at Volk, she needed to move to the fishing yawl. She whispered a prayer to Ogoun—the loa of war—for strength and that her bullet would find its mark. Her spirits buoyed, she rose and sprinted toward the yawl.

CHAPTER SIXTY-FIVE

Mango watched Ryan kick the gun over the railing and, with arms raised, step down into *Dark Water*'s cockpit. Mango tried to anticipate the next move in the play.

Something landed at Ryan's feet. He bent down and picked up a pair of handcuffs.

Mango pulled away from the scope and blinked. Then he jammed the stock tighter into his shoulder and refocused his eye on the glass. Ryan was manacling himself with the cuffs, wrists in front of him.

"Hang tight, bro," Mango said. He slid off the table, leaving the Dragunov resting on its bipod. He stepped to the canvas bag he'd transported the rifle in and unzipped it. There was one more weapon he'd obtained when Joulie had driven him to Toussaint's armament cache. He slid the steel and wood tube of an RPG-7 from the bag. He'd planned to use it if they needed a distraction. Now was the time.

Squatting on the bridge deck, Mango loaded the RPG round into the tube. He stood, walked the four steps to the port bridge wing and aimed the rocket-propelled grenade at Toussaint Bajeux's Carver.

The little boat bobbed on the choppy waves as it slowly circled the narrow entrance between the commercial quay and the small spit of land occupied by the private dock. Toussaint had told Mango and Ryan he would stay in place to prevent them from running away once they'd liberated Greg. To arm his meager blocking force, he'd brought several RPG rockets and the crewmen carried AKs. These he had also shown them to emphasize the point that they were not to attempt an escape.

But Mango had brought a contingency plan for dealing with Toussaint. The Haitian warlord would be the distraction. He focused the iron sights on the Carver, hoping that when the Carver detonated, Ryan could use the brief seconds of commotion to take out the bounty hunter.

Mango pulled the trigger.

Unlike the movies, he saw no streak of smoke as the rocket screamed across the water. The boat was there one moment and the next it was a raging ball of fire. Twisted fiberglass, metal, wood, and bodies flew into the air to come raining back down.

For a moment, he stood watching the fury subside. Then he bolted back to his Dragunov and pressed his eye to the scope.

CHAPTER SIXTY-SIX

Joulie was halfway across the yawl's deck when she saw the white Carver explode. She clamped a hand over her mouth to stifle a cry. More tears burned her cheeks. Toussaint was dead. Ryan had kept his promise. She must repay the favor.

She moved again, feeling the exhilaration of freedom wash over her. From the corner of her eye, she saw Ryan launch himself off *Dark Water*'s railing and land awkwardly on the deck of the fishing vessel. Bullets chased him, ricocheting off metal and showering him with rust and flecks of paint.

The shooter did not reveal himself. Joulie prayed to the loa, Erzulie, to deliver Volk to her. Erzulie was the goddess of love, but a goddess who could be spoiled and jealous. Right now, Joulie felt jealous. Jealous for the life of a man who had come to save her, and jealous for her new freedom. She was free for the first time since she'd been a child. No one was going to take away her ride to America.

Joulie pressed herself against the bowsprit and aimed. Erzulie would deliver the target, but it was the hand of Jean Lafitte that steadied her gun.

CHAPTER SIXTY-SEVEN

Volk rose from behind his hostage and stared at the blazing ball of fire rising from the middle of the harbor. Ryan leaped for the fishing boat. Volk brought his pistol up and fired until the slide locked back. The two million dollars was payable dead or alive. Alive could be worth a bonus, and there was the pleasure of seeing his bounty tortured by the ruthless Aztlán cartel. He'd thought Russians were the masters of torture, but the Mexican cartels took it to new levels with their witless victims.

He rapidly changed magazines and watched as his bounty scrambled on his belly behind a hatch cover. Volk aimed and fired a round that ricocheted off the deck just inches from Ryan's face.

Ryan bounced up and dove behind the protection of the bridge's steel walls and the electronic consoles inside.

Volk laid his lips back to expose his canines in his trade-mark grin. He screamed, "I am tired of playing this game!"

He grabbed the handles on the back of Greg's wheelchair and shoved him into the cockpit.

"Let's play new game!" Volk shouted. "You come out, or I shoot."

He pressed the warm pistol muzzle to Greg's temple, palming Greg's head like a basketball with his beefy hand.

With a sadistic smile on his face, Volk watched Ryan Weller step out from behind the trawler's bridge with his hands in the air.

Volk growled, "Get into the boat."

CHAPTER SIXTY-EIGHT

Joulie saw a massive Russian push a man in a wheelchair into the Hatteras's cockpit. She lined up the sights as Mango had instructed, the small blade of a front sight centered between the divot of the rear. Volk's head sat like a pumpkin on a post.

Instead of Volk's head, she saw Toussaint's toothy grin, the high forehead, and wide-set eyes. She hated him. Her hands trembled as she held the gun out straight, finger drawing tight around the trigger.

She nearly dropped the gun when it discharged.

The bullet went wide of its mark. Joulie stood rooted to the spot, unable to move. In slow motion, she watched as Volk turned, bringing up his gun to target her.

Then Volk's head exploded.

CHAPTER SIXTY-NINE

Ryan had just stepped out from behind the bridge. His job was to lure the Russian bounty hunter out into the open. With arms raised, he walked around the front of the bridge and onto the fishing boat's narrow side deck. He grinned at Greg.

A second later, a gunshot rang out. Volk started to spin toward the sailboat behind them. Ryan took a running step to the rail and vaulted it. His legs had just cleared the railing when Volk's head exploded.

The Russian just stood there behind Greg, his arm half raised, head split open like a ripe melon. In slow motion, his gun slid from his hand and then his knees buckled. He toppled over, smacking face first into the gunwale with an impact that shattered his spine. Blood from the head wound oozed across the white fiberglass.

Ryan lost focus on his landing as he saw Volk's head explode and he fell in a crumbled heap in *Dark Water*'s cockpit. He scrambled to his feet and squatted beside Greg.

"You okay?"

Greg nodded. "Glad that's over. What about Toussaint?"

"That was his boat that just blew up. Be right back. Get the engines started." Ryan crossed back to the fishing boat and jumped down to the dock. "Joulie!"

As he ran along the dock, he saw his body double struggling up the muddy bank at the edge of the water. He appeared wet but unhurt.

Ryan found Joulie leaning against the sailboat's bowsprit. The pistol lay in a puddle of vomit at her feet. He wrapped an arm around her shoulders. Her skin felt like it was on fire. "Are you okay?"

She shook her head and buried her face in his chest. Hot tears soaked into his shirt. She trembled as she cried.

"We need to go," he said softly.

He felt her head bob.

Ryan guided her off the yawl and across the fishing boat to *Dark Water*. Greg was already on the bridge.

Ryan called out, "I'll get the lines as soon as I get her inside."

Joulie sank into the settee behind the table. Ryan fetched her a bottle of water as the diesels snorted to life. He handed her the water and ran out to the dock. Kneeling down, he grabbed the line tied to the rebreather and hauled it up.

"Get the bow line," Greg yelled.

Ryan put the rebreather in the cockpit and ran forward to work the rope loose from the cleat before tossing it onto the Hatteras. He was untying the stern line when Greg engaged the drives and began to swing the bow around.

"Cast off!" Greg shouted.

Ryan pulled the line loose and tossed it onto the boat before jumping aboard. He scrambled up the ladder to the bridge and pointed across the bay at the commercial docks. "Mango's over there. We need to pick him up."

"What's he doing over there?"

"Sniper overwatch. Who do you think shot Volk?"

"I didn't think it was the girl." Greg ramped up the throttles, and they shot across the choppy bay.

Ryan punched on the radar, sonar, and GPS screens. "Where we running to? That hurricane has to be getting close."

"We have to go north and east. The eye has already crossed the Mona Passage between the DR and Puerto Rico."

Ryan dropped down the ladder to the cockpit as Greg brought the Hatteras alongside the boat that had served as Mango's overwatch position.

The blustery wind tore at Mango's clothes as he stood on the long liner's deck. He tossed a green canvas bag to Ryan before he jumped to the Hatteras. Greg had them roaring away before Mango could get his feet under him.

The two men bumped fists. "Saved your ass, bro."

Ryan grinned. "It's like déjà vu all over again."

Greg shouted, "Quite playing grab-ass and get the fenders."

Ryan went forward to pull the bow fender while Mango retrieved the rear. They stored them in the cockpit locker before Mango carried his bag into the salon. Ryan followed him to check on Joulie. She was still at the table. Mango paused, set the bag down, and unzipped it. He pulled out a pair of jeans, a T-shirt, and a sweater. All of which, he tossed on the table.

"Thanks," she said.

"You're welcome. Watch out for this one." He pointed at Ryan.

"I just came to see if everything was all right," Ryan said. "I'm going up to the bridge to help Greg."

"I'm fine," Joulie said, rising to gather her pile of clothes. "Is there a place I can change?"

"I'll show you," Mango said. "I'll be up in a minute, Ryan. I'm serious, Joulie, watch out for him."

She smiled and shook her head. Ryan gave her a devilish grin and went up to the bridge.

Greg had *Dark Water* up on plane, charging toward open ocean when they passed Toussaint Bajeux's former house on Rival Beach. The small barrier islands along the eastern entrance to the bay were blocking six-foot waves marching in from the storm. Rain began to pelt the boat.

"It's going to be a rough ride," Greg yelled.

Ryan scrambled to close the spray curtains the Russians had opened. He zipped the front one last. He looked out to see Fort Picolet passing on their port side. The nose of the boat hit the big waves, beginning their yo-yo ride.

Joulie and Mango joined them on the bridge.

"Are we going to make it?" Mango asked.

"Yeah, but it ain't gonna be fun," Greg said. "I'm heading to Matthew Town on Iguana Island. We've got enough diesel to make a full power run, but I don't think I can push very hard in this weather."

Ryan glanced up from the radar screen. "Storm track says it'll run right along Hispaniola and cross to Cuba."

"Why not go to Jamaica?" Mango asked.

"I don't have enough fuel. The guy at the marina refused to give me a full load and I burned some trying to find you guys. Plus, we'd be crossing right in front of the hurricane. If something happened to the boat, we'd be screwed."

"Power on, bro," Mango said.

EPILOGUE

Hurricane Irma savaged everything in her path. Islands once green with vegetation were laid bare. The wind stripped away leaves and grass to leave behind naked trees and eroded rocks. The lower Florida Keys were the hardest hit part of the United States. Sections of U.S. Highway 1 had been washed away, houses demolished, bridges damaged, boats flung onto dry land, and channels reshaped as the storm moved around coral and sand. Even shipwrecks shifted on the sea floor.

People who had run from the storm, thinking they would be safe in Tampa or Orlando, were surprised to find the storm chasing them up the western coast. This shift was good news for the crew of the sixty-three-foot Hatteras GT sportfishing yacht, *Dark Water*. Their anchorage on North Eleuthera Island in the northern Bahamas remained unscathed, save for heavy rain and high winds.

After they'd arrived at Dunmore Town, they'd checked into a small hotel. Ryan called Landis from the privacy of his room and gave him the whole story.

"Another job well done, Ryan," Landis congratulated.

"We didn't accomplish much. Kilroy is still out there, and Mango and I still have a bounty on our heads."

"We'll keep an ear out for any word about you guys and the shipwreck in case Kilroy tries to recover the gold."

"I think the gold will bring people in droves."

"How many people know about it?" Landis asked.

Ryan thought for a minute. "Me, Mango, a couple of guys on the *Santo Domingo*, Kilroy, Toussaint, and probably a few of Toussaint's men. Most of those guys are dead."

"I'd forget about it if I were you."

Ryan shook his head. "It'll be hard."

Twenty-five million dollars' worth of gold was not easily forgotten, especially when he'd seen one of the steel strong boxes break loose from the pallet and spill gleaming bars across the cargo deck. He would be the first to admit he had gold fever.

"Think about all the bounty hunters who will start chasing you again if they know you're alive and going after gold."

"Yeah," Ryan agreed half-heartedly.

"Look, don't do anything hasty. Stay dead for a while and we'll see how things shake out."

"I can do that. What are you going to do? You'll have to hire a new goon for your ops."

"Well," said Landis. "Since you went off the reservation, the DHS has put a damper on DWR's operations."

"It's probably for the best. I think the hurricane cleanup is going to keep them busy. I've heard Greg on the sat phone talking to Shelly and Admiral Chatel about it."

"What about you, any plans?"

"Put some distance between myself and DWR. Jennifer is meeting *Dark Water* in the Gulf on their sailboat, so she and

Mango can start their cruise together. I hear you're working on new passports and paperwork for them."

"Yes, I'm also trying to arrange asylum paperwork for Joulie. It's a difficult road with the current political climate, especially with the president considering deporting Haitians." He sighed. "That's my problem, not yours, and you haven't told me what you're planning."

"I'm going to hang out in the Keys and spend some time with Emily."

"Uhm ... she's ... uhm," Landis stammered.

"What?"

"She gave me a message for to you."

"She did?" Ryan sat up, eager to hear news of his girlfriend.

"I can't repeat half of what she said because it was pretty foul, but the gist of it is that she's done with your relationship, and she doesn't want you to call her, or to go see her. I'm sorry, man."

The news stunned Ryan. He'd survived multiple hits on his life, stopped a tyrant from starting a war, and swam out of a sunken ship, only to be blindsided. *No wonder she hasn't returned my phone calls.*

"I'm sorry, Ryan," Landis repeated to fill the dead air.

"I know. I'll call you later." He hung up the phone in a daze. *Why doesn't she want to see me?*

Two hours later, Greg found Ryan at the outdoor bar, chain smoking and drinking straight tequila.

"This can't be good," Greg said, motioning for the bartender to pour him a shot. "You okay?"

"I'll be all right," Ryan said. They clinked shots and kicked them back. "Emily broke up with me."

"You sure you're okay? I mean, she was *the one*, right?"

"Yeah." Ryan shrugged. "I thought she was."

"We're pulling anchor tomorrow. The hurricane is

crossing into Georgia and we've got a clear window to get gone."

"Cool." Ryan threw back another shot.

Greg started to turn away.

"Is everything good with you?" Ryan asked. "I mean, you about got plugged by that Russian bastard."

"He's feeding fish now. I'm good." Greg rubbed the side of his face where Volk had slapped him. Most of the bruising had disappeared.

"I'm sorry I got you into this."

"Don't be an asshole. You didn't get me into anything I couldn't handle. Besides, we've been through worse."

Ryan nodded and took a pull on his cigarette.

"That shit will kill you, bro," Mango said, walking up with Joulie. The two had become fast friends.

Ryan flipped him the bird.

RYAN KNELT IN THE SAND, staring up the knifing edge of the U.S.S. *Spiegel Grove*'s bow. Named for President Rutherford B. Hayes's estate in Fremont, Ohio, the vessel had served with distinction for thirty-four years before being sunk as an artificial reef. Coral grew all long the five-hundred-and-ten-foot length of dock landing ship thirty-two (LSD-32). At its sinking, the LSD had been the largest artificial reef in the world. The U.S.N.S. *Vandenberg*, off Key West, and the aircraft carrier, U.S.S. *Oriskany*, twenty-two miles off the coast of Pensacola, Florida, now placed the *Spiegel Grove* in third, but it was still one of the most visited wrecks in the Florida Keys, and one of Ryan's favorites.

He rose slowly along the bow. A goliath grouper eyeballed him as Ryan came to foredeck. He swam leisurely toward the stern and turned on his dive light. He kept his arms close to his body as he entered the upper superstructure. Much of the interior had been removed before sinking, but the crewmen had left strange things, like a row of urinals. His light played across the painted image of Charles Schulz's cartoon dog, Snoopy, wearing a sailor's cap and riding an alligator under the words "Top Dog." The image lent the ship the nickname, *Spiegel Beagle*.

For the last six months, Ryan had lived in the Florida Keys. He'd hired himself out to work cleanup from Hurricane Irma, demolishing the interiors of water-damaged homes, cutting up downed trees, and recovering sunken boats. He worked for cash and room and board while making his way north from Marathon to Key Largo, where he took a job as a dive instructor.

He'd tried calling Emily, despite Landis's message, but she never answered. He tried to see things from her point of view. His job was dangerous, and it had dragged her in both times. The first by her choice and the second unwillingly. He enjoyed the thrill and the challenge. It was addicting, and anyone not used to the danger would want off the ride. Emily elected to exit the carousel, and he was okay with that. He had to be okay with it. He was still trying to see it from her point of view.

As he came out of the *Spiegel Grove*'s superstructure, Ryan looked up at the American flag, hanging limp in the calm water. Four, five and six-foot-long great barracudas hovered at the base of the flagpole.

He checked his computer and finned toward the ascent line.

A shadow flashed over him. He glanced up to see a hammerhead shark swim past and disappear into the gloom.

Ryan grinned into the mouthpiece of his rebreather; glad he'd rescued it from under the dock before casting off *Dark Water*'s lines. Seeing an elusive hammerhead made this dive even more special, but what kept crowding into his mind was the sight of two pallets lying in the hold of the *Santo Domingo*. Just over a half-a-ton of gold bullion in twenty-seven-pound bars. He thought about them every day. They were calling his name.

ACKNOWLEDGMENTS

I had several terrific alpha and beta readers who critiqued this novel and helped shape it into what it is now. Thanks for your help and comments. It's hard to take sometimes, but it really helps, and

it keeps me down to earth.

George Schlub is one of my best friends. He's an actual detective sergeant. We started diving together more years ago than I want to think about, and we've had many wild adventures, both diving and traveling together. George is also an accomplished musician and trumpet maker for Schlub Brass.

ABOUT THE AUTHOR

Evan Graver has worked in construction, as a security guard, a motorcycle and car technician, a property manager, and in the scuba industry. He served in the U.S. Navy, where he was an aviation electronics technician until they medically retired him following a motorcycle accident which left him paralyzed. He found other avenues of adventure: riding ATVs, downhill skiing, skydiving, and bungee jumping. His passions are scuba diving and writing. He lives in Hollywood, Florida, with his wife and son.

Can you do me a favor and leave a review? I appreciate it as reviews are the social proof that others have read the book.

If you would like to follow Ryan Weller's adventures and learn more about him, please subscribe to my newsletter to receive a free short story *Dark Days*. Click here to tell me where to send your copy.

Made in the USA
Coppell, TX
11 April 2020